Jungfrau

Jungfrau

A selection of works from the Caine Prize for African Writing

First published in 2007 by
New Internationalist™ Publications Ltd
Oxford OX4 1BW, UK
www.newint.org
New Internationalist is a registered trade mark.

First published in 2007 in southern Africa by
Jacana Media (Pty) Ltd
10 Orange Street
Sunnyside
Auckland Park 2092
South Africa
+2711 628 3200
www.jacana.co.za

Individual contributions © the Authors.

Cover: Four Seasons by Diana Ong/Getty Images.

Printed on recycled paper by T J International Limited, Cornwall, UK, who hold environmental accreditation ISO 14001.

British Library Cataloguing-in-Publication Data.
A catalogue record for this book is available from the British Library.

Library of Congress Cataloguing-in-Publication Data.
A catalogue for this book is available from the Library of Congress.

New Internationalist ISBN: 978-1-904456-62-9
Jacana Media ISBN: 978-1-77009-367-6

Contents

Introduction

At the first Caine Prize Award Dinner, in Oxford in July 2000, Ben Okri, speaking as Chairman of the Judges, decried the way in which bookshops treated African writers as an exotic, 'special interest' category, relegating them to remote corners under varietal headings, diversely appropriate, such as 'Black Literature'. He even castigated those who bought them, for housing them apart in their bookshelves at home. (I bit my lip at that point, worrying about the African section among my own books – though Ben Okri, as a Booker Prize winner, was happily filed elsewhere, with the mainstream. In fact I still have a shelf devoted to Caine Prize writers, but perhaps I may claim special dispensation for that.)

The criticism is still often voiced; but I believe it is less and less just. The last ten years have surely seen African writing moving into the mainstream in the UK; and if the case is not quite the same in the US, that is perhaps because 'Afro-American' is a characterisation to conjure an American readership, free of patronising implications.

What evidence can one point to? A glance at the publishers of novels subsequently produced by Caine Prize winners is indicative: Leila Aboulela (winner 2000) – *Minaret*, Bloomsbury 2005; Helon Habila (2001) – *Waiting for an Angel*, 2002 and *Measuring Time*, 2007, Hamish Hamilton/Penguin (the latter longlisted for this year's Booker); Segun Afolabi (2005) – *Goodbye Lucille*, Jonathan Cape, 2007. And at the agents who have taken them on: for example, David Godwin has Binyavanga Wainaina (winner 2002) and Yvonne Adhiambo Owuor (2003) in his stable as well as Helon Habila and Segun Afolabi. In terms of mainstream acclaim perhaps most telling is the fact that Chimamanda Ngozi Adichie (Caine Prize shortlist 2002) has not only since been twice shortlisted for the Orange Prize – for *Purple Hibiscus*, Fourth Estate, 2004 and for *Half of a Yellow Sun*, Fourth Estate, 2007 – she also featured this year in the Richard and Judy show's Book Club Choice. That is the distinction perhaps most coveted by UK fiction publishers; and it places *Half of a Yellow Sun* at the very centre of the commercial literary fiction mainstream today. Such books do not get hidden away among esoterica in the bookshops.

I think with the Caine Prize we have helped this process, at least by putting our effort in the right place at the right time, and I am sure the writers whose work you can read in this volume – the Prize's 2006 shortlisted candidates and the participants at this year's workshop – will be able to carry it further along.

Last year's Caine Prize winner was Mary Watson, whose family was classified Coloured under the absurd apartheid system, and who herself now teaches film and media at the University of Cape Town. Her story, *Jungfrau*, appeared in her collection, *Moss*, published by Kwela Books (Cape Town) in 2004, of which Andre Brink said, 'Our literature will be the richer for accommodating a voice of this calibre, persuasive power and exquisite beauty'. Another South African on the shortlist was Darrel Bristow Bovey, whose *A Joburg Story*, from *African Compass – New Writings from Southern Africa 2005*, published by Spearhead, was particularly commended for its dialogue by J M Coetzee. The Nigerian writer Sefi Atta's story, *The Last Trip*, came to us from the Cape Town magazine, *Chimurenga*. Her novel, *Everything Good Will Come*, was first published by Interlink Books in the USA and subsequently by Double Storey Books in Cape Town. Like Sefi Atta, Laila Lalami (Morocco) teaches in the USA and her story, *The Fanatic*, comes from her collection, *Hope and Other Dangerous Pursuits*, published by Algonquin Books of Chapel Hill in 2005. Finally, for the first time, a story written at one of our workshops, and published in a Caine Prize anthology, made it to the shortlist: Muthoni Garland's *Tracking the Scent of My Mother*, from *Seventh Street Alchemy: A Selection of Writings from The Caine Prize for African Writing 2004* (Jacana Media, Johannesburg, 2005). It was a great joy to have the synergy between the Prize and the Workshops underlined in this way.

The Celtel Caine Prize African Writers' Workshop 2007

For the second year in succession, our workshop for African writers was sponsored by Celtel International BV; and it was the third successive workshop to be held at Crater Lake, near Naivasha, Kenya, a perfect venue with wonderfully welcoming personnel. With the help of the incomparable Kairo Kiarie from *Kwani?*, Celtel Kenya organised an Open Day for the participants, who were joined on an excursion into the countryside and then in a filmed debate by a couple of dozen writers and journalists from Nairobi. The same organising partnership brought together an audience of over 100 for a reading by workshop participants at the conclusion of the workshop, hosted by Celtel, which was televised at the Godown Arts Centre in Nairobi.

Celtel's sponsorship still has a year to run and has been a tremendous benefit to our writers. This year's stories are printed below.

Once again, Air Kenya provided tickets for some of the workshop participants. Once again, the promise of publication of the workshop stories kept the participants at work – for which we warmly thank our publishers.

And once again we record our very warm thanks to our principal funders, the Ernest Oppenheimer Memorial Trust and the Gatsby Charitable Foundation, on whose generosity the Caine Prize has existed for the past five years.

Nick Elam
Administrator of the Caine Prize

Caine Prize Stories 2006:
Winner and Shortlist

Jungfrau
(Winner)

Mary Watson

IT WAS THE VIRGIN JESSICA who taught me about wickedness.

I once asked her why she was called the Virgin Jessica. She looked at me with strange eyes and said that it was because she was a special person, like the Blessed Mary.

"A virgin is someone who can do God's work. And if you're very, very clean and pure you can be one of the one hundred and forty-four virgins who will be carried in God's bosom at the end of the world. And if you're not –"

She leaned towards me, her yellow teeth before my eye. I thought she might suck it out, she was so close. She whispered, "If you're not, then God will toss you to the devil who will roast you with his horn. Like toasted marshmallows. You don't want the devil's evil horn to make a hole in your pretty skin, now do you?"

She kissed my nose – my little rabbit's nose, she called it – and walked away, her long white summer dress falling just above her high, high red heels. Her smell, cigarette smoke and last night's perfume, lingered around my eyeball. I wanted to be like the Virgin Jessica. I wanted a name like hers.

We called her Jez for short.

My mother Annette was the Virgin Jessica's adopted sister. She was older and tireder. The Virgin had no children while my mother had forty-three. She was a schoolteacher in one of those schools where the children wore threadbare jerseys and had hard green snot crystallized around their noses and above their crusty lips – lips that could say poes without tasting any bitterness. Or that secret relish of forbidden language.

Sometimes my mother would have them – her other children, her little smelly children – over at our house. They would drape themselves around our furniture like dirty ornamental cherubs and drink hot pea soup. The steam melted the snot, which then ran down into the soup. It did not matter to them because they ate their boogers anyway.

I hated my mother's other children. I glared at them to let them know, but they stared back without much expression. Their faces had nothing to say – I could read nothing there. Jessica found them amusing.

"Sweet little things," she mumbled, and laughed into her coffee. Her shoulders shook epileptically.

After the Virgin told me how important it was to be clean, I tolerated them in the haze of my superiority. I was clean – I bathed every night – and they were filthy, so obviously God wouldn't want to touch them.

The Virgin spent hours in the bathroom every evening. Naked she walked to her bedroom, so lovely and proud she seemed tall; I followed faithfully, to observe a ritual more awesome than church. With creams and powders she made herself even cleaner for God. How he must love her, I thought. She spread his love upon her as she rubbed her skin until it glowed and her smell spread through the house, covering us all with the strength of her devotion. Then she went out, just after my father came home, and stayed out until late.

The Virgin Jessica had a cloud of charm twenty centimetres around her body. Strangers hated her because they thought that anyone that beautiful could only be mean. But it was not her pretty black eyes or her mouth that made her beautiful. She was beautiful because she was wrapped in a cloud of charm. And when you breathed in the air from the cloud, you breathed in the charm and it went down your veins and into your heart and made you love her. If you came close enough, she would smile her skew smile, pretending to love you with her slitted eyes, and the charm would ooze out like fog from a sewer and grab you and sink into your heart and lungs. Even I who had known her all my life would feel the charm with a funny ache. She had a way of leaning forward when she spoke, claiming the space around her with her smell, her charm. And my father, who didn't speak or laugh, he too would be conquered.

"What's the old man up to tonight?" she would say, leaning towards him with a wink, her eyes laughing; and he would fold his newspaper and look pleased, even grunt contentedly.

I tried saying those same words, leaning forward the way Jez did, and he looked at me coldly. So cold that my wink froze halfway and my laugh caught in my throat. Embarrassed, I transformed the laugh into a cough and rubbed my eyes like a tired child. I think it was then that I realised that his love for me was bound to me as his little girl. And my love for him bound me to my little girl's world.

I took pains to keep my girl's world intact after that. When boys teased me at school, I felt the walls of my father's favour tremble. One of them phoned and sang a dirty song into my hot ear. My head burnt for days after that. I felt the fires of hell from that phone call. I feared that the fires would start inside me, catching my hair and eating the strands like candlewick, melting my skin like wax, dripping and staining mommy's carpets (she would be very cross). The fire would eat the horrid children in the schoolroom, then crawl towards my mother, burn her slowly and then finish with her chalk-stained fingers. Her glasses would shrivel up and her mouth crease with silent screams. Unsatisfied, the fire would move towards my father, crackling his newspaper; the smoke would cloud his glasses. Beneath them, his eyes would have that same cold look – but not cold enough to douse the flames. The fire would then stagger towards the Virgin. Leering, it would grab her ankles and eat her white frock, turning it to soot. She would cry out and her head would toss, her hair unravel and she would scream from the force of the flames. The Virgin Jessica's screams in my head made me put a knife on the window-sill of her bedroom so that she could undo the burglar bars and escape.

The image of flames and screams resounded in my head for several days. They surged whenever the other girls in their shortened school dresses lit cigarettes in the toilets. They could not see how the flames would get bigger. I checked all the stubs carelessly tossed into the sink and bin to make sure that the fire did not escape. The slight thrill I had once received from the boys teasing me in the safety of the schoolyard, away from my father's fearsome eyes, faded. I spent my intervals at the far end of the yard, eating sandwiches and talking to the dogs through the wire fence. I had to coax them across the road with my milk and the ham from my bread. I was found one day, squatting on my haunches and telling Nina and Hildegarde about a garden of moss. I felt a shadow; it made me shiver, and I looked up to see if God was angry. Instead I saw Ms Collins above me, her eyes made huge by her glasses. I was scared that she'd be cross. I wanted to pee; some dripped down my leg, so I crouched and shut my eyes tightly, praying fervently that I would not pee. She reached out for my hand and asked me to make some charts for her in exchange for some biscuits and cool drink. From then on I spent my breaks helping Ms Collins in her art room and she would give me yoghurt and fruit and sometimes chocolate. I never ate these. Instead I put them on the steps of the white Kirk on the way home. Ms Collins tried to ask me questions, but I was shy and would only whisper, "I don't know." She would speak relentlessly. She told me about her baby daughter who ate grass.
I preferred just to look at her. I liked looking at her big ugly eyes and her pretty hair. But I think she got tired of me: maybe my silence wore her down; maybe the

sound of her own voice scared her, for it must have been like talking to herself. She probably thought she was going mad, talking and talking to still brown eyes. But the day I went into her art room and found a boy from my class helping her with the charts, I remembered the fires of hell and ran away. Maybe she wanted me to burn; maybe she wasn't a virgin either.

It must have been the sound of midnight that woke me. The house without my mother felt unguarded. It seemed her presence warded off a fury of demons. I sat upright in my clean girl's bed, trying to feel the pulse of the night. I slipped my feet over the side of the bed and listened. The darkness is covered by a haze that makes the still corners move.

I knew that my mother had not returned. The wild child with snot streaming from his nose and eyes, he had her still. I sat at the lounge window, watching the sea, hating the wild child. He had come after supper, his little body panting like a steam engine. He ran up the hill in the rain, he had run all the way from the settlement. He sobbed, buried his head in my mother's trousers.

"Please, please, *asseblief*, please," his broken voice scratched.

Wishing so very hard that he hadn't come, I watched the boy cry until my mother barked, "Evelyn, get out of here."

I prayed that the wild child would leave: go back to your plague, I screamed silently. It was too late. He had brought his plague with him. It wandered about our house and muffled my warnings. So she did not hear me, and let the child take her away.

Her trousers soiled with tears and mucus, she rushed into her bedroom, where I was watching one of those endless sitcoms about silly teenagers. She grabbed her car keys.

"Don't wait up for me."

I would not have waited for her. Even now, in the dark hour, I was not waiting for her.

I must have stayed at the window for at least an hour. I saw the sea roar-smash-roar against the rocks. I saw the stillness of the midnight road, the white line running on towards the mountain. The road was empty; but then I saw two people walking up the hill. They walked slowly and closely in their midnight world. The walk was a stagger.

They fell pleasantly against each other. I saw them walk towards the house and only then did I see who they were.

When Jessica and my father entered the house, quietly and with the guilty grace of burglars, they were glowing from the wind and walking and waves and the wildness of the night's beauty. The haze inherent in the darkness was centred around them. I looked on with envy, for I too wished to walk the empty night with them. Jessica let out a startled sound when she saw me curled up on the window-sill.

"Look at you," she fussed, "hanging around dark windows like a sad little ghost."

Her face was close to mine and her breathing deep.

"Have you been watching for your mother? Has she come home yet?"

I shook my head. I had not been waiting for my mother.

She held my hands in her cold, cold fingers. "Your hands are freezing," she said.

"You need some Milo. How long have you been sitting here? Long?

"Your father and I went to see if your mother was coming home. I wish she'd phone, but then they probably don't have one. I really don't understand why Annette involves herself in other people's business. But I suppose you should count your blessings. When we were small, Annette and me, all we had to play with was scrap metal."

Jessica chattered on, repeating the stories I had heard so many times.

My mother came home while I was clutching my Milo. I was playing the mournful ghost, the sick patient, and all the while glowing in the attention of both my father and Jessica. Jessica was chattering brightly, so bright that she made the darkness her own while I huddled in its shadows. My father was silent, his eyes as dark as mine. Jessica's words tripped out of her mouth and drew circles around us.

Then Annette stepped into our enchanted circle. She asked for tea. As Jessica made the tea her words stumbled then stopped. My father went to bed, taking my hand as he left the kitchen. I did not want to go to bed. I wanted to be in the kitchen with just my father and Jessica and me.

I stood on a rock in the garden and stared down at the people watching my sea. They were dotted across the small beach, the wind twisting their hair around their necks and forcing them closer into their jackets. They lifted their fingers to point, just like in a seaside painting.

Their mouths were wide with laughter and their eyes bright, yet all the while I knew that they were posing, as if for an invisible artist. Their minds could sometimes glimpse his black beret, his paint-splattered smock in this idyllic scene.

I went down to the sea. There were too many whale-watchers trampling the sand, my desecrated temple, with their flat feet and stubby toes. I glared at the fat children who clung to their parents, hanging on to their arms and legs.

"Beast with two backs," I muttered.

They smelt suburban. Their odour of white bread and Marmite drifted unpleasantly into the sea air. They huddled into their wind-breakers and yawned at the ocean.

"It's just a dark blob," they whined, their winter-paled faces cracking beneath the noon sun. They shivered from the wind nuzzling their necks.

I sat near the water's edge and buried my pretty toes in the sand. The crowd, the people who came to see the whales, were noisy and their noise ate into my ears as they crunched their chips and the packets crackled in the wind.

"Go home," I hissed to a solitary toddler who wandered near me.

I turned to see a woman scoop him up and pretend to eat his angel curls. My coward's face smiled at her.

I stayed there for a while, watching the people watch the whales. Then I noticed some of my mother's children playing in the water on the other side of the beach. They shrieked and laughed; some played in their dirty clothes, others in varying stages of nakedness.

They sang a ditty with filthy words while roughly shoving and splashing each other with the cold water. They knocked down their friends and made them eat sand. The suburban children's parents shook their heads, pulled their young ones and walked away, still shaking their heads, as though the shaking would dispel the image from their minds. They soon forgot all about those children who haunted the corners of my world, my mother's chosen children.

She came to call me for lunch. She did not see her young ones, who had moved towards the tidal pool, and I did not tell her about them.

I sneaked my mother off the beach, chattering too brightly. We walked towards the hill. Someone came running behind us, but we carried on walking, for my mother didn't seem to hear the foot steps – maybe I was too bright. I walked faster and we crossed Main Road. When we reached the other side, I felt a light strong-hard knock like a spirit just made solid. I turned to see the wild child hugging my mother, her arms wrapped around him. He gave her a flower and ran back. When the wild child crossed the road, he was hit by whale people in a blue car. The driver got out, my mother ran to her child. The driver, annoyed and red, complained that he hadn't seen anyone, there was nobody there.

"Just a shadow flitted across my eyes," his wife wailed. "Just a dark shadow."

The driver said that he would fetch help. He and his wife drove off in their blue car – the dent was slight – and didn't come back. Perhaps to him there really was nobody there: the dent was so very slight, and those children are so thin, after all.

My mother lifted the wild child in her arms. She waited and while she waited, her mouth got tighter and tighter and she wept. When one hundred blue cars had passed by, she slowly got up from the pavement. With the wild child in her arms, she walked up the hill. She did not speak to me, her mouth was tight and her hair unbound from its ponytail.

At our house Jessica and my father hovered awkwardly around her, their legs and arms looking wrong on their bodies, as if they had taken them off and put them back the wrong way. They moved slowly and clumsily, like they had wound down. My mother lay her child on my clean girl's bed and stayed by his side.

"Stephen, get the doctor quickly," she barked at my father.

I ate my Sunday roast. I paid little attention to the doctor's arrival or the child's crying or my mother's pacing. Her tight face had shut me out. I sat in the lounge and watched the sea, picking at the meat. When the violet hour came, the beach was empty and my room smelt of the wild child and the barest hint of my mother's love. But they were both gone.

I stayed in the lounge with my father and the Virgin, who brought us tea. We played cards and laughed the soft, covered laughs of forbidden frivolity. We munched biscuits and watched the Virgin's teasing eyes as she tried to cheat, as she toasted marshmallows over a candle flame, as she spoke, smiled, sighed. The wild child and my mother were forgotten. I did not think of the bruised bundle on my bed.

Then the quiet beneath our laughter became too insistent. It was guilt that sent me in search of her. It was the guilt of the betrayer for the betrayed, because guilt is more binding than passion.

There was not a trace of my mother and the wild child in my bedroom. There was no mark of my mother's care or her chosen child's blood staining the sheets. There were no cup rings on my dressing table, no dent on the pillow. I looked for my mother in my bedroom. I hunted in every corner but could not find the slightest whisper of her smell.

I could find nothing of her in the lounge – that was my father's room. Their bedroom was green and clinical and did not contain either of them. The kitchen was heavy with the Virgin's presence, which smelt of rose water with a burny undertone. I sat down on the floor, perplexed.

Agitated, I realised that I could not remember if her smell had been in the house the day before. Or the previous week. I went to the garage, which she used as a schoolroom. As I opened the door, a fury of smells came screaming towards me. There were the wild children's smells of pain and fear and anger. And she was there, entangled in this foul mix. Nothing of her remained in the house because it was all concentrated here. Delicately it cushioned and enveloped the rawness of the children as it wove itself into them. The force of this beauty, this tenderness made me want to weep with jealousy. Such sadness, such terror. I left the dim garage knowing that my mother had been gone for a long time. I had not noticed because I had been coveting the Virgin. I went back to the house.

Jessica tilted her head slightly and focused her skew eyes on me. I had not seen her standing in the doorway, slim and graceful (she was so beautiful), watching me.

"What are you sniffing around for? Does something smell bad?" She seemed anxious.

"Not in here," I replied. "I was just smelling. Smelling to see where my mother has gone."

"You funny, funny child," she said, wrapping her precious arms around me. I pretended to squirm. "What else can that incredible snout of yours sniff out? Can you smell where your father is?"

I was surprised, because she didn't understand me at all. I looked at her and saw an odd dullness in her pretty face.

"It doesn't happen with my nose," I tried to explain. "It happens inside somewhere, same as when Daddy and I go to the moss garden. I don't see it with my eyes."

She regarded me with a slight frown shadowing her eyes and making her face sulky.

"What moss garden?"

"Secrets."

I smiled sweetly at her and she lost her frown and said, "Don't you trouble your pretty little head about your inner eyes and ears, you are much too young for such worries."

She coaxed me into helping her make sandwiches, which was easy because I loved doing anything with her. But she still did not know what I meant.

I sought out my mother after that. I lavished attention upon her, for I felt that I had betrayed her. I betrayed her with my unholy, selfish love for the Virgin. I placated her with tokens of love, with tea and wild flowers picked along the road to the beach. I feared that the Blessed Mary would not be pleased that in my heart of hearts I had turned my love from my flesh mother to another. My guilt was augmented by my jealousy of her chosen children, and because I denied her my love yet begrudged her theirs. As my guilt grew so her nocturnal visits to the township increased.

"There's so much fear out there, you couldn't imagine it, Evie. You're a lucky, lucky girl. I remember being so poor that my hunger nearly drove me insane. We were like wild flowers growing on the side of the road."

I resented my mother's childhood poverty. I resented her hunger and I resented being made to feel guilty about not being hungry.

"You could so easily have been one of those children, look at Auntie Carmelita, the way her children run around, that's the inmates ruling the asylum. So you just be grateful that you're not like them. You think about that if it makes you sad when I go out at night."

It did not make me sad when she went out at night. I was jealous but not sad, because her absence set my nights free. I would stare at the midnight sea; I would walk the moss garden with my father.

I sought her greedily with endless cups of tea and awkwardly asked her how her day had been – did she not think the weather was fine for this time of year? – smoothed her hair, kissed her cheek with my Judas lips and fussed about her as much as Jessica did.

And she would be propped in her chair, my mother, my failed heroine, and I would talk and talk and she would say, "Not now, Evie, I'm tired, tired," and my guilt would grow and I would leave unhappy yet relieved. Her eyes would hold mine and she would say, "Thanks Evie," and the guilt grew and grew because there was trust and affection in her eyes, doggy brown eyes that I did not want to love.

Those eyes changed one day and she became cross. Her breath was thin and tinny, like she did not want to take air in, let air out. The tedium of breathing seemed to offend her, so she resisted it. That was when she started smoking cigarettes. She took some of Jessica's cigarettes, shrugged like Jessica and laughed.

"Makes breathing interesting," she tittered. "Besides, we're all going to die anyway," she cackled, looking at the danger signs on the box. She laughed and laughed but it was a cross laugh.

It crept out of the silences, was born between a glance held, then turned away. This guilt would not be contained. It was in the air as plain as the tingling cold of sunny winter days. It kept me awake those cold August nights. So cold that my fingers would ache as I lay awake, feeling the ice in the walls, the breathing of the house, the numbness of my mother's nocturnal absences. I sighed and turned the other cheek, hoping to find sleep with my back to the wall, then my face, then my back again.

There is no rest for the wicked.

"Be a good girl," my father had said as he kissed me that night. "Be a good girl for your old father."

He kissed me again and pulled the covers up to my chin. When he got up from the bed, the mattress rose as the weight lifted. I felt safe then, as the rain and wind struck down on the roof.

It was still raining as I lay staring at the ceiling in the small hours of the morning.

There is no rest for the wicked.

Sighing an old woman's sigh, I kicked my tired sore legs to the right, the side where I always raised myself from the bed. I wandered to the kitchen seeking leftovers from the Virgin's dinner, because I was famished. Trying to be the good child exhausted me and then left me sleepless. I could hear my father snoring. He sounded like a wailing wolf. I was surprised that he slept. When I wandered around the rooms at night, I felt the alertness of a house that did not slumber nor sleep.

I found the Virgin in her kitchen. She was eating. She stuck her fork into the mince and rammed it into her mouth. Again and again she stuffed forkfuls into her mouth, sometimes pausing to mix the mince with spaghetti, her delicate fingers swiftly swirling it around the fork. The apple-pie dish lay empty before her.

When she looked up and saw me, spaghetti was hanging down the side of her mouth, from those sweet red lips. She let go of the fork. She seemed embarrassed, but she had no need to be because I knew that she had been fasting. The Virgin often fasted to deny herself the pleasures of the flesh. I admired her for that because I could not fast no matter how hard I tried. But looking at her with spaghetti on her chin and mince on her white nightgown, I felt ill. Surely she would make herself sick, eating like that. She looked up and saw me, and it frightened me because she looked old. The guilt had etched itself there too. I was frightened because I thought that the Virgin was pure. I chased those naughty thoughts from my mind. I chased them until my beloved Virgin seemed young again. Then unbidden, the words came to my mouth.

"There's no rest for the wicked," I said.

My words hurt her; she placed her head in her hands. The guilt was what made me do it, the guilt, it made words come to my mouth. My secret joy at releasing suppressed words sank into my flesh and I felt my skin tauten. My hands were wet so I wiped my mouth, but it would not be clean. When she left the room, my mind screamed for her mercy, for forgiveness. She did not hear me; she took none of that with her. I sat in her chair and waited and waited.

I longed for my mother then. I longed to press my burning face, my wet nose into her trousers and sob. I wanted her to leave her bed at night and come to me and to choose me as her child and I would choose her as my mother and the guilt would go away and we would be happy. I went to where I knew I would find some of her.

The schoolroom door creaked slightly and my white slippers upon the cold cement floor made a featherlight crunch. I stood in the dark waiting to feel her and the children, waiting for sounds that were long gone. I crossed my arms around myself and waited. And then they came to me – the sighs, the hushed tinkles of laughter, the moans and the whimpers. The room was drenched in sorrow. I listened excitedly as the ghosts of yesterday came to me. The sounds grew less and less faint. They were calling to me. The shadows started taking shape and I saw that everything had fallen into a woven mass, a moving tapestry in the corner of the schoolroom. I saw my mother as a she-wolf, her hair tangled and glowing, licking her young ones, her tongue moving over furry flesh. I wanted to join her pack and have her lick my sins away. I moved towards them, then stopped, for the shadows changed again. My mother now had Jessica's face, an unfamiliar Jessica face with enormous slanted glowing eyes, feral biting teeth that dipped to the whimpering flesh beneath her. My mother was gone.

"Mommy?" I whispered. "Mommy?" It was shrill and anxious. I did not know what magic I had conjured.

"Mommy?"

Everything stopped moving. The tapestry froze and then unravelled.

And then I saw them. I had not imagined the moving tapestry in the corner of the schoolroom, nor had I imagined Jessica licking the furry flesh. As my eyes accustomed themselves to the dim light, I saw that it was my father with Jessica. They were clumsily covering their bodies, hiding themselves, and I thought that was silly – I had seen it all before. But I had not known that he shared the moss garden with her. I left the garage. I heard them calling after me and I walked away.

Mary Watson was born in Cape Town, South Africa. Her collection of interlinking stories, *Moss* (Kwela 2004), explores themes of innocence, human cruelty, loss and belonging, distorted through the prism of apartheid Cape Town. Watson is currently lecturing Film Studies at the University of Cape Town where she received a Meritorious Publication award for *Moss*. She completed her Master's degree in Creative Writing under the mentorship of Andre Brink in 2001, and studied Film and TV production at Bristol University in 2003. Her film, writing and research interests all arise from an obsession with stories and with alternative ways in which reality can be represented through art. She has contributed several short stories to published anthologies (including in translation in Afrikaans and German). She is currently working on her first novel and on a collaborative novel together with a group of other South African authors.

The Last Trip

Sefi Atta

THIS TIME, HE WANTS her to deliver a hundred and twenty-seven balloons of heroin to London. He counts them on her table to make sure there is no question about the number. The balloons are multicoloured, a little smaller than her thumb. She is capable of swallowing every one of them, but she bargains for extra pay, a thousand US dollars more.

"I'll do it for five," she says.

She speaks in broken Yoruba because she has to be careful about eavesdroppers. The room she rents for her trips has thin walls. It contains the wooden table, a couple of collapsible iron chairs, and a new mattress that smells vaguely like urine because she sweats more than usual on the nights before she travels. Her son, Dara, is asleep on the mattress, face up. He rubs the eczema patches around his eyes and wheezes. A miniature oscillating fan blows dust over him. She has considered leaving her windows open to give him some relief. The heat indoors is unbearable, but the air in this part of Lagos has a sour taste. For now, she is more worried about sounds that escape her room. Even on afternoons like this, with the horns and engines of the traffic on nearby streets, she can hear her neighbours talking. She guarantees they are listening. They know she has a man in her room.

"Since when five?" he asks.

He goes by the name of Kazeem. He has a lisp that is amusing, potentially. In the past, he has hired killers to dispose of difficult couriers, couriers who have double-crossed him. After thirteen years of loyalty to their organisation, she is not worried about the consequences of betrayal. She is scared of him the way people are of little dogs that jump and bite. His eyes are a sickly shade of pink and the sun seems to have roasted him, the fat in his body melting to oil. His skin is too shiny and clings to his bones. The veins in his arms protrude. He crunches on kola nut and occasionally stops to smack his lips. This habit of his irritates her.

"You can't just demand five like that," he says.

"Why not?" she asks, sitting up. "My life is not worth five?"

She is taller than he is, robust, especially with the brocade boubous she favours for international flights. They give her stomach enough space to expand and make her chest look as sturdy as a shelf. Many times before, she has concealed bags strapped around her torso. She eats well to keep her weight up, bleaches her skin with hydroquinone creams to freshen her complexion. In her latest passport photograph she appears much younger than she is, and can pass for her fake age. Her alias is Simbiyat Adisa.

He sucks a piece of kola nut out of his teeth. "I pay you in kind, nothing more."

"No!" she says, waving her hand. "Not in kind!"

She tells him in a whisper, even though he already knows this about her, that she does not push drugs.

He shrugs. "So, it's four as usual."

"Five," she repeats, spreading her fingers.

The man sees her as walking storage. He will pay her more only if she swallows more.

"Take it or leave it," he says. "There are many where you came from."

She is one of his best. He will have trouble finding anyone willing to swallow this many balloons. He is testy because last week the drug law agency arrested more of his couriers at Murtala Mohammed Airport. These ones did not even make it past check-in. They were novices, 200-gram mules. He has had to drop his prices because of seizures like this, and is trying to sell more within Nigeria now, but wealthy Nigerians are not easy to hook: they get high on Mercedes Benzes. He wants to target their children who depend on pocket money, or the masses that would have to give up their meals for one hit.

She has seen addicts like this in her neighbourhood. One walks around the marketplace naked and scratches his crotch. Street hawkers pack up and run when he begs for food. Heroin makes people mellow, Kazeem says, but the rumour is that when this addict can't find a little to lace his hemp, he shivers as if he has malaria and vomits on himself. He will steal from his own mother to buy an ounce. What will he do to a stranger?

"Use the boy if you want more money," Kazeem says, "I will pay you well for that. It is not as if he will know what he is carrying, with his mental condition, and no one will bother to check him at the airports. You'll see."

She taps the table. He has never had tact. "This is between me and you," she says. "Never mention my son again."

* * *

Kazeem leaves her room muttering about her audacity. Everyone is making life difficult for him of late: his couriers, the drug law agency in Lagos, his shippers in Bangkok, the Turks in London, Colombians in New York. The entire universe is conspiring to make life difficult for him and deprive him of business.

There was a time when he would brag that their organisation was the largest in Africa, that he had established their trade routes from Thailand. He even claimed to have taken over South Africa after apartheid, colonised the whole country with cocaine, he said, and spread heroin use in countries as far off as Russia, New Zealand, South Korea and Saudi Arabia. She used to be in awe when she didn't know a poppy seed from an Asian brown or white. Then she discovered that Kazeem was just a middleman, and not even a high level one at that.

He reports to bigger men in their organisation, and fears them. He is rich in naira terms, but they are wealthy in foreign exchange, these men. Barons they are called. She calls them cheats out of common sense rather than a sense of moral superiority. The balloons she carries are worth over a thousand times more than the amount Kazeem pays her, and packed with a pretty consistent mix. At a time like this, when he needs reliable couriers, if she travels with half a million dollars of heroin in her stomach, is it too much to ask for five thousand?

"Foolish man," she says.

* * *

She drinks a bottle of Swan Water to settle her stomach, and lies next to Dara. His body is warmer than hers. Every drop of water she has had seems to be leaking out of her pores. Is she menstruating early or falling sick? She pats her neck to monitor her temperature and checks her watch. The minute the hour hand reaches twelve, she gets up and pours palm oil into a plastic bowl; then she dips each balloon in before putting them into her mouth.

She has to be cautious with the oil: too much might get her stomach juices going again and dissolve the latex. The balloons are bulky to swallow. They block her ears as they go lower, and hurt her chest, so she pauses in between to rest. All things considered, they are easier to get down her throat than the surgical glove fingers she trained with, and anyway, it is like losing virginity: eventually one becomes accustomed.

When she first started swallowing, she would gag as if someone was strangling her. Her nose would stream with mucus and her eyes would well up with tears. Kazeem would yell, "You'd better keep it down!" If she threw up, he would remind her of how he had given her a plane ticket, passport and spending money, handed her a suitcase and driven her to the airport. He sent her to Douala, Accra and then to Amsterdam. She travelled with Indian hemp back then. When Indian hemp became less profitable, he gave her cocaine. Heroin is popular these days. He calls it the big H or H, depending. She swallows the last of the balloons. Her stomach is bloated and hard, as if she has been constipated for weeks.

When Dara gets up, his height overwhelms her, and so does his heavy breathing. Her room is not meant for two. There is not enough space to have a private thought, or smell.

As he dresses, she notes the hairs above his upper lip and in his armpits. He has muscles like a teenager but still has the heart of a child. He sobs whenever she travels, does not like staying with his grandmother, and even his grandmother will not keep him this time. "Take him to his father's," she said, clapping her arthritic hands. "After all they're both men. Go on. I can't control him anymore. Let his father take responsibility for him... for a change." In her desperation, she left her mother's house and headed for her ex-husband's to ask if he would look after Dara while she was away. That one stood in his doorway, in his dirty string vest and said, "Don't bring that boy anywhere near me! He's not mine!" She explained that Dara had never been on a plane, and she was nervous about how he might cope. "I told you," he said, finally acknowledging Dara, "to let the nurses smother him." She cursed him. His new wife, barely twenty years old, and pregnant again, ran out of the house, and pleaded on her knees, "Ni suru," have patience.

Patience she has: she had no home or job when the man threw her out days after Dara was born. She was almost considering prostituting herself when Kazeem came along. She taught Dara how to dress himself, feed himself and helped him to adapt to his handicapped school. She was there when he learnt how to weave baskets and kick a football. This month, she has been training with him for his favourite event on sports day, an obstacle race, parent and child. They run through hoops and jump over buckets. He wants to win every time and jeers at the losers. His headmistress is delighted with his academic progress. His report sheet is full of teachers' comments like: "Omodara is an exemplary student" and "Omodara is a credit to our school." She will continue to work for Kazeem to make sure Dara remains a student there. The school is not one of those where teachers beat or neglect their students. They are Christian-based; evangelical. They believe in the healing power of prayer, but their fees are expensive.

* * *

It is early evening, and the sky bleeds a light shade of orange. She leaves her room with Dara carrying only a handbag, inside of which are their passports and plane tickets. The car that will take them to the airport is parked outside the gates of the tenement, a Peugeot 504 that reeks of lemon air-freshener. The driver informs her that her suitcase is in the boot. She doesn't look too long at his face, in case he is one of those who don't approve of women couriers. She does notice how he stares at Dara.

"BA," she says, startling him.

"British Airways," he confirms.

They drive over potholes, past rubbish piles almost as tall as palm trees. The houses are mostly unpainted. The gutter that runs parallel to the road is thick with slime that resembles boiling tar. Pedestrians cross over it on wooden planks leading to their cement verandas. Street hawkers have already perched kerosene lanterns on their stalls on the roadsides, ready for the night market. Children walk around barefoot. A group of old men have gathered to play a game of ayo. One of them, his eyeglasses secured with Sellotape, cries out in triumph. A rooster flaps its wings and scampers.

The driver continues to sneak peeks at Dara through his rearview mirror. He takes the Third Mainland Bridge to the airport and drops them off in the parking lot. One good thing about the new government is that they have cleaned up the place. The last government was lax; the airport was teeming with touts, from the parking lot to the departure gates. She would have to forge her way through crowds, and was always worried about being mugged.

Now, the police have erected barriers, and they patrol the airport with guns. They will stop anyone who attempts to cross the barriers without evidence to prove that they are travelling, or accompanying someone who is. The drug agency is also on the lookout, but Kazeem worries more about them than she does. Couriers who get caught look like they are couriers: they appear desperate for a start. One eyeball from an official and they begin to twitch.

They don't lack guts; they lack imagination. She always ties her headscarf with the aplomb of a Lagos fabric trader, wears conspicuous colours. Her flamboyance helps her to get through passport control and customs. Dara's presence can do her no harm either, since people are too busy gaping at him.

What she fears most are flight delays. An hour is nothing to worry about, two hours and her heartbeat will rise; three, and they will leave the departure gates and find their way back home. She knows couriers who have convulsed and died when balloons burst inside them. That is why she refuses to travel Nigerian Airways. British Airways flights are fairly timely.

* * *

Dara keeps playing with the rope that leads to the check-in desk. "Please," she says. "Leave that thing alone for heaven's sake."

25

People are looking at him as if he is unearthly. His hand drops immediately. One warning is usually all he needs.

Customs officers ahead are preoccupied with a teenage boy who is travelling business class. They open his suitcase and ruffle his belongings, mostly jeans and T-shirts. The only questionable items they can find are two small ebony carvings.

"Have you got written permission for dis?" one customs officer asks.

"Pardon?" The boy says in an English accent.

"Have you got written permission?"

"Why would I need written permission?"

"You're not allowed to travel with national antiquities."

"But I bought them at Hotel Le Meridien. Daddy?"

The boy waves at a grey-haired man who has been talking to a woman at the first class check-in desk. The man is definitely his father. The father has a pot-belly and the boy is lanky, but they have the same prominent widow's peak.

"What's going on?" the man asks the customs officer.

The boy explains. The customs officer fidgets with the carvings. Perhaps he thought the boy was alone and could get away with hustling him.

"Come on," the boy's father says. "They're just souvenirs."

The customs officer shakes his head. "They're national antiquities, sah."

"I don't believe this," the boy says. "Book ends?"

"He is a student," his father says. "He is going back to school. Now, see how you've scattered his suitcase for no reason, eh? They're common souvenirs for tourists. You can even buy them here at the airport. What is wrong with you people? The work you're supposed to do, you don't do. The one you're not supposed to do, you do, eh?"

"I'm following directives," the customs officer mumbles.

He has to be careful. He doesn't know whom he is addressing. The elite are so well-connected that if this man is not someone important, he will certainly know someone who is.

The commotion is convenient for her. She checks in without scrutiny. The customs officer, still sore about his dressing down, beckons impatiently. "Step forward," he says, and then lifts his hand and orders, "Step back."

Customs checks are not for drugs, or terrorist weapons, or precious artwork anyway. They are for bush meat, stock fish, smoked herring, live snails and all the other foods that people slip in their luggage, knowing that they are prohibited overseas.

* * *

Between passport control and the gate, she loses sight of the boy with the book ends. He is probably in a special lounge, not in the row of seats by the gates with faulty air-conditioning. There are two Nigerias, after all, two ways to enter and two ways to leave: one for people with a lot of money, and the other for everyone else.

She stops at the airport café to buy Dara a cold Maltina and tells him he deserves one for being good. He laughs; he loves to be praised.

A waitress, in an over-sized waistcoat and trousers that are too tight, pours his Maltina into his glass. Dara claps to congratulate himself, and then spits out froth after his first gulp.

"Behave yourself," she says, as she pays the waitress. "You're not a baby anymore."

The waitress says through her nose, "Burt it is nort his fault."

She does not defend herself. First of all, does this waitress imagine she is living overseas because she works in an airport? Why else would she speak with such an odd accent? And who is she to judge? If she cares so much for the handicapped, doesn't she wonder why there are so few of them around, or is there a special country for them too? Stray dogs are more prominent in Nigeria.

"He's making a mess," she says.

Dara knows how to behave in school to impress his teachers. He knows how to frustrate his grandmother so that she will tire of him. He certainly knows how to get the attention of a pretty girl.

"Burt he's nort doing it on purpose," the waitress insists.

"He is an intelligent boy. He knows exactly what he is doing."

Showing off, she thinks, womanizing like his father. Just wait. Wait until he grabs that high backside of yours, then you will know why I discipline him.

* * *

Their flight boards twenty minutes late. She stops sweating as soon as the air-conditioning on the plane is on full blast. They settle in two window seats by the left wing. Across the aisle, a bald man clears his throat and snorts. She helps Dara to fasten his seatbelt and then loosens hers.

If she presses her stomach hard enough, she can feel the balloons. She must not eat or drink, and since the flight attendants are on the look out for passengers who don't, she will have to switch her tray with Dara's. He can easily eat enough for two. Normally, she hides portions of her meals in her handbag and flushes them down the toilet. For now, she watches Dara as he studies the signs: exit, no smoking, and then the long line of heads ahead.

The most trying part of being his mother is the guessing – not prompting him

27

to feed and dress himself, not his allergies and ointments and wayward limbs, not even trying to restrain him whenever he gets excited over women. Just as she thinks she has a good sense of what is going on in his mind, it tightens and shuts her out like a knot.

He is fascinated not frightened as the plane takes off. The sky is pure indigo. Soon she is able to see the horizon, and the flight attendants walk down the aisles to offer drinks. Tonight, they are serving beef stew or tarragon chicken for dinner. The smell reminds her of baking meat pies. Her mouth waters. The passengers behind her choose the chicken. A flight attendant, blonde with coral lipstick, asks in a chirpy voice, "Chicken or Beef?"

She chooses the chicken for herself and the beef for Dara. He plays with his fork. She makes a show of helping him to lift the foil cover of his packed meal. Close up, the beef smells like a burp.

The bald man across the aisle protests, "I specifically requested a meal without salt."

"Give me one moment," the attendant says.

"I specifically requested," the man says even louder. "No salt."

"Just a moment, please," the attendant says in a pleasant voice, as if she is speaking to a wilful child.

"For medical reasons," he says and snorts.

The attendant turns to her with a conspiratorial smile and asks, "All right?"

"Oh, yes," she says.

Distractions are perfect for her. Dara is gobbling carrots. The attendant tilts her head as if she is observing a puppy.

"He's got a good appetite, hasn't he?" she says.

"Oh, yes."

You with your skinny self, she thinks, just don't lean too far over him if you know what is good for you.

The attendant carries on up the aisle. She exchanges Dara's beef for her chicken and whispers, "Well done. When you finish, we'll go to the toilet before you sleep."

* * *

He pees on the toilet seat and forgets to wash his hands. She sends him back in and he does as she tells him, but emerges with his head bowed. She ignores his sulky face and follows him down the aisle.

As usual, she bites off corners of the blanket bags before tearing them open. She spreads his blanket over him, and hers over her lap. Dara raises his over his head. She lowers the window shutter, places her pillow against it and shuts her eyes.

He begins to snore and she realizes how long it has been since she's had company on a flight. In the days of cocaine, Kazeem would fill a plane with carriers. Sometimes, twenty of them would be on board, smuggling in their luggage, in their clothing, or in their stomachs. Kazeem recruited grandparents, government officials, mothers travelling with their children. In those days, whenever a courier was caught, it caused a scandal. The newspapers would go wild with their reports – "An Epidemic of Drug Mules," and such. There was the case of the woman who stuffed cocaine in her dead baby and cradled the baby as if it was sleeping, and the other case of the society woman who swore she thought she was carrying diamonds. That woman had been smuggling when British Airways was British Caledonian, when British Caledonian was BOAC. Princess so-and-so, famous for cramming a condom of cocaine into her vagina.

These days, Kazeem sends only one courier per flight. He uses just as many men as women, and oyinbos from England and America. The oyinbos are rarely stopped. He pays them twice as much, and will use children as mules with their parents' consent. There was that eleven year-old boy who was caught at La Guardia with God knows how many grams of heroin in his stomach. The boy was charged as a juvenile. In England, Kazeem said, the boy would have been handed over to social services and placed with foster parents. "The English are more civilized," he said, "far more advanced than the Americans when it comes to these matters."

He makes assurances like "Confess if you're caught and they'll give you a lighter sentence," or "They have no space in their prisons. They will deport you back home," and oh, oh, his best one is, "They're not looking for people like you after 9/11."

So many of his own couriers have ended up as John or Jane Doe of No Fixed Abode. One was stopped at Heathrow and sent to Holloway Prison for her first offence. She discovered a whole community of Nigerians there. Another was stopped at JFK. She refused an x-ray, so federal agents chained her to a bed and waited for her bowels to move. She got five years with no probation. Then there was that other man, Lucky or Innocent something or the other, who, after spending time in an American prison, was deported, only to spend another nine years in Kirikiri Maximum Security before he was pardoned. He came out swinging his hips like a woman, eventually died of tuberculosis. She has heard of other couriers who were executed by firing squad in Nigeria, publicly beheaded in Saudi Arabia. Granted, none of them are flying angels, but given their work hazards, five thousand is not too much to ask for.

She sighs and shifts her headscarf to a more comfortable position. After this trip, she can afford to pay her rent. It is paid two years in advance. Her carburettor needs to be replaced, or so her mechanic says. She does not move in circles where last year's iro and buba are no longer fashionable, but she does like to take care of herself. She will buy herself some lace and a few silk scarves, maybe matching shoes and bags from Liverpool Street Market. Of course, she has Dara's school fees to consider first, but in less than twelve hours, she will have earned more money than most Nigerian women spend in a year. She has often wondered what it would be like to be one of those who come to England to work. She sees them at Gatwick Airport, on the Gatwick Express and at Victoria Station, walking with the same hurried gaits, and recognises them by the shapes of their lips and noses. They are all jacketed up like English potatoes and their skin and hair are dried up from the cold. They have more education than she has. Some are even university graduates, but how legitimate can their work be if they are living here illegally?

No, to come and go as she pleases is still the better option for her, even if she ends up spending one night in some cold hotel in North London, with a narrow staircase and worn-out carpet, in a room that doesn't have enough corner space to lay her suitcase down. When she gets there, she will take a dose of laxatives, and hopefully pass the balloons before her contacts arrive. She is humiliated by their expressions whenever they have to wait for her to finish up in the bathtub. She herself cannot stand the smell, or sight, as she rinses her faeces off. She wonders who would smoke a substance, knowing that it has come out of a stranger's bowels, or sniff it up their noses, or inject it into their blood.

She doesn't expect sympathy from the world like the addicts who waste their money getting high. But each trip she makes she plays with death; each trip is her last, until the next. So she, too, is dependent on the drugs she carries. She, too, is living with a habit, after all.

Dara keeps elbowing her, Mr. No Salt across the aisle continues to snort. She has several more hours to go, and wonders what it would be like if the plane were to crash and she never has to work again.

* * *

After midnight she falls asleep. She dreams of death by plane crash, car accident; sees herself drowning in Lagos Lagoon, Dara peering over the Third Mainland Bridge, and her mother unable to stop him from slipping in because her hands are so crooked from old age they look like a couple of crabs.

When she wakes up it is breakfast time. The lights are on and the attendants are walking down the aisles again. Her eyes are swollen and sore. She shakes

Dara's shoulder and he coughs.

"Take it easy," she says rubbing his back.

The air-conditioning is no good for his lungs. She checks his socks are still on. The blonde attendant stops by them with a trolley and offers two trays of food and half a smile. Her lipstick has faded.

"Had a good rest?" she asks bending over Dara.

Dara reaches up and pulls her hair. She struggles to free herself. He drags her lower. She pries his fingers apart and straightens up with a red face.

"Gosh," she says. "He's got quite a grip there, hasn't he, Mum?"

"Sorry," Mum says. Maybe now you'll leave him alone, she thinks.

The attendant smoothes her hair back. As soon as she rolls the food trolley past them, Mum hands her sticky pastry to Dara, and then raises the window shutter.

The ground below looks like geometric shades separated by green bushes. Roads curve through clusters of red brick homes. From the ground level, the red brick homes are the colour of dried dirt, a few of them defaced with graffiti, and their gardens are so tiny, so chinchini. She would not like to live in England. She wants to remain here, above the country, suspended.

Dara eats his pastry after hers. The blonde attendant collects their trays and is more careful about keeping her distance. In no time at all the pilot announces they are about to begin their descent.

"Nn," Dara moans when the plane dips.

"Hm," she responds in his language.

Taking off is easier than landing. She clutches her armrest and braces herself. The balloons in her stomach feel as if they are about to drop.

* * *

Only Nigerian passengers clap and cheer when the plane lands with a bump, she is certain of this, and they also get up and remove their hand luggage from the overhead compartments before the seat belt signals are switched off. At Gatwick Airport there is a rush, as usual, through the corridors towards passport control. She would like to keep up with the rest, but Dara lags behind. He is preoccupied with the clusters of trolleys, and the lit signs saying emergency exit, arrivals and baggage reclaims.

They reach the hall and join the long queue. Her heart beats on her eardrums and she tries to focus on a sign to keep calm: We. Take. Extremely. Seriously. Any. Attempt. To. Inti. Midate. Our. Staff. Either. By. Threats. Or Assaults. We take. Extremely seriously. Any attempt. To intimidate. We take extremely seriously. Any attempt to intimidate...

She takes hold of Dara's hand, just in case it strays again. When they stop at the line on the floor that they can't cross over, she mentally pokes fun at the man behind the immigration booth so she can speak to him with confidence. The man's head is shaped like a boiled egg. His cheeks are as blotchy as half-ripe paw-paws. His mouth is no bigger than a kobo coin.

"Morning," she says, looking at his forehead.

"How long will you be staying?" he asks.

"Too weak..."

"Sorry?"

"Too. Weak."

"Two weeks?"

She nods. This one can't understand her. She herself finds it difficult to decipher what oyinbos are saying especially when their mouths are as small as his, but he enunciates as the flight attendant had.

"What is the purpose of your trip?"

"Holiday."

"Visiting friends or family?"

"Friends."

He stamps their passports after a few generic questions. She has found that white immigration officers are more lenient than blacks, and men are more lenient than women are.

"Have a nice stay," he says, nodding at Dara.

"Thank you," she says.

Again, she has to remind herself to take even breaths. At Baggage Reclaims, she concentrates on the carousel to avoid making eye contact with those on surveillance. Her clothes don't matter because they can't differentiate between Nigerians. They can only rely on telltale signs like shiftiness and sweating.

She is sweating again, under her arms. People continue to break from the crowd around the carousel to retrieve their luggage. She panics when she doesn't see hers. She will not make this journey again, she tells herself. She should not and cannot. Her nerves will not survive another trip.

"Wait for me," she says to Dara.

She walks around the carousel to stop her legs from trembling, and spots her suitcase with a pink and grey tapestry pattern. She reaches for it, as if it is drifting down a river, and grabs the handle. The suitcase is lighter than she recalls and she loses her balance. She backs into someone, and discovers it is Dara.

"I told you to wait," she says, without raising her voice.

She is not upset. He has been the perfect diversion. Here in England, people glance rather than stare at him, as if they would rather be fake than rude, but he is shivering. Is he nervous or just cold?

"What?" she asks, leading him away from the carousel. "What is it?"

She is using the opportunity to check that there are enough people passing through Nothing to Declare. Two customs officers are on duty. One of them steps forward and her heart beats so loud it deafens her: *please, not now, not us.*

The customs officer stops someone else behind them. She takes steady steps before she is round the corner, and is relieved to see the shop, the one with all the colourful socks. They walk into the crowd on the other side, past people who are waiting for arriving passengers. An elderly woman kneels to embrace a toddler. A row of men display hand-written name cards. Dara raises his fists and cheers. Everyone watches as he runs a victory lap and returns to her.

"Iwo," she says, shaking her head: You.

This is the last time she will travel with him, but he has given her so much trouble she has almost forgotten hers. He claps as if he knows she is pleased with him, and she is glad he has no idea why.

Sefi Atta was born in Lagos, Nigeria. She trained as an accountant in London and began to write while she was working in New York. She is a graduate of the creative writing program at Antioch University, Los Angeles, and has won prizes from Zoetrope (3rd prize, Short Fiction Contest, 2002), Red Hen Press (1st prize, Short Story Award, 2003) and the BBC (2nd prize, African Performance for plays, 2002 and 2004). In 2005, she was awarded PEN International's David T K Wong Prize and her debut novel entitled *Everything Good Will Come* was published (Arris Books, England, Interlink Publishing, USA, Double Storey Books, South Africa and Farafina Books, West Africa). She has just written her second novel, entitled *Swallow*. She lives in Mississippi with her husband Gboyega Ransome-Kuti, a medical doctor, and their daughter, Temi, and teaches at Mississippi State University.

A Joburg Story

Darrel Bristow-Bovey

"WHAT'S THIS STREET CALLED?" said Rob.

We looked at the street and then we looked at Rob.

"Seventh," I said.

"I know seventh," said Rob. "Obviously seventh. Seventh what?"

We thought about that. It was a good question. "Seventh Street," said Mershen. "The streets go down, avenues go across."

"Right!" said Rob triumphantly. "But then why's that programme called *Sewende Laan*? *Laan* means avenue!"

"Maybe it's a different sewende laan," I suggested.

"No!" said Rob, more triumphant. "At the credits, they show *this* street." He jabbed his finger streetwards. "In fact, the overhead shot starts just about exactly *there*."

"So what's it, then? Seventh Avenue?"

"I don't know," said Rob. "That's why I'm asking."

"When we go," I reasoned, "one of us can walk up and see what the sign says."

"Good idea," said Rob.

"Not me," said Mershen. "I'm parked down the road."

"Me too."

"Me too," said Rob, which seemed to more or less end the conversation.

"Maybe," said Mershen slowly after a while, "the Seventh Avenue on *Sewende Laan* isn't supposed to be a real street. Maybe it's a fictional street that just *looks* like this street."

"Mmm," said Rob.

"Uh," I said, and with that we took another drink.

There was nothing very unusual about that night. We were out too late at the Ponta Linga Linga, Rob and Mershen and me, and there were no girls left in the place and Seventh Street or Avenue was closing down but we were still drinking

35

more in that tired, sorry way when you think that maybe if you stall a little longer, get a little more drunk, something will happen. That's the thought: if only I were a *little bit more drunk*, something fun might happen.

I know it was a weeknight because we all had work the next day and also because we only ever sat around drinking that late on weeknights. Down the street the other bars were closing and the waiters across the road were putting chairs on tables. Cas was at a table in the corner, talking with some girl who'd seen one of his plays once. The Ponta Linga Linga Bar and Restaurant is Cas's place. We asked him once what Ponta Linga Linga means and he said it's a place in Mozambique, which makes sense because there's a tatty map of Mozambique prestiked to a wall, and a potted banana tree, and a mural of some palms and a beach and there are some Mozambiquan bank notes sticky-taped behind the bar.

If Cas hadn't been talking with that girl who'd once seen one of his plays he'd probably have shooed us out because it was way past closing time. Rob was drunk. I knew Rob was drunk because every time Cleo passed us he looked at her breasts as though it was the first time he'd noticed them. Cleo wasn't her real name but everyone called her Cleo because the first night she worked at the Ponta Linga Linga the other waitress's name was Chloe. If that makes any sense to you, you're probably a regular at the Ponta Linga Linga.

So we were sitting there at the bar, just talking a little, and that not much, when the guy came in. He was just a guy, not especially tall, head shaved bald, but he was wearing a kind of oversized shiny tracksuit and that attracted our attention. It was shiny purple and he wore it with new white Nike trainers, so he looked like a drug dealer. Not a real drug dealer, not a Joburg drug dealer, but like in a Spike Lee movie or a rap video. I'd guess we all thought, *Why does this guy want to look like a drug dealer?*

Cleo looked up from wiping a table and said, "Sorry, we're closed."

The guy raised his hands with his palms open toward her and said, but mock shocked: "My sister, no!"

He wore a big smile and he said something to her in Sotho or maybe Sepedi – I know it wasn't Zulu or Xhosa because I know a little Zulu and Xhosa has more clicks – and she said something back in, I suppose, Sotho or Sepedi, and he said something again and she said something again and then she let him in.

He came up next to us at the bar. We nodded and he nodded and Mershen said, "Heita," and the guy nodded again and said " 'ta". I could see Mershen filing that away. Next time, I knew, he would just say " 'ta." The guy ordered a drink and rolled the ice in the glass, looking at it, like you do.

By this time I had lost interest in the guy, but Rob was squinting at him and rubbing his forefinger and his thumb together, like he does when he's trying to think of something.

"Don't I know you?" said Rob. The guy raised his eyebrows.

"I don't think so," said the guy and held out his hand, and they shook hands so we all shook hands. We said "Hi, I'm David" and "Mershen" and "Rob", but he didn't say his name, which I thought was a little bit odd, even then.

"Didn't you work on *The Early, Early Breakfast Show?*" Rob persisted, still squinting. "Don't I know you from there?"

"I'm not in television," said the guy, which made me like him even though he was wearing a shiny purple tracksuit and – I could hardly believe it – around his neck in the open V of his tracksuit a gold chain with big gold links. Now, I'm not trying to be funny, but come on.

"Oh," said Rob. "I thought I knew you from *The Early, Early Breakfast Show.*"

Then I knew he was very drunk, because Rob doesn't ordinarily like people to know he was involved in producing *The Early, Early Breakfast Show. The Early, Early Breakfast Show* was not a success. People laughed at it, but not in a good way. Rob always said that it was the only TV show in the history of TV shows that never got any of its producers laid. It never actually got anyone involved with it laid, which is unusual because in my experience it's not how good the thing is that gets people laid, just whether it was on TV.

So we sat there and drank some more of our drinks. The guy finished his and ordered another with a hand movement that I thought was very cool. Some people are cool – I'm not, and Mershen isn't really and Rob only is sometimes – and this guy was. We didn't say anything for a while, mainly because we'd run out of things to say.

Finally Rob said: "Are you sure you weren't on *The Fast, Fast Breakfast Show?*" Weren't you the guy who dressed up like a piece of toast?" and the guy shook his head with what looked to me like honest regret and said, "Sorry."

"So what do you do?" I asked, to keep the conversation going.

"You should be on TV," said Rob.

The guy just smiled and shrugged and took another sip of his drink. He gulped the first one but this one he sipped. I noticed he had a gold watch. I hadn't seen a gold watch since my father's gold watch. The guy noticed me staring at it while I tried to remember what my father's gold watch looked like.

"Nice watch," I said.

The guy nodded and smiled again. He was a good smiler, it was an easy smile.

"You're not a drug dealer, are you?" said Mershen all jokey, sitting next to Rob, furthest from the guy.

The guy threw up his hands like he did with the waitress. "I'm not from Nigeria," he said and we all laughed, also him.

"Pity," said Mershen and we all laughed again.

We finished our drinks and debated whether we should have another and I said I had to work tomorrow but then the guy ordered drinks for all of us, again just by moving his hand. Ordinarily Cleo likes to pretend she hasn't seen hand movements, especially late at night when she wants to go home, but this time she served up. We looked sneakily at Cas to see if he would object but he was leaning across the table, speaking low to the girl who'd once seen one of his plays. He was touching her hand with his finger, making a point, and I heard him say something – I swear - about deconstructing bourgeois conventions. He glanced at us and looked a bit embarrassed, not because he was touching the hand of a girl who wasn't his girlfriend, but because he thought we might have heard him say something about deconstructing bourgeois conventions. Then he lowered his voice even more.

When a guy buys you a drink you should make some conversation with him, but we didn't really know what to say. I was about to say to Rob, "Why did someone dress up like a piece of toast?", just for conversation, like, when Rob said to the guy, "So if you're not in TV what do you do?"

I thought the guy might get annoyed but he just smiled again, big and easy, and turned sideways to face Rob.

"I do jobs," he said.

"Jobs?" said Rob.

"Right," said the guy.

"Yuh?" said Rob encouragingly.

"Yuh," said the guy.

"What kind of jobs?" said Mershen. It wasn't like any of us to take such an interest in what a guy did for a living, but this guy had a way that made us curious.

"Jobs," said the guy again.

"Jobs, like ...?"

The guy smiled into his glass then he raised it to his nose and sniffed at it.

"I kill people," he said.

I wished he hadn't said that.

In the silence that followed I thought maybe I hadn't heard right, but then I felt a little lurch in my stomach and I thought, *I don't like this guy.* I still think that.

I don't know if any of us really wanted to say anything more, but when someone says something like that you can't just ignore it.

"What sort of people?" said Mershen.

The guy smiled kind of proudly. "Anyone," he said. "All kinds."

I'd had enough of talking to the guy in the shiny purple tracksuit. I don't like that kind of joke. Outside I could hear the car sounds of Seventh emptying and I remembered I had work to do tomorrow and I started to feel tired and my clothes smelt of cigarette smoke.

"Whoever I get told," said the guy.

"Fuck off," I said to that, half like a joke and half meaning he should fuck off. But Rob and Mershen seemed to find him funny.

"You're a hit-man?" whooped Mershen.

The guy shrugged again. Besides smiling, he was also a frequent shrugger.

"So you, what, you get told to, uh, to, uh, to *whack* someone," said Rob, and I don't think he was believing him, but you could see he really liked using the word `whack'. "And then you – what? – you go and you, you *whack* them?"

"Then I go to his driveway and –" he made a gun shape with his forefinger and thumb and jerked his wrist to indicate the recoil. "Like a hijack."

By now Mershen wasn't finding the joke funny either. He frowned and leant back on his stool. But Rob, gee. Rob was drunk.

"So do you know these people?" he asked. "Who you whack?"

"Not at first," said the guy. "But then I get to know them. Watch the house, see when they come, when they go."

I looked around for Cleo to call for the bill but she must have been outside in the stockroom.

"Sometimes," said the guy, "I meet them before."

"You meet them?"

"Pass them on the street, sure, maybe ask directions. I like meeting them before. To get a –" the guy rubbed his palms together in a circle, "a feeling." He looked across at Rob.

"Look," I said to Rob and Mershen, levering myself off my barstool, "I'm going to get going."

"Just wait a minute," said Mershen, "we're going too ..."

"I'm not listening to this."

"Just hang on a second, let me finish my drink and we'll ..."

"Sometimes," said the guy conversationally, "I maybe bump into them in a bar."

If I could I'd just leave this part blank to show the silence then. It wasn't total silence, there was still Cas's voice low at the table behind us and the sound of Cleo clinking bottles out the back and a car going by outside, going by, going home, but it felt like it. It felt like total silence. We looked at the guy, me and Rob

39

and Mershen.

"What?" I said, not friendly.

"Sometimes I maybe bump into them in a bar. Say hello. Buy drinks." He shrugged and rubbed his palms together, looking at nothing in particular.

"What're you saying?" I felt myself getting properly angry.

He shrugged again.

"No, fuck you, what are you saying?" I said and I stepped toward him so I was standing right over him.

"Dave," said Rob grabbing my arm.

"Fuck you," I said to the guy, and my voice was getting louder. "If you want to say something, *say something*."

I don't usually get aggressive when I drink and I don't usually want to get into fights, which is good because I can't fight, but I wanted to fight this guy. No, I wanted to hit him.

"Hey!" said Cas from his table but I didn't turn around, I kept staring at the guy's face although he wasn't looking back at me, I kept staring at him like maybe Joe Pesci in *Goodfellas* or like one of those Latino gang movies with Edward James Olmos, but I wasn't trying to be like in a movie, I was wanting to hit this guy, just hit him, just keep on hitting him until I couldn't see him any more. The guy just carried on looking away, all casual, and I couldn't tell if it was because he was scared or because he really wasn't. Rob stood up between us and said, "Dave, leave it, leave it," and he steered me down onto his barstool and he sat down on mine. I looked at Mershen and his eyes were open wide but not because of me. He was staring at the guy.

"What *are* you saying?" said Rob, and although he still sounded drunk he sounded a little bit less drunk.

The guy just shook his head and shrugged and raised his hands again, palms open, like to say, "I'm not saying anything, I'm just sitting here."

"So when you get your – your orders," said Rob, all casual, "who are they from?"

"A guy," said the guy, "who gets calls from people."

"What sort of people?"

"People who don't want other people around any more."

"Like what sort of people?"

"People." His eyes flickered. "Say, someone who doesn't like you."

"Me?" said Rob, his voice suddenly very high.

"Anyone."

I thought this was all bullshit and I said so, I said this is bullshit, and Rob looked at me but he looked back at the guy. The skin around Rob's eyes was tight and grey and he was holding his glass so tight his fingertips were white. I hated this. I hated this fucking guy coming into our lives in five minutes and doing this to us, I hated it, because of course it was bullshit, of course it was, but how could you not be scared, this guy in his purple tracksuit, this guy?

"So what do you do after you've bumped into them in a bar?" said Rob softly.

"Sometimes I buy them a drink, and then I go home and then we only meet again one more time."

"And other times?"

"Other times ..." the guy pursed his lips then sucked them then pursed them again. "Other times, sometimes, we make a plan so we don't meet again."

"A plan, like ..."

He spread his hands, just slightly. "I am a businessman."

"For Chrissake!" I said. "We're not listening to this shit."

"How much?" said Mershen.

The guy seemed to be counting something in his head. He said "Six."

"Six?"

"Two each."

"Guys!"

"Is that an offer?" said Mershen.

"Guys!"

"Is that an offer?"

"It's an offer."

It was a nightmare.

"When?" said Rob.

The guy said "Now."

"My ATM limit is a thousand," said Rob.

"Me too," said Mershen. "And I've already drawn today."

"As much as you can now," said the guy. "I'll collect the rest tomorrow."

"From where?"

"I'll come to your house," said the guy and his voice and his eyes were very flat.

"You don't ..." Rob started, then stopped.

"Where you live in Auckland Park," said the guy to Rob. And then: "I won't worry your wife," he said to Mershen.

They just stared at him. Mershen's mouth was slightly open.

"I'll let you decide," said the guy. "Five minutes." He got up and walked out the back door to the little concrete courtyard where the toilets are. He passed

41

Cleo in the doorway and as she came in I asked her for the bill. Behind us at the table Cas and the girl were kissing, leaning into each other, like goldfish. One of Cas's girlfriends once told me he only ever kissed her in public. "He's afraid of intimacy," she said. Rob and Mershen were looking at each other.

"What?" I said when I saw this look going on. "What? You're not!"

They kind of raised their eyebrows and didn't say anything.

"Come on!" I said. "Some fucking guy walks off the street and says he's been hired to kill you and you give him money? What are you, children? Come on!"

"You're very fucking confident," said Rob.

"If some white guy had sat down next to us and said he was a hitman, would you give him a second thought? Guys, now, come."

"I would if he was Eastern European," said Rob, thinking. "Like, Russian, or, you know, Bulgarian."

"Or Lebanese," said Mershen.

"Or that kind of Afrikaner," said Rob, "that kind, like, from Pretoria."

"With blue eyes," agreed Mershen.

"Joost eyes."

"So anyone, basically," I said, "who isn't white and speaks English?"

"Who'd ever choose us to be a hitman? We'd be fucking useless," said Rob, which was a good point.

"I wouldn't believe an Indian guy," said Mershen thoughtfully. "Indian guys, not really."

"I don't know," I said there. "Those guys in Durban who run the clubs, I wouldn't ..."

"Are you telling me I don't know Indian guys?" said Mershen, who is himself an Indian guy.

"You're from Joburg, you prick," I said. "You don't know them in Durban ..."

"Look," said Rob, "what are we going to do?"

"We're not giving him fuck-all," I said. "This is a scammer. He's an actor. He's the guy who dressed up like a piece of fucking toast, and you want to give him money." It pleased me to hear the words I was saying.

"He knows where I live, Dave!"

"And that I'm married!"

"You're wearing a wedding ring, you knob, and as for you, if he worked on *The Early, Early Breakfast Show* he'd easy know where you live. You're always slipping home next door from the set because you've forgotten your cellphone or you're fighting with Leigh-Ann or something."

"You think he planned this?"

"No," I said. "I think he walked in for a drink and saw you and thought, 'Ha, ha, there's a cunt'. I'll tell you this, if you give him money now he's not stupid enough to come to your house tomorrow when you're sober and've thought about it. He'll just go home and laugh with his buddies for the rest of his life about what a cunt you are."

"But what if it's not me who's his job? What if it's you?"

I wished he hadn't said that.

Just for a moment the breath stopped in my chest, just a moment, but for that moment it was harder to fight down what I'd been fighting down, this big thing, this fear that came from nowhere and made me want to cry or beg or something. This wasn't just being afraid, it was *fear*, like something there, something actually inside you you didn't know about, not even a part of you, just using you to come out.

"I'm not his job," I said, "and nor are you. He hasn't got a fucking job, the fuck."

I hated the guy in the purple tracksuit. I'm not an afraid person but now this fear, this *thing*... I couldn't tell if it'd been there all along and he'd woken it or if maybe it's not from inside at all, maybe it runs through this town under our feet and through our skin and the air like dark electricity and this guy just conducted it, just brought it down and focused it in one place. I hated him for it.

"You're right," said Rob.

"Fuck right, I'm right."

But none of us moved. Outside Seventh was dead, the cars were all gone. Seventh is too dark with no people in it, the yellow streetlights aren't enough. I tried to remember the guy's face. If I had to describe him for the police I wouldn't be able to. He was just an impression, a shiny tracksuit, a shaved head, a smile, a pair of spread hands. He was more an idea than a guy.

"You can stay if you like," I said to them. I dropped two hundreds on the bar. "Are you staying?" I said.

Something passed between them.

"No," said Mershen.

Rob got up too and they left money and we all hurried outside onto the dark sidewalk. We stood there a moment, the three of us, and breathed the air.

"Fucking scammer."

"Fuck 'im."

It was dark out there, we couldn't see each other's faces.

"We shouldn't, like ..."

"What?"

"We shouldn't, like, do something? Teach him a lesson?"

"Oh for fuck's sake, who are we? *Teach him a lesson?* We couldn't teach

43

ourselves a lesson. Let's just fuck off."

"Right."

Even in the dark we were looking away from each other, looking at our feet, over our shoulders.

"OK," I said, "my car's down there," and we shook hands like we always do and I took off down the road. I turned at the corner with Second where I'd parked and when I looked back Rob and Mershen were still standing on the sidewalk outside the Ponta Linga Linga. They were standing there, and it looked like they were saying something to each other, then at last they turned and walked together up the road, and I went into Second and found my car and drove home.

It felt good driving home. The lights on the freeway were good and bright and the wide, empty lanes felt safe, like day. It felt good because I'd beaten down the fear. My heart felt light, I thought: *I can live in this town. I've got what it takes.*

But that was a couple of weeks ago and since then my heart's not so light, because the next morning I remembered that conversation I had with Rob and Mershen before the guy came in, about the name of the street and the sign up the road. I remembered that their cars were down the road, the same way as mine, not up the road where they walked. The only thing up the road was the corner café but that was closed, and also the ATM machine and that was still open. And I wondered whether maybe they'd drawn money so that they could buy a pie from the all-night Shell shop on the way home, or just maybe whether they'd taken their money back into the Ponta Linga Linga.

And I know it's nothing, but I haven't spoken to Rob or Mershen since then, or maybe it's that they haven't spoken to me. I've driven past the Ponta Linga Linga a few times and I even went in but I haven't seen the guy again. And the thing is I want to see the guy again because I know it's just the fear but two nights ago when I came home I saw a blue car parked a little way up the street and I don't know if I've ever seen a blue car parked there before, and although it didn't look like there was anyone in it, still I'm thinking maybe of going tomorrow to my bank in Sandton City and drawing out some money and keeping it on me or maybe in that alcove in the dashboard behind the gearstick because, look, I know it's just the fear, I know it's just the fear but it's two grand, right? Right? I mean, what's two grand? What's two grand, anyway?

Darrel Bristow-Bovey was born in Durban, South Africa, in the 1970s. He studied at the University of Cape Town under JM Coetzee and Andre P Brink and worked for three years as editor of children's fiction at a publishing house in Cape Town. He moved to Johannesburg in 1997, where he became television columnist for *The Sunday Independent*, and a popular columnist in a range of publications and on the radio. He has won four Mondi Awards for Best South African Columnist, and has published four books: two books of humour, titled *I Moved Your Cheese* (2001) – which was translated into four languages – and *The Naked Bachelor* (2002); a collection of his columns titled *But I Digress* (2003), and his first book for younger readers, *SuperZero* (2006), which won a 2006 Sanlam Prize for Youth Literature. He currently writes for television, having been head writer on the first three series of the popular South African drama series, *Hard Copy*.

Tracking the Scent
of my Mother

Muthoni Garland

MY FATHER WOOED MY mother in a 1200 Datsun pick-up that was sold so soon afterwards that it must have felt to her like a false promise. Senior-mother, his first wife, whose tight religious clothes constricted her breathing, had already borne him five daughters – Mercy, Charity, Faith, Hope and Grace.

His five acres grazed the River Sagana in Ihwagi, on the outskirts of Karatina, where the old Mountain-of-God loses its shadow. By day my mother tilled the land, and by night my father tilled her. She birthed me and my brother in quick succession.

While my brother scowled at us, or napped on a khanga under the shade of a Mugumo tree, my mother and I washed the family's clothes by the banks of Sagana, whipping them against the rocks in frenzy. If I held back, my mother was just as liable to ignore as launch a slapping attack on me. She was difficult to predict.

She walked with eyes downcast and the sharp wedges of her cheeks on her broad face pointed to squashy lips that she constantly bit to bleeding. Her pleated dresses, passed on by Senior-mother, grazed her ankles. Still she hunched her body as though to further blur the curves. But when roused, my mother unfolded herself and it would come as a shock to realise she was as tall as my father.

After we had spread the washing on large boulders to dry, we would waddle in to the depths, me naked, she in her billowing petticoat. We would stretch our bodies in the water and drift with the current. Even during the rainy season when the rush of water hid the boulders that formed our boundaries, we would dare the current to deliver us past the patchwork of tea, potato, maize and cabbage farms, past the facing ridges of Mukuruweini and Ithanga; beyond the old Mountain-of-God, and further west of the Yatta Plateau where Sagana became the crocodile-infested Tana.

Afterwards, I would dry in the sun while my mother applied soap to her long damp limbs like a lotion. Tucking a khanga around her waist, she would bare her breasts to feed my brother. After a while, I would take off to explore and determine the owner of the hidden eyes staring at us.

My half-sister, Faith, hid behind fig trees and wild-gooseberry bushes, and spied on us. When I caught her spying, she ran away. I chased her. I knew she wanted to steal my mother.

I remember the roar of water during the rainy season, and the rickety plank-and-rope bridge on which Nairobi City relatives swayed and groaned under the weight of the flour, sugar, Tree Top orange squash and Cadbury Cocoa they brought us that last Easter.

I also remember the roar of water during the rainy season, and the rickety plank-and-rope bridge because it was there a couple of years later that I pushed Faith into Sagana's rushing waters. It was not my fault that she had never learnt to swim.

At Easter, our Nairobi city relatives had to park their car on the other side of the river under a roughly constructed awning of sisal sacking. While the men slaughtered a goat by a distant clearing, the women pounded mukimo, gossiped about the latest city fashions – flares and curly-kits, and practised rolling out sentences in the nasal English-English spoken by my cousins.

After the feasting, the men meandered off to baptise a half-drum of muratina, or in the words of Uncle Erasmus, "To partake of the fruit of the hog-dog tree, otherwise known as Kigelia Etiopica."

My father had never been to school because in the old days when leopards and buffaloes roamed, at least one son remained behind to herd the goats and cattle. Uncle Erasmus, a lecturer at a private university in Nairobi, always made the effort to visit and advise us. In his presence, my father chewed his mswaki stick to curtail his tongue, but when Uncle Erasmus was gone, my father said, "Life speaks in proverbs; anyone who is intelligent will understand."

Seventeen-year-old cousin Wangui's stellar KCSE results punctuated her mother's every other sentence. Nobody complained when Wangui slipped a cassette into father's player, tied a khanga around her hips, and wriggled to the spiky notes of Congolese lingala as though attacked by red ants. Of course, I joined her, and discovered that even at six, my limbs were looser than hers.

My mother hovered on the fringes of the group, and her darting eyes kept lighting on me. She laughed that afternoon for all of Karatina, but the hollow in her tone confused me. I did not realise then that my mother was only four years older than Wangui. I didn't understand that a woman who gives birth is like a tall

48

and leafy banana tree that breaks under the weight of its own fruit.

There must have been a time when earnings from tea and four grade cattle were good because my father's house, a rectangle with three rooms, was built with cemented bricks. The veranda, whose sloping roof darkened the rooms inside, served as his lounge and observation point. Sun glinted off the roof, but when it rained the rat-at-tat hammered the corrugated iron sheets, and later, water would sneak its way in through rusted corners. When we looked up during bible meetings, I wondered if the echoes of our deafening prayers for wealth – we were already rich in spirit – would lift the room and float our house to the sky, or if patched gaps in the ceiling would leak their potency.

Senior-mother insisted that, along with her disciplined five, my brother and I attend these services, while my mother tended to more practical demands like cooking.

The mud and cowpat orphan of a kitchen squatted by itself in the furthest reaches of the compound. Stabbing mukimo with a wooden spoon by the fire, my mother hummed funereal hymns, "Woii, woii gugika tia ati ninia datigwo" *Oh dear, what will I do now that I'm the one left behind.*

I would sit by her feet on the hard-packed earth and root out jiggers from her toes with the sharp nib of my father's penknife while she wept. The tears and wood-smoke reddened her eyes, and the stale smell lingered and stiffened her hair, but her singed shins gleamed.

As the river of practical demands – for meat, school fees, clothes, cotton wool..., rushed its course, the veins on my father's forehead throbbed like rustling snake hatchlings. He regularly visited Sagana Co-operative Society and Kenya Co-operative Creameries and The Co-operative Bank of Kenya to beg for his tea and milk dues, and to negotiate for fertiliser, school fees and tide-me-over loans.

When the chairman of the former, in the Nyayo-grabbing tradition of his predecessors, emigrated to South Africa with all the proceeds of the 1988 tea auction, my father broke. That night, and every night for six days, while Senior-mother wailed and beseeched God to let her know how they were going to feed and educate Mercy, Charity, Faith, Hope and Grace, my father cut down every tea bush. He said, "Where there is a shortage of figs, don't birds survive on the bitter fruit of the Mugumo?"

Senior-mother appealed to The Extension Officer when he brought a red tractor to plough the farm because my father wanted even deeper roots uprooted. From his shrug and the eyes he widened at Senior-mother, I sensed The Extension Officer sympathised with her plight. But he cranked the tractor when my father said, "Nobody regrets what he leaves, only what he does not find when he comes back."

Twanging the elastic on our catapults, my brother and I went hunting for birds. We liked to collect the long dark feathers of Widow Bird tails. My brother followed me, and sometimes drove me crazy by claiming he had downed my bird. No matter how much I hit him, he would state, 'I shot it' as though declaring a fact made it true.

When a bird dropped, we would watch it crazily flap or rotate on an injured wing. I cut the neck with the penknife stolen from my father, and plucked off the feathers, gutted the stomach, and cooked the bird in a Blue Band tin over a three-stone fire. We would munch the meagre mouthfuls of meat, and also crunch and swallow the bones.

When my mother stopped working on what became a maize and potato farm, her new happiness was as fascinating and unfathomable as my father's proverbs.

She would plonk herself on a stool in the shade of the compound and thrust in my hands a broken wedge of mirror. Peering into it as though she were a stranger to herself, my mother would style her thick hair using a pick with several missing teeth, and scold me in an indulgent voice for dancing from one foot to the other.

The volume of Senior-mother's complaints and prayers increased as Mercy, Charity, Faith, Hope and Grace dropped in and out of school due to lack of fees. My father sold the cows but the money never lasted. Eventually Mercy left school altogether to work as a maid for an Indian family in Thika. Soon after, Charity eloped with The Extension Officer.

Against the background of Senior-mother's prayers and wailing, my father observed my mother's preening from his veranda perch, and concluded, "Two wives are two pots of poison." But he would then descend and yank my mother by the hand to his room to taste her brand of poison.

I would stop sweeping the compound, and run to our room – the middle one in the line of three that before our time had served as the sitting room. When important visitors came, like the pastor during bible meetings, the stiff and cracking black plastic sofa and its matching chair squashed against the wall, still served their duty.

I'd lie on the Vono mattress, stained with my brother's urine, on the bed we normally shared with my mother. I'd close my eyes, my knuckle rubbing my mound to the squeaking of my father's iron bed behind the wooden door. I'd listen past my father's grunts and the slap of bare skin to hear my mother's gasping.

By twisting my ear, my mother encouraged me to scramble up the overgrown climbers that grew wild on border fences, to fill a debe with wrinkled purple passion fruit. We gouged out the phlegmy insides with spoons she bent into shape for the job, and sieved the black seeds from its dense juice. My mother added water and stirred in the turmeric powder that my half-sister Mercy had brought home on her day off, to intensify the yellow colouring.

Four miles into Karatina we walked, with plastic containers balanced on our heads like Luo women. Trailing behind her, neck throbbing too much to turn, my eyes traced the rise and fall of my mother's big buttocks. I was conscious my eyes were not alone in this enterprise.

At the sausage and chips shop, a Mkorino with a white headscarf tied low on her forehead, sniffed the juice and accused that we'd either diluted it or used unripe fruit. She added that while she did not want to be unreasonable, only God knew the cost of the sugar needed to sweeten the juice would leave her with nothing.

Using a handkerchief drawn from the depths of her bosom, my mother wiped the sweat from her forehead, and let her towering silence do its work. My father would have said, "One keeps silence with people one does not like."

With the proceeds my mother bought me a Fanta. I sipped it while a hairdresser in Veeginia's Hair Salon cooked my mother's head with chemicals.

At the sight of my mother's shiny curls and their insinuation of foreign ways and squander, words failed my father. He attacked her on the iron bed in his room.

With my collection of Widow Bird tail feathers, I bribed my brother to take off his clothes and lie on top of me to listen to my mother's gasping.

A different type of gasp alerted me to hidden eyes spying on us. I pushed off my brother and chased Faith all the way to the bridge. She was fourteen to my nine, but her attention was divided between her fear of the swaying bridge and my angry kicking. I jumped up and down vibrating the rope with my hardened palms while Faith cried, "For God's sake, why do you want to kill me?"

When she tumbled over, only a flash of her thin legs flailing under her long polka-dot skirt appeared in my view because the bridge was rocking. Clutching the rope, I glued my eyes on the facing ridges of Mukurweini and Ithanga, and the snows of the old Mountain-of-God until the bridge and the hammering in my head were still again.

I vomited every time my frowning father, or crying Senior-mother, or location chief, or sub chief, or policeman questioned me about Faith. My mother rocked

51

me on her lap, and wiped my mouth. My brother went to see them investigate the scene, test the planks and ropes of the bridge, study the boulders and rushing waters. But I burrowed into my mother until the policeman in his blue, shiny-button uniform, concluded that Faith, in the careless ways of children, had died playing on the bridge with me, that it was a most unfortunate accident.

The turbaned pastor from the New Deliverance Church led the service for Faith's funeral, but Senior-mother insisted that nobody had ever seen Faith play with me, and refused to let me, my mother or brother attend.

My father bought my brother a uniform and found for him a place in the New Deliverance Church Primary School. When I asked and what about me, my father said, "One clears the bush, the other eats from it."

So my mother twisted my brother's ears and instructed him to teach us. We could soon sing, 'ABCD-el-emu upto zee', and 'Inky-pinky-ponky. Father had a donkey...' I also learned to read, 'See Rabbit Run.'

I never again beat up my brother, and when I shot a bird, I let him claim it.

After another Luo-style walk balancing passion juice on our heads, my mother bought herself some bangles from a street hawker, and Hairglo Curl Activator Gel. She rubbed it into her hair to fluff out the curls. Jangling the new bangles, she placed the gel in the paper bag and pushed it towards me along with a shilling, and instructed me to wait for her by the Ihwagi turnoff.

On the main Nyeri-Karatina-Nairobi road that sliced through the centre of town, matatus kicked up dust and clamour as they spilled over the verges to avoid potholes. Lurking behind a red phone booth, I watched my mother remove the khanga from around her waist to reveal a flowery skirt I thought I'd never seen before. On longer scrutiny, I realised she'd removed the pleats and chopped off the ankle-inches.

Drawn to the Congolese katika music twanging from within Three-In-One Bar, Restaurant and Lodgings, she lingered on the threshold. Two school girls, sweaters tightened around their buttocks, emerged from a Peugeot 405, and were escorted in by a man in a large cowboy hat and another man who looked like the location chief. My mother tightened her belt and slipped into the bar behind them.

Three hours later, my mother staggered to the stage, slurring, "Where are you my daughter?" and jerking her finger at onlookers, "Inky-Pinky-Ponky, your father he is a donkey!"

I wanted to hide from the sniggers of sweat-stained farmers, and the pitying glances of market women on their way back home with empty baskets, but my mother fell. Her legs splayed out from her like the vee of a catapult.

As the clicking of tongues and wagging of heads and scandalised comments turned into curses, my mother laughed. This changed into a braying sound that broke off after each long gulp of breath, changed pitch and rose to a scream.

People shuffled back, sniffed the air in exaggerated fashion, staring at her as though she had turned into a gorilla right in front of them. Ripples of,'Ngai Fafa!' 'What is that smell?' and 'Haiya, Devil Worshipper...' tainted the dusky air.

When my mother quietened, I held her hand and guided her into the matatu.

Drivers never refused to carry her. In fact they'd insist we sat in front, with my mother in the middle. As her pale yellow thighs came into view, the temperature in the vehicle rose. I'd fidget. When I could not stand it anymore, I'd pretend to be jogged by bumps, and place the paper bag of Hairglo on her lap.

My mother would somehow brush it to the floor. And old Gakuru, who could barely see over the wheel, or Muriuki, with his brown teeth and severely receded hairline, and even Nehemiah, who preferred to speak in English because his wife taught at my brother's school, would flash me triumphant looks. A wonder none of the vehicles veered over the banks of the parallel Sagana!

As we neared home, my mother punctuated the country music playing on the cassette stereo with her own sorrows:

"I took the diamond ring you gave me and threw it way out in the sea," Skeeter Davies sang.

"Shu-a-ray, this is too mush" my mother moaned.

"And I had this awful feeling." Skeeter countered.

"Enough is enough" my mother cried.

"That's just where I ought to be."

"Braaday herro."

My father was not normally a loud or violent man, but the chest contains a beehive full of pride. His flailing arms greeted us the moment we emerged at the bridge. He shouted that neither my mother, "...drunken prostitute and devil's messenger nor her useless daughter would ever leave the farm again."

My mother shielded me with her body and urged me to run, run away, before unfolding herself to turn the attack on him. They fought all the way to his room, and all night their wrestling rumbled the ground.

The next morning my mother was gone.

My father did not look for her. He sat on his chair on the veranda, chewing a mswaki, staring at the spot where my mother once styled her hair. Sometimes he lit his eyes on me, but he said nothing. Later, he'd cough a lot. At the clinic, the doctor told him he suffered bronchitis. But I suspected my father was either emptying his chest or choking on the memory of my mother.

Senior-mother said that my mother probably fell into the river, floated away to where the Sagana became the Tana, and where, God help her, she was most likely consumed by crocodiles. My half-sisters Hope and Grace said that I would now come back to earth, as though I had flown off it in an aeroplane like the one we'd heard delivered cousin Wangui to America.

To distract my brother who now urinated in bed every night, I read him his 'Hadithi za Abunuasi' books. Even though I had not yet been to school, my brother relied on me for help with his homework.

Tracking the scent of my mother, I criss-crossed the streets of Karatina, but no-one claimed to have seen her, not even in Three-In-One, or Veeginia's Hair Salon, or the Mkorino woman's sausage and chips shop. I wandered as far as the ridges of Mukurweini and Ithanga, and shading my eyes, scanned the Mountain-of-God and westwards to the Yatta Plateau squatting on the horizon.

I described her, layer upon layer like the topographical contours I'd later cover in school, even though forming the words caused me pain. It forced me to see her as another, separate and different from me. To basket-weaving market women, and bushy-haired men, and bent tobacco-chewing old people, shiny-buttoned policemen, vaselined schoolgirls, bow-tied waiters, loud matatu touts, I said, "My mother is tall. Her skin is the soft yellow of mashed cooking bananas, and her lips are tinged with pink. She has big breasts and hips and buttocks, but when she tightens her belt, her waist is narrow. Muscles bunch up in her calves like isolated potatoes, but her legs are slender. Unlike Cousin Wangui, my mother's voice trips over certain letters, but it is deep and rare. Her hair is in the latest curly kit fashion. She likes beads and bangles, and the itchy music of Congo. But the Western music makes her cry."

I discovered that in a house full of women, motherless children often sleep hungry. Sometimes food brought with it diarrhoea. Once, broken glass in water cut my tongue. But when a snake appeared in my and my brother's bed, and Senior-mother cried about the invasion of Evil Spirits in her house, and brought the New Deliverance pastor to cleanse us, it dawned on me that I would have to halt the search for my mother.

Even then I sensed that beauty and truth are the privileges guaranteed to bite themselves in time. At eleven, wasn't I as enticing as an almost-ripe mango, firm to the touch yet yielding, and bursting with juiciness inside? Wasn't my skin Ambi-light and Johnson's powder soft? Didn't my breasts shout, 'Hello, Hello' from across Mukurweini ridge to the facing ridge of Ithanga? Wasn't my back straight and my legs strong from ploughing the land of my father? When I crossed the Sagana, didn't the frogs croak, "Kairitu, but you're beautiful, Kairitu, but you're beautiful!"

I was hoeing my father's fields one dusty afternoon, glad to be away from Senior-mother and her twin chorus, when my father came to work his jembe. He hammered it into me, then twisted and turned over my ground. He hurried away to hide in his room.

It took me a long while to stagger to mine, and on the way the twins glared at me like I was faking pain to get off from digging. Senior-mother smelled the air and disappeared into the kitchen. It was not yet dark when she knocked on my father's wooden door to deliver him his food. He ignored her.

"Jesus Christ!" She beat her head against the door. "My house is falling."

I lay on my and my brother's bed, the rags from my mother's cut-off skirts soaking up my bleeding, and vomited. Nobody came to wipe my mouth.

It took me a week of hiding and hunger to decide that if this is what had to happen, I would milk its truth to feed mine. On my mother's spot in the yard, I styled my hair and taught my eyes to flutter promises.

So my father ploughed a pliant daughter, gratefully and repeatedly slithering his sperm into my bitter receptor. In turn, he enrolled me in school with money earned from Senior-mother's, Hope's and Grace' maize and potato-digging. And my father said, "The offspring of a leopard scratches like its mother."

On weekends I resumed the search for my mother. I came home with meat that everybody ate, and it dulled the volume of their complaining. I let the matatu drivers plough me – Muriuki with his stained teeth, English-speaking Nehemiah, whose wife now taught me in school, and even wiry old Gakuru. For two years, I let them plough me until Nehemiah finally confessed that he had driven my mother one early morning.

Such a meticulous man was Nehemiah. Exactly three-and-a-quarter miles between my home and the homestead of his teacher-wife and children, he'd wedged his matatu into the bushes at such an angle that no glint of it could be seen from the road. He'd collapsed the rear passenger seats, folded his clothes, and cushioned the floor beneath our naked bodies with a Raymond blanket.

Like pebbles cast in water unaware of the ripples or even the depth they'd sink,

Nehemiah's English words landed. That on their way to Nairobi, he had stopped to fill his matatu at the Shell BP station near the River Chania in Thika. That she'd slipped away and when he'd caught up with her crossing the bridge near the Blue Post Hotel, she'd waved him away despite his pleas. That he had sat in his car at the parking lot only to see her disappear with a cowboy-hatted man who drove a white Peugeot.

Though there was a measure of guilt in his voice, Nehemiah insisted that he had only done what she wanted, and that if I continued to be good to him, he would do the same for me.

How was I to swallow the words of a man who'd helped steal my mother? Gooseberries raised their heads on my naked flesh. I had to snatch breath in tiny sips. Later when I read about the slave trade, I recognised how ancient my anger, but at the time, I rustled in my clothes, and drew out my father's penknife.

Perhaps it was shame or shock or fear, or just too dark for him to see, but all Nehemiah did was tremble as I unfolded my body to slash his carotid artery.

I was not even suspected for Nehemiah's murder.

When I passed my primary school certificate with top grades the same year as my brother, my father wasn't that pleased because secondary school for us meant a sharp increase in fees, and reduced the opportunities for his ploughing. From his coughing I also sensed he feared I'd disappear from him. But he sold an acre of land because having a bone to lick is better than having to gather up limbs in hunger.

In my third year of secondary school, I gave birth to my daughter. She was retarded, of course, being that she was my father's.

With her suspicions confirmed, Senior-mother beat her flustered wings to spread the gossip. Her disciples spread the Word and it multiplied.

When the elders and the location chief and his sub-chief and the shiny-button policeman came to mediate over the matter, I refused to talk.

I could deal with my father's renunciation of me as though the incestuous devils had only plagued me. I could deal with being thrown out of home with my blank-face daughter as though the sight of us reminded them of their own vulnerability. I could stomach the spitting and hissing at the market where I tried my hand at hawking, my daughter drooling on the khanga next to me. After all, retribution dates to the beginning of time. And weren't these the biblical weapons of condemnation by a mindful, church-going public eager for me to exit their domain?

If I sound bitter, it is only because this bend on my road had delivered another surprise. My daughter moved her toothless mouth to gurgle at the sky in crooked ways, and her tender limbs spasmed. But she so intensified the scent of my mother that I sometimes fainted with gratitude and yearning.

It was Uncle Erasmus who finally said, "What a waste of good brain" and used his connections to find us a home. We moved into the mission of Our Veiled Sisters of Mercy. Why should I have been surprised that so many teenage fruits of incest, homelessness, and murder incubated in this home of red brick and hard-waxed floors, heavily decorated with sacramental votives, crosses and candles? After all, what girl walks freely wherever and whenever she wants?

Of course we wore pious faces for the nuns, and they in turn taught us skills. With my daughter beside me, I learnt to sew and bake and even took mechanic classes. Two years later, I departed with a KCSE certificate and a just-in-case paper in my hand that declared me a competent maid, mechanic or wife-in-waiting.

A flat, wide space existed between the dark expressive islands of my daughter's eyes. Her face was broad and brown, her head as thickly haired as my mother.

Only I understood her, but not all the time. It was though she kept losing words, and the more formed the thoughts, the more the words escaped. Despite my encouragement, she could barely string three together. Trying to capture the depth and breadth of her thinking, my daughter's hands flapped like the wings of captured widow birds. I sensed how beautiful her wordless thoughts, how sophisticated. I frustrated her most when I was closest to understanding, and she broke things or hit me.

My daughter needed help to express herself and soothe her body, so I begged Uncle Erasmus for more help. He raised the funds through a family Harambee to put me through a Teachers' Training College. Most of the money came from his daughter Wangui in America, but even my born-again father contributed.

I enrolled my daughter in St Clementine's Boarding because the headmistress explained that while I should not expect miracles, my daughter was not an idiot just mentally challenged.

A Luo lecturer from Maseno, rubbing his steel-wool hair on my breasts, claimed my smell intoxicated. He added that his passion was psychological not just a physical feeling. When I laughed he frowned, and invited me to 'Come-we-Stay'. And since lightning did not strike at the same place twice, he added, he would accept my child, and expected me to bear him many children. He was a stout man who drank too much Pilsner Lager, but spoke with the assurance of one used to being heard. So I heard him.

I had already confessed the bitter portions of my background, but my Luo man began to sulk over my missing pregnancy as if I had deliberately misled him. In fact, he had often asked me to repeat details, and had once concluded that my history served as a tragic metaphor for Africa just before he turned me over to plough me.

I offered to leave him because of this sulking. He replied that it was too late as I had clearly applied on him a powerful Mganga's concoction that bound us.

But that was not the reason I followed him to the lecturers' dining room hiding a knife in my sleeve, trembling. I found him bowed over a bowl of tomato soup, white bread and a Pilsner Lager on the side, and slashed his neck.

My daughter's school had called to find out when we expected to send a payment. Using his commanding voice to convince them of his good intentions, my Luo man collected my daughter from school. In our two-bedroom house, he sat her on a dining chair and stared at her until she had vomited on herself.

When I arrived she was gurgling at the ceiling. As I tried to gather her and wipe her mouth, my Luo man prodded my stomach. His words reminded me of my father, "It seems a dried-up tree cannot bear a green one."

I took my daughter back to school in a hired taxi, where I told the clear-spoken headmistress the version of the story that I thought most likely to secure the padlocks of the school-gate in future. Then I returned to seek my Luo man because I feared what might happen. And I killed him because despite the intimate things he knew that bound us, he had terrified my daughter.

When she heard the news, the clearly-spoken headmistress contacted the Legal Aid for Women (LAW). The LAW arranged for my legal defence. But on the wings of my brutalised history, they also wanted to raise awareness of the terrible plight of the girl child, and the issue of domestic violence.

"As a representative of over 300,000 teachers in the country," said a tired-looking lawyer in a striped suit, though I was yet to qualify in that profession, "your voice is bound to cause ripples, and furthermore, the publicity will help your defence."

"You are to be admired, after all," added her colleague who wore a maroon suit, "because instead of taking the easier route of abortion, you took on the burden of mothering your – she had coughed at this point to delicately swallow the word 'father's' – baby?"

But to the microphones and photographers, the interviewers and lookers-on,

I appealed for news of my mother. I said, "My mother is tall. Her skin is the soft yellow of mashed cooking bananas, and her lips are tinged with pink. She has big breasts and hips and buttocks, but she when she tightens her belt, her waist is narrow. Muscles bunch up in her calves like isolated potatoes, but her legs are slender. My mother's voice trips over certain letters, but it is deep and rare. Her hair is in the latest curly kit fashion. She likes beads and bangles, and the itchy music of Congo. But the western music makes her cry."

I wondered about the accuracy of my description – maybe she had changed – because when I said these words, people looked at me without answering. Their eyes searched me up and down, and then lingered on mine as though puzzled that I could not see the answer.

Perhaps I landed in Kamiti because of the confusion that followed this publicity. Every time I emerged from the back of the police land rover during the trial, people pointed, sniffed, hissed, or kissed the air at me. Even in court, Judge Kipketer kept banging his gavel to restrain the commotion.

Listeners called in on Citizen and Capital and Kameme FM to comment on my story. Some said I was desperate or unfortunate. Some said the publicity was a clever ploy to avoid the price for murder. Women said it was unjust that men got away with rape and defilement. Men said women should not equate rape with murder. Kikuyus said it proved nothing good resulted from consorting with an uncircumcised Luo man. Luos cried for my blood to avenge theirs. But the only comments that hurt my ears are those that said I had no mother.

In my years lived amongst the condemned in Kamiti prison, I have read every letter sent to me by the clearly-spoken headmistress who said that the lawyers of LAW had raised the funds to keep my daughter in school.

Sometimes I ask myself, what if my mother had not run away, what if my father had not raped us, and what if my daughter could speak clearly. I even ask whatever happened to Mercy, Charity, Hope and Grace.

But then I realise that this pondering is just as useless as the question my Luo man in college asked in his examination paper, "How might Africa have developed if white people had never appeared on the scene?"

Or the questions they asked in those interviews arranged by the suited lawyers – "Why do you seek your mother? At what cost?" and, "If you find her, what will you do with her?"

When they bring my daughter to visit, the prison guards shake their heads at the tremors of her body and her drooling. They look away. But with every visit, my daughter so intensifies the scent of my mother that I sometimes faint with gratitude and yearning. That's when a foolish thought visits – I wonder if my mother is hiding in her. She giggles when I tickle her armpits and back and buttocks searching for my mother.

After I tickle her, she sits on the floor opposite me. Her hands flutter less and the islands in her eyes reflect deeper. She grasps my elbows, her body jerking only a little, searching to see if I understand her meaning. Gooseberries raise their heads on my naked flesh. I have to snatch breath in tiny sips because when I look inside her eyes, we are floating on the Sagana, she naked, me in a billowing petticoat, daring the current to deliver us past the facing ridges of Mukuruweini and Ithanga; beyond the old Mountain-of-God, and further west of the Yatta Plateau where the Sagana becomes the crocodile infested Tana. In my fear I thrash, but she grips me hard as we return again and again to brave the crocodiles of the Tana.

Muthoni Garland was born and bred in Kenya. She is married to an Englishman, and between them they have four children. She writes stories for children and adults. Her work has been published in *Kwani?*, *Chimurenga* (SA), *Absinthe Review* (USA); *Memories of Sun* (anthology for children published by HarperCollins USA) and is forthcoming in *The Reading Room* (USA); and *Sex and Death* – an anthology edited by Mitzi Szereto (UK). She was highly commended in the 2002 BBC Commonwealth radio competition. Muthoni is working on her first novel.

The Fanatic

Laila Lalami

LARBI AMRANI DID NOT consider himself a superstitious man, but when the prayer beads that hung on his rear view mirror broke, he found himself worrying that this could be an omen. His mother had given him the sandalwood beads on his college graduation, shortly before her death, advising him to use them often and well. At first Larbi had carried the beads in his pocket, fingered them after every prayer, but as the years went by he had used them with decreasing regularity, until one day they ended up as decoration in his car. Now they lay scattered, amber dots on the black floor mats. He picked up as many as he could find and put them in the cup holder, hoping to get them fixed later. He eased the Mercedes down the driveway and into the quiet, tree-lined street. Traffic was unusually light, even when he passed through the crenellated fortress walls at Bab Rouah.

In his office at the Moroccan Ministry of Education, he opened up the day's *Al-Alam* and asked the *chaouch* to bring him a glass of mint tea. In a few minutes he would tackle another pile of dossiers, deciding where newly graduated teachers would perform their two years of civil service, but for now he took his time reading the paper and sipping his tea. The headlines announced a train workers' strike and yet another hike in the prices of milk and flour, so he skipped to the sports page. Before he could read the weekend football scores, his secretary buzzed him to announce that he had a visitor. Larbi put the paper away and stood up to welcome Si Tawfiq, an old friend he had not seen in fifteen years. (Or was it fourteen?) They had lived next door to each other in a new apartment complex in downtown Rabat, but after moving out to the suburbs they had lost touch. Mr. Tawfiq entered the room cloaked in his white burnous, even on this warm September day. After salaams and other pleasantries had been exchanged, Tawfiq cleared his throat. "It's about my niece. She's finishing her degree next summer." His protruding eyes, the result of a thyroid condition, made Larbi uncomfortable.

"Congratulations," he said.

"And she wants a job in Rabat." Tawfiq smiled knowingly.

Larbi tried to conceal his annoyance. The greatest need for teachers was in smaller towns or in one of the forgotten villages of the Atlas Mountains.

"I was hoping you could help her," Tawfiq added.

"I wish I could, Si Tawfiq," Larbi began, "But we have so few jobs in the city these days. The waiting list is this thick." He held his fingers wide apart, as if he were talking about the phone book.

"I understand," Tawfiq said. "Of course, we would try to do anything we could to help you."

Larbi stroked the ends of his thin moustache, twisting them upward. He was not above taking the occasional bribe, but he recalled the morning's omen. "Please," he said, holding up his palms. "There's no need." He cleared his throat, and added weakly, "I'm happy to serve all teachers. It's just that when so many people want the same thing, it becomes impossible to get all of them the assignment they want."

Tawfiq looked disappointed, and he stared at Larbi for a long minute. "I understand," he said. "That's why I've come to you."

Larbi sighed. He did not want to disappoint his friend. And anyway, what sense did it make to refuse a favour to a department head in the Sûreté Nationale? "I'll see what I can do," he said. Moving Tawfiq's niece up the list would require creative handling of the paperwork. He would have to be discreet.

Afterwards, Larbi swiveled in his chair and put his feet up on the desk, crossing them at the ankles. He looked out the window at the row of eucalyptus trees outside, and thought again about his mother, her benevolent face appearing in his mind's eye. He lit a Marlboro and inhaled slowly. Times were different now. He did not create the system; he was just getting by, like everyone else. He turned to face his pile of dossiers.

When Larbi got home that night, there was a nice surprise waiting for him on the console – a rare letter from his son, Nadir, who was studying electrical engineering in Québec. He stepped inside the living room, and sat on one of the leather sofas, moving a white-and-pink silk cushion out of the way. Two years ago, Larbi's daughter Noura had taken up silk painting, and, besides cushions, had made scarves, handkerchiefs, and watercolours. The results of her labour were scattered around the house. Larbi had thought that she had taken a serious interest in decorative arts, but it turned out to be nothing more than a high school fad, and all the brushes and bottles of paints she had insisted on buying were now in a plastic bag somewhere under the kitchen sink.

Larbi opened the letter. These days, Nadir sent only hurried e-mails with scant details of college life. Whenever he wrote real letters, it was to ask his parents for money. This one was no different – he wanted 10,000 dirhams to buy a new laptop. Larbi shook his head. Nadir would probably spend it on CDs or a weekend out of town. But he did not mind, so long as the boy did well in school, and he always did. Larbi loved to think of his son's future, and of the position Nadir would be able to get with an engineering degree, especially one from abroad.

Larbi walked through the corridor to Noura's room. He thought for a moment that she wasn't home, because her stereo was not blaring rock music, as it usually did, but he heard voices and so he knocked. Noura opened the door. She wore jeans and a black T-shirt with glittery letters spelling out the name of a rock band. Her hair fell in curly cascades on her shoulders. She looked at her watch. "It's already six-thirty?" she said, sounding surprised.

"Look what I got for you," Larbi said, handing her some magazines he had bought on his way home.

"Thanks, Papa," Noura said. She took the magazines from him, and when she stepped aside to drop them on her desk he saw her friend, a girl who sat on the chair by the window, her hands folded on her lap. She wore a grey, pilled sweater and an ankle-length denim skirt, and her hair was covered in a headscarf. Noura introduced her as Faten Khatibi, one of her classmates at the university in Rabat. Noura was supposed to have gone to NYU, but her scores on the standardized TOEFL exam were not high enough, and so she had to take a year of English at the public university. She was going to apply again in December. The delay had left her somewhat depressed, and the feeling was compounded by her loneliness – most of her friends from the private French lycée she had attended had gone on to universities abroad.

Larbi stepped into the room and cheerfully extended his hand to Faten, but Faten did not take it. "Pardon me," she said. Her eyes shifted back to Noura and she smiled. Larbi dropped his hand awkwardly by his side. Well," he said. There was an unpleasant pause; Larbi could think of nothing to say. "I'll leave you two alone."

As he went to the kitchen to get a drink, Larbi heard the key turn in the lock. His wife, Salma, walked in, her leather satchel on one arm and a set of laundered shirts on the other. "Sorry I'm late," she said. "The judge took a long recess." Larbi took the shirts from her, dropping them on a chair in the foyer. He asked her who Noura's friend was. Salma shrugged. "Someone she met at school."

"She's not the type of girl I've seen her with before."

"You mean she's not an *enfant gâté?*" Salma gave him a little ironic smile. She had little patience with Noura's friends, private-school kids who spent most of their time worrying about their clothes or their cars. Years ago, Salma had disapproved of the idea of Noura's going to a French school, and Larbi himself had occasionally felt guilty that his own daughter was not part of the school system he helped to administer. Yet he had insisted; his daughter had so much potential, and he wanted her to succeed. Surely even an idealist like Salma could understand that.

"I just don't want her to mix with the wrong type," he said.

"She'll be fine," Salma said, giving him that woman-of-the-people look she affected from time to time and which irritated him supremely – just because she took on several cases every year for free and was active in the Moroccan Association of Human Rights did not mean she knew any better than Larbi.

So it was that Faten became a regular visitor in Larbi's home. He grew accustomed to seeing her hooded figure in the corridor and her shoes with their thick, curled soles outside Noura's door. Now that Noura spent so much time with her, Larbi watched Sunday-afternoon football matches by himself. This week, his beloved Raja of Rabat were playing their archrivals, the Widad of Casablanca. Salma, for whom football was only slightly more exciting than waiting for a pot of tea to brew, went to take a nap. When Larbi went to the kitchen at halftime to get a beer, he heard Faten's voice. "The injustice we see every day," she said, "is proof enough of the corruption of King Hassan, the government and the political parties. But if we had been better Muslims, perhaps these problems wouldn't have been visited on our nation and on our brethren elsewhere."

"What do you mean?" Noura asked.

"Only by purifying our thoughts and our actions..."

Larbi walked a few steps down the hallway to Noura's open door, which she promptly closed when she saw him. He retreated to the living room, where he smoked cigarettes and drank more beer, and barely paid any attention to the rest of the match.

Immediately after Faten's departure, Larbi knocked on Noura's door to ask what their conversation had been about. He stood close to her, and she wrinkled her nose when he spoke. His breath smelled of alcohol, he realized, and he stepped back.

"Nothing, Papa," she said.

"How can you say 'nothing'? She was here for a while."

"We were just talking about problems at school, that sort of thing." She turned around and, standing over her desk, stacked a few notebooks.

Larbi stepped in. "What problems?"

Noura gave him a surprised look, shrugged, then busied herself with inserting a few CDs in their cases. On the wall above her desk was a silk painting of a peony, its leaves open and languid, its centre white and pink. Larbi stood, waiting. "She was just telling me how last year some students didn't even sit for final exams, but they passed. I guess they bribed someone on the faculty."

"What would she know of such things?" asked Larbi, frowning.

Noura heaved a sigh. "She has firsthand experience. She flunked last year."

"Maybe she didn't work hard enough."

Noura looked up at him and said in a tone that made it clear that she wanted him to leave after this, "The kids who passed didn't, either."

"She can't blame her failure on others."

Noura pulled her hair up into a ponytail. She took out a pair of lounging pants and a T-shirt from her marble-top dresser, flung them on the bed, and stood, arms akimbo, waiting. "I need to take a shower now." Larbi scrutinized his daughter's face, but it was as impassive as a plastic mask. He left the room.

Salma was still napping when he entered their bedroom. He sat on the bed, facing her. Her eyelids fluttered. Without waiting for her to fully awaken, Larbi said, "Noura can't see this girl anymore."

"What?" Salma said, opening her eyes. "What are you talking about?" She was already frowning, as though she was ready to analyze the situation and construct the right argument.

"I don't think it's a good idea. I caught them talking politics just now."

"So?"

"Don't give me that look of yours, Salma. You know exactly what I mean. I don't want her involved in anything. If someone heard them talking that way about the king at school, there could be trouble."

Salma sighed and got up. "I think Faten is good for her, frankly. Noura needs to know what's going on around her."

"What do you mean?"

"The world doesn't revolve around fashion and movies."

"She can look around for herself! What does she need this girl for?"

"Look, Noura's going to be leaving at the end of the school year anyway, so I doubt they're going to see each other after that." Salma adjusted her dress and tightened her belt. "You're making a mountain out of a seed," she said. She was the sort of woman who liked to end discussions with a proverb.

Larbi shook his head.

"By the way," Salma said. "You won't believe who called this morning. Si Tawfiq, remember him?"

"Of course," Larbi said, getting up. He had already made up his mind to help him with his niece's situation. "I'll give him a call back."

As the weeks went by, Noura seemed to be increasingly absorbed by her books. One Saturday afternoon in October, Larbi asked her if she wanted to go to the theatre. The performance was by a stand-up comic who had been banned for a few years and only recently been allowed to perform again. The show was sold out. He thought it would be good if she took a break from all that studying.

"I have to write an essay," she said. The soft sound of Qur'anic chanting wafted from her CD player.

"You're missing out," Larbi replied. This was not the first time Noura had declined an outing. The week before, she had turned down an invitation to go to a tennis finals match, and two weeks before that she had refused to join them at the betrothal of her second cousin. She had always been a good student, but he didn't understand why she worked so hard now. This was supposed to be an easy year, to improve her English. There would be plenty of time to study next year in New York. "Come on," he said. "Spend some time with your father for a change."

"Fine, Baba," Noura said.

On the way to the theatre, Larbi glanced at Noura in the rearview mirror. "You're not wearing makeup," he observed.

Salma laughed. "Don't tell me you cared for her eyeliner."

"I'm just saying. It's the theatre, after all."

"Why should I paint my face to please other people?" Noura said indignantly.

Salma pulled down the passenger-side mirror and stared at her daughter in it. "I thought you liked to do it for yourself."

Noura bit at her unmanicured nails, tilting her head in a way that could have meant yes as much as no, then shrugged.

The comedian's routine was a mix of biting satire and musical numbers, but although everyone around him laughed, Larbi found he could not relax. He wanted to talk to Noura, though he feared she would again say it was nothing.

The next day, Larbi waited for his daughter to leave for school before slipping into her room, unsure what to look for. The windows were open and the sun was making tree spots on the floor. Larbi sat on his daughter's bed. It struck him that it was made, the crocheted cover pulled neatly on all sides. She had always been messy, and he had often joked that he would need a compass to find his way out of her room. Now he felt silly for finding her sudden neatness to be suspicious. Salma was right, he worried for no reason. He got up to leave, but the garish colour of a paperback on her nightstand caught his eye and he reached for it. It was a book on political Islam. Leafing through it, he saw that the print quality was poor and that the text was littered with typographical errors. How could Noura bother with this? He tossed it back on the nightstand, where it hit another tome, this one a leather-bound volume. Larbi tilted his head sideways to read the spine. It was *Ma'alim fi Ttariq* by Sayyid Qutb, the Egyptian dissident and member of the Muslim Brotherhood. He doubted that Noura, who had been schooled at

Lycée Descartes, could even read the complicated classical Arabic in a book like that, but its presence on her nightstand made him look frantically around the room for other clues. Next to her stereo he found a stack of tapes and when he played one it turned out to be a long commentary on jurisprudence, peppered with brief diatribes about the loose morals of young people. He couldn't find anything else out of the ordinary.

When Noura came home for lunch he was waiting for her in the living room. "What's this?" he asked, holding up the Sayyid Qutb book.

"You were looking through my things?" Noura said, looking surprised and hurt.

"Listen to me. I'll only say this once. You're not to see this girl Faten any longer."

"Why?"

"I don't like what she's doing to you."

"What is she doing to me, Baba?"

"I don't want that girl in my house anymore. *Safi!*"

Noura gave him a dark look, turned on her heel, and left the room. When the maid served lunch, Noura said she was not hungry. Larbi didn't mind. Better a sulking child than one who gets in trouble.

It was only a few weeks later, the day before Ramadan, that Noura made her announcement. Salma was shuffling back and forth from the kitchen, where the maid was roasting sesame seeds in the oven for the *briwat* pastries she would make for the holy month. Larbi was looking at pictures Nadir had sent of the apartment he had just moved into with a friend, and he was more amused than upset to see no trace of the laptop the boy had claimed he needed.

"You're spoiling him," Salma said.

"He's going to get a Master's Degree," Larbi replied.

Noura walked into the dining room and sat down at the breakfast table. "I've decided to start wearing the hijab." Salma tried to reach for her daughter's hand and knocked over her cup of coffee. She pushed her chair away from the table and used her napkin to blot the stained tablecloth.

"What? Why?" Larbi asked, dropping the pictures on the table.

"Because God commands us to do so. It says so in the Qur'an," Noura replied.

"Since when do you quote from the Qur'an?" he said, forcing himself to smile.

"There are only two verses that refer to the headscarf. You should take them in context," her mother argued.

"Don't you believe that the Qur'an is the word of God?" Noura asked.

"Of course we do," said Larbi, "but those were different times."

"If you disagree with the hijab, you're disagreeing with God," she said.

The confident tone in her voice scared him. "And you have a direct phone line to God, do you?" he said.

Salma raised her hand to stop Larbi. "What has gotten into you?" she asked her daughter. Noura looked down. She traced the intricate geometric pattern on the red rug with her big toe. "Those verses refer to modesty," Salma continued. "And besides, those were the pagan times of *jahiliyya*, not the twenty-first century."

"God's commandments are true for all time," Noura replied, her brow furrowed. "And in some ways, we're still living in *jahiliyya*." Larbi and Salma glanced at each other. Noura drew her breath again. "Women are harassed on the streets in Rabat all the time. The hijab is a protection."

Salma opened her mouth to respond, but no sound emerged. Larbi knew that his wife was thinking of those young men with hungry eyes, of how they whistled when they saw a pretty girl and how they never teased the ones with headscarves. "So what?" Larbi said, his voice already loud. He stood up. "The men can't behave, so now my daughter has to cover herself? They're supposed to avert their eyes. That's in the Qur'an, too, you know."

"I don't understand why it's a problem," Noura said. "This is between me and God." She got up as well, and they stared at each other across the table. At last Noura left the dining room.

Larbi was in shock. His only daughter, dressed like some ignorant peasant! But even peasants didn't dress like that. She wasn't talking about wearing some traditional country outfit. No, she wanted the accoutrements of the new breed of Muslim Brothers: headscarf tightly folded around her face, severe expression anchored in her eyes. His precious daughter. She would look like those rabble-rousers you see on live news channels, eyes darting, mouths agape, fists raised. But, he tried to tell himself, maybe this was just a fleeting interest, maybe it would all go away. After all, Noura had had other infatuations. She had been a rabid antismoking advocate. She had thrown his cigarettes away when he was not looking, cut out pictures of lungs dark with tar from books and taped them to the refrigerator. Eventually she gave up and let him be. She had also had a string of hobbies that she took up with astonishing passion and then abandoned a few months later for no apparent reason – jewellery making, box-collecting, the flute, sign language. But what if this was different? What if he lost her to this... this blindness that she thought was sight?

He thought about the day, a long time ago now, when he had almost lost her. She was only two. They had gone to the beach in Temara for the day, and Nadir had asked for ice cream. Larbi had called out to one of the vendors who walked back and forth on the beach. He had paid for the cones and handed one to Salma and one to Nadir, but when he had turned around to give Noura hers, he realized she had vanished. They had looked for her for hours. He remembered his face burning in the sun, the vein at the base of his neck throbbing with fear and worry, his feet, swelling from walking on the sand. He remembered the tears that continued to stream down Salma's face as they searched the beach. Eventually an old woman brought the disoriented but unharmed toddler to the police station. Noura had gone to collect seashells and it took the old woman a while to realize that the girl who had sat quietly on the rocks was alone. He had promised himself then never to lose sight of her, but the terror he felt that day came rushing in, and the weight of it made him sit down in his chair, his head in his hands.

Moments later, Larbi heard Noura's footsteps in the corridor. He could see her in front of the mirror, her freckled face turned to the light coming from the living room, placing a scarf on her head, tying it under her chin so that her hair was fully covered. Before he could think about what he was doing, he lunged at her and took off the scarf. Noura let out a cry. Salma stood up at the dining table but did not come to her daughter's rescue.

"What are you doing?" Noura cried.

"You're not going out like that." Larbi threw the scarf on the floor.

"You can't stop me!"

Larbi didn't say anything. He knew that she was right, of course, that he couldn't keep her under lock and key just because she wanted to dress like half the city's female population. Noura picked up her scarf and quietly resumed tying it on her head. She said her goodbyes and left. Larbi turned to look at his wife, whose face displayed the same stunned expression as when Noura had first spoken.

On the first night of Ramadan, Salma took out her best china and set the table herself. She had sent the maid home to celebrate with her own family. One by one, she brought forth the dishes they had prepared that day: *harira* soup with lamb, *beghrir* smothered with honey, sesame *shebbakiya*, dates stuffed with marzipan, and a tray of assorted nuts. Larbi called out to Noura that it was time to eat then sat down to await the *adhan* of the muezzin, the moment when day became dusk, the fast would end, and they could eat. At last, Noura poked her head in and stood listlessly at the entrance of the dining room. Larbi looked at her beautiful hair, its loose curls reaching her chest. It was a reminder of what she had chosen to do.

The TV announcer came on to say that the sun was setting; the call for prayer resonated immediately after. Salma gestured to Noura. "Sit, so we can eat."

"I'll only break the fast with water. I'll eat after I've done the *Maghrib* prayer."

69

Salma glanced at Larbi. "Fine," he said.

Noura added, "We're supposed to have frugal meals during Ramadan, not this orgy of food." She pointed to the festive table her mother had prepared.

Larbi felt his appetite melt away. Instead, he craved a cigarette and a stiff drink. Preferably Scotch. Of course, there was not a place in the city that would sell alcohol for another twenty-nine days. He swallowed with difficulty. It was going to be a long Ramadan. "We'll wait for you," he said.

Noura turned to leave, but then turned back. "Well, maybe just a little bit of *shebbakiya*," she said. She took a healthy bite out of the candy.

"Didn't you say this was too much food?" Salma asked.

The family ate without talking. In years past, this first night had been special; friends and family would sit around the table, sharing stories of their fast and enjoying their meal, but there had been too much on Larbi's mind lately to think about inviting anyone.

It was yet another drought year – the end of November and no rainfall at all. Looking at his desk calendar, Larbi noticed that the NYU application deadline was approaching. At least he had Noura's future to look forward to, he thought, even if the present was difficult. Since she had taken on the hijab, he had stopped mentioning her at work. He felt it was beneath someone like him to have a daughter in a headscarf, and he provided only terse answers to anyone at the Ministry who asked him about his daughter.

After work he found her in her room with her mother, busy hanging new curtains. He asked her if he could read her essay before she sent it out.

"I'm not applying," she replied. She slid the last curtain tab onto a mahogany pole.

Larbi glared at her. "Why not?"

"Because I want to transfer out of university at the end of next year. I'm going to be a middle-school teacher."

"What happened to your plans to study economics?" Salma asked, sitting down.

"Morocco needs me. You two always talk about the shortage of teachers," Noura said.

"Have you lost your mind? You're not going to solve the shortage problem..."

"Am I crazy to want to help my country?" She turned away and climbed onto her desk to place the pole on the brackets.

"Look, you'll be of more help as an economist than as a schoolteacher," Larbi said. "It's that friend of hers," he added, turning to his wife. "She's filled her head with these ideas and now she can't think for herself."

"No one is filling my head," Noura said, standing next to the window, the late afternoon light in her hair. "There's too much corruption in the system now, and I want to be a part of the solution." Larbi wondered if she was referring to him. No, that was impossible. He had always kept his deals secret from his wife and daughter. Still, he thought it best not to respond. Noura jumped down from the desk. "Besides, why go to school in the States when I can just as easily study here?"

"For the experience, child," said Salma.

"And you think people in America are going to want me?" Noura said, raising her voice. "Americans hate us."

"How would you know if you've never been there?" Salma asked. "Your brother has never complained. Why don't you talk to him?"

"He's in Canada," Noura said, as though her mother couldn't tell the difference.

"Doesn't your Islam tell you to listen to your father?" Larbi asked.

"Only if my father is on the right path."

"Congratulations, then. You alone are on the right path," he said.

"*Baraka!*" Salma said. She got up. "What about all those years you spent learning English? All the plans you had?"

"I really want to be a teacher," Noura said.

"Think carefully about what you're doing, ya Noura. People your age would do anything for an opportunity like this, and you squander it."

"I want to stay," Noura said, and she pulled the new curtains shut.

It was Salma's idea to invite Faten to dinner. Larbi had agreed, reluctantly at first, then resignedly, thinking that perhaps he might be able to talk some sense into his daughter if he understood her friend a little better. It was a Saturday evening, and the table had been set with a new service Salma had bought. Larbi sat at the head of the table with Noura to his left. Salma sat to his right, under the framed silhouette of a younger version of herself. During their honeymoon in Paris some twenty-five years ago, they had gone to Montmartre, where an artist had talked them into getting their silhouettes done. Working with his scissors, the old man had made Salma's bust more generous, and she'd laughed and left him a good tip.

Faten sat across from Larbi, at the other end of the table, looking calm and content. She had amber-coloured eyes, plump lips, and skin so fair that it seemed as though all the light in the room converged on it. She was, in other words, beautiful. This maddened Larbi. God is beautiful, and He loves beauty, so why hide it beneath all that cloth?

71

The maid brought the main dish, a stew of chicken with black olives and preserved lemons. "Thank you, um..." Faten said, looking up.

"Mimouna," the maid said, glancing at Larbi.

"Thank you, Mimouna," Faten said.

"To your health," Mimouna said, smiling.

Larbi started to eat, periodically glancing at Faten. He was mildly satisfied to notice evidence of less-than-genteel upbringing – she had placed her knife back on the table even after using it. After a decent amount of time had been spent eating and the expected compliments had been made about the food, Larbi cleared his throat. "How old are you, my child?" he asked, affecting as gentle a tone as he could muster toward the girl.

"Nineteen," Faten replied.

"Noura told me you're repeating this year," he said.

Noura shot her father an exasperated look.

"That's true," Faten said.

"I was sorry to hear that. It must have been tough."

Noura slammed her fork on the side of her plate and dropped her chin in her hand. She stared at her father angrily.

Salma intervened. "And are you from Rabat?" she asked Faten in a pleasant tone.

"I was born here, but I grew up in Agadir. I've been back only four years now."

"So where do your parents live?" asked Larbi.

"I live with my mother." Faten's voice dropped an octave. "In Douar Lhajja."

Salma picked up the bread basket and offered it to Faten. "Have some more," she said.

"Let me ask you something," Larbi said. "If someone offered you a chance to study in New York, would you take it?"

"Not again," Noura sighed. Yet she seemed interested in what her friend would say, for she turned and waited for an answer.

Faten blinked. "No one is offering me anything."

"But if someone did."

"I would want to know why they made the offer. No one gives anything for free. That is the trouble with some of our youths."

Larbi felt another lecture coming from Faten, and so he called the maid to ask for more water. Mimouna brought another bottle of water and refilled Faten's glass, but she left without refilling Larbi's. "What do you plan to do after graduation?" he asked Faten.

"I'm not sure yet. It's all in God's hands."

"My daughter here wants to leave school, give up going to NYU, and go teach in the villages."

Faten smiled with approbation. "She will do a lot of good."

"Don't you think that a degree from abroad would be better for her?"

"No, I don't. I think it's a shame that we always value foreign degrees over ours. We're so blinded by our love for the West that we're willing to give them our brightest instead of keeping them here where we need them."

"If you think teaching middle school is so good, why don't you join Noura?" Larbi asked.

"I may well do that," Faten said cheerfully, "although, to tell the truth, I'm not very good with children." The dismissive wave of her hand as she spoke made Larbi's heart sink. He was losing control of his daughter to this girl, who didn't even seem to care enough to want to go with her. Faten pushed her plate away. "You must be so proud," she said. Of all the things she could have said, this made Larbi angriest. He didn't say anything for the rest of the meal, rudely getting up from the table before the tea was served.

He was outside smoking cigarettes when Salma slid the glass doors open and joined him on the terrace. She sat on the wrought-iron chair next to him, and they stared at the blooming jacaranda trees that lined the far end of the backyard. Salma spoke at last. "What are you going to do about this?" There was a hint of accusation in her tone that made Larbi want to scream.

"*Now* you want something done?" he said.

"I didn't know it was going to get to this."

Larbi pulled on his cigarette. "What do you think I should do, then, *a lalla?*"

"I don't know. Just do something," Salma said.

He did not have the heart to tell her that he'd already asked Si Tawfiq for help, and that his friend had said there were no police records on Faten. She was a member of the Islamic Student Organization, but the investigation had not turned up anything illegal. Tawfiq said he'd keep an eye on her. All they could do now was wait.

Months went by. Exam season was a busy time at the ministry, so when Si Raouf rang the doorbell at the house, Larbi thought it was because of some work matter and he hoped to settle it fast and have him leave before the subject of Noura came up. Larbi knew Si Raouf from his days as an education inspector. Raouf had been a schoolteacher, but eventually he had finished his Ph.D. and now he was a lecturer at Noura's college. Today Raouf had the exhausted look he always had this time of year, when he had to grade hundreds of undergraduate papers. Salma served the tea herself, but neither man touched his glass.

"It's Noura, Si Larbi," Farid said, his eyes looking intermittently away, his voice tinged with nervousness. "She passed a note to someone."

Larbi felt his stomach tighten. "I-I don't understand," he whispered.

"One of the students – Faten Khatibi is her name – she passed a paper to Noura with questions and Noura sent her back the answers."

"She cheated?" Salma sounded incredulous.

"She helped someone cheat," Farid said, in an effort to lessen the blow. "This is grounds for expulsion. But we're friends, and I thought I'd warn you. If it happens again with another proctor, there could be a problem."

Larbi walked the professor out. He turned around, marched to Noura's room and flung open the door without knocking. Salma was beside him. Noura was at her desk. He grabbed her by the arm. She stood.

"Cheating at the exams? This is how you repay us after all the sacrifices we've made for you?" Larbi said.

"W-what?"

"How will I ever be able to show my face at the ministry?" he shouted. "My own daughter is caught cheating at the exams!"

"I was just trying to help Faten. She didn't know the answers-"

"Help her? You think this is a word game?" Salma asked. "You didn't help. You cheated."

"I-I couldn't say no. She begged me."

"You lecture us about right and wrong and then you cheat at your exams. Have you ever opened the Holy Book or do you get everything secondhand from Faten?" Salma asked.

"If I ever hear one more word about that damn girl, by God, I'll lock you up in your room," Larbi said. "I won't have a word said about my reputation, do you hear me?"

"Everybody cheats. Everybody." Noura looked him straight in the eye, and he could not hold her stare. He had always kept the favours he did for his friends quiet, but now he suspected that she somehow knew.

"That doesn't make it right," Salma said.

Noura disappeared in her room for two days after that, reappearing only to watch a TV program on religion and jurisprudence called 'Ask the Mufti.' She'd never missed an episode. She would come in and sit in the family room when the program was on, her eyes riveted on the screen. People phoned in with various questions, from the serious ("What is the proper way of calculating the zakat alms?") to the simple ("How do I complete the pilgrimage?"), but Noura watched it all. Today someone phoned in to ask, "Is the use of mouthwash permissible even though it contains alcohol?" Noura looked at the old mufti with great anticipation.

Salma abruptly took hold of the remote control and changed channels. When Noura called out in surprise, Salma said, "I can't believe you're interested in silly details about mouthwash when you can't even see anything wrong with cheating at exams." Larbi laughed, but he was overcome by bitterness. If only he could get that damn girl away from his daughter, perhaps he might be able to convince Noura to go visit her aunt in Marrakech – a stay in the southern city might do her some good. But first he had to deal with Faten once and for all. He picked up the phone. The exams were still being scored, and there was still time to act. He needed someone trustworthy to deal with Faten, and he knew Farid would not let him down.

Larbi sat at his wife's vanity, trimming his moustache, while Salma folded the laundry. He suddenly felt nostalgic and wanted to ask her about those heady days in the seventies when they were both young and the world was open before them and they had big dreams of setting it right. He had started out as an educator and she as a lawyer, but while she still spent her days trying to help clients, he had moved on to administrative positions, and he had been unable to resist the temptations that came with them. What had happened to him, he wanted to ask. He felt he had failed, though he didn't know when that happened. He heard a knock on the door. It was Noura. "I passed my exams," she announced, smiling.

"*Mbarek u messud*," Salma said flatly, then resumed folding the clothes. Normally, she would have hugged Noura; she would have put her hand around her upper lip and let out several joy-cries, but now she sounded no happier than if her daughter had told her she had successfully hung a painting.

"Baba, I have a favour to ask," Noura said. Larbi put down his scissors and turned to face her. "There's been a problem. Faten flunked her exams..." Her voice trailed off.

"And?" Larbi asked, unsurprised.

"Well, she'd already flunked them last year, so this means – she's expelled now. She doesn't know what she's going to do."

Salma stood, hanger in hand, and pointed it at Noura. "Where are you going with this?" she asked.

"What's going to become of her? There are so many unemployed college graduates, but without a diploma, her chances of ever finding a job... it's so unfair–"

"I don't understand what that has to do with me," Larbi said.

"I thought perhaps you could sort it out. You have connections, and she asked me to see if you could help out," Noura said. Her eyes shifted away from him for a moment and then settled on him again.

75

Larbi smiled bitterly. Here she was, the purist, the hard-liner, the anticorruption activist, but in the end, she wanted her friend to get special treatment, just like everyone else. "No more talk of meritocracy?" he asked. Noura looked down. He paused to savour the moment, however fleeting he knew it would be. How many times had she rebuffed him when he asked her to take that damn scarf off and go back to the way she was? What of his dream to see her in cap and gown at NYU? His heart ached just to think of it. Now it was her turn to be on the asking end. "I don't think it'll be possible. It would require breaking the law. Utterly un-Islamic, as you well know," he said.

"When you play with fire, you get burned," Salma said as she closed the wardrobe doors. Noura stared at her angrily and then left the room.

Larbi turned around on the stool and looked at his reflection in the mirror for a while. He, too, had played with fire, but maybe he'd already been burned. When he reached for the scissors again, he noticed a velvet pouch tossed in the middle of the perfume bottles. He took it in his hand and opened it. In it were the prayer beads that had broken, years ago it seemed, and which Salma had saved here for him. He could not help but think about his mother, for whom virtue and religion went hand in hand, about a time when he, too, believed that such a pairing was natural.

"I know I shouldn't be happy about someone's misery," Salma said. "But I'm glad Faten was expelled. At least now Noura won't be seeing as much of her at school."

Where had he gone wrong? He had always had Noura's best interests at heart. What was so bad about her life before? She had it all, and she was happy. Why did she have to turn to religion? Perhaps it was his absences from home, his fondness for the drink, or maybe it was all the bribes he took. It could be any of these things. He was at fault somehow. Or it could be none of these things at all. In the end it did not matter, he had lost her again, and this time he did not dare hope for someone to return her to him.

"Do you think that'll help?" Larbi asked his wife.

Salma shook her head. "I don't know."

Laila Lalami was born and raised in Morocco. She earned her BA in English from Université Mohammed-V in Rabat, her MA from University College, London, and her PhD in linguistics from the University of Southern California. Her work has appeared in *The Los Angeles Times*, *The Oregonian*, *The Boston Globe*, *The Nation*, and elsewhere. She is the recipient of an Oregon Literary Arts grant and a Fulbright Fellowship for 2007. Her debut book of fiction, *Hope and Other Dangerous Pursuits*, was published by Algonquin in October 2005. She is also the founder and editor of Moorishgirl.com, a blog about books and culture.

Celtel Caine Prize African Writers'
Workshop Stories 2007

Christianity Killed the Cat

Doreen Baingana

MY FATHER WAS FIERCE sometimes, a coward otherwise, and that is why he married my mother. One day, he was the worst sinner ever, three wives, overdrinking, you name it, and the next, he switched to his father's religion, Christianity, but exaggerated it to the point of obsession, that is, he became born-again. When he saw the light he chased away all the family except my mother and me, and married her in his new church that week. Why her? Because it was her kiosk and garden we lived on, and because she threatened him all the way to the altar. Why him? I can't answer that. He was already married to booze, and perhaps she was stimulated by competition. His excuse for his love for the bottle was that his father was a gifted and true medicine man from a long family of *basezi*, but he had not passed on his secret and powerful knowledge because the whites came and confused him into Christianity. And so my poor father, with nothing to inherit but a borrowed religion, drowned his sorrows. No son too, was his other excuse, pointing at whomever of us girls were nearby, as if it was our fault. I was as frightened and confused as my sisters were by the babble of tongues of all the church people who came to the house to help him clear out the evil of polygamy. I was jealous too, because I thought my sisters were packing for a long trip, until I discovered I would have my father all to myself.

The conversion stopped his sorrowful drowning for about a month, and then he took to wading into it now and then. After school, it was I who went and secretly bought crude Waragi for him from Obama's bar. We understood that a saint should not be seen in bars, especially a brand new one. Obama knew whose it was, but you couldn't expect him to refuse money. I got there early enough, five o'clock, before the regular drinkers came, and he filled my plastic bottle of Orangina with the clear firewater. We would sit outside, my father and I, leaning on the far wall of the house, away from both the main road and the kitchen, me on my little bamboo stool now the shape of my small bum, he on a worn smooth wooden one. I scratched the dust with a stick while he sipped in silence,

79

or murmured to himself, mostly about good and evil. "The demon's got me." "Ah, just a little won't hurt." "All gods may be one." As the evening wore on, there was less murmur and more silence, and he relaxed into himself, the ropes of religion loosening off him.

From the other side of the house, I could see and smell wisps of smoke from the *sigiri* rising into the air, mixing with my mother's complaining conversation with our neighbour Lidiya. Maama went on about my father being at home the whole day, doing nothing but praying and reading his Bible, just sitting there and calling it The Work of the Lord. Lidiya would take over with wails about her man who she didn't see the whole day, work, work, work, he said, but who knew what he was doing? They sighed heavily, sinking comfortably into their womanly burdens, while my father and I sighed with more important weight.

One evening, the air heavy with smoke from many houses' suppers, my father interrupted his silence by shuffling into the house, and I heard him move their metal bed, and pull and shift around something heavy. I guessed he was rummaging in those old baskets he kept under the bed. Maama had threatened to throw them all out, but my father growled, "I'll throw you out first," but of course he had not. Instead, he had stopped talking to her, and to me too, which I thought was unfair. He had retreated into himself, and not just physically. Hunched over and brooding, he had become a cold ghost at the table, one that moved from room to room in our three-roomed house, filling it with a bitter smell. But after a week, he suddenly smiled at her when she silently put food on the table. "For all your faults, you are a good cook," he said, as he shaped a small white lump of *posho* in his thin fingers, rolling and rolling it before dipping it in the bean sauce. Our mouths formed wide white smiles, and we wouldn't have stopped even if we had been slapped. I would have fought my mother over those smelly bags.

He came back outside with a tattered, grey, long, hairy sack. It was a cow's leg, the dark hoof weighing it down at the bottom, the long sack made of dry old skin with most of the hair missing. He sat down and put his arm deep inside, searched around in it, and came out with crumbs that looked like soil and lint. From his coat pocket, he pulled out a pipe that seemed just as old, and sprinkled the particles into the pipe, hardly filling it. "Nothing," he murmured, "Nothing, that's all." He lit the pipe as I stared; I knew he wanted me to watch him. He must have smoked the skin itself. The smoke curled up and disappeared into the thin air with a faint but somehow familiar scent. "I'm not giving you any," he said, not looking at me but out at the blue-black shadows that had been trees and houses a moment ago. The dark made the known shapes mysterious. When I looked back at him, tears glinted faintly on his face, perhaps from the smoke.

"Okay – I'll teach you to kill, at least."

I was jerked out of an almost trance-like silence. "What?"

"Don't eat anything tomorrow. That's how I was taught."

"To kill what?"

"For your size, a bird. But you have to be hungry for it."

I kept quiet. My father didn't make much sense on these evenings of ours, but this was worse. I sometimes wished he wouldn't talk at all.

My mother came round the corner of the house. "Have you Christians drunk enough? Come and eat," she called, cheerfully.

We could not bask in silence forever. My father got up wearily, and I got up like him, pretending weariness. "Women," we both muttered under our breath, but followed her, her huge swaying buttocks an affront to our spirit.

The next day, Saturday, was a good day not to eat because there was no school. Mother was the fussy one, "What? Not eating? It's fish for lunch."

"No. Taata said so." He was always my way out. But today of all days, when fish was so rare, obeying him was painful.

"What is your fool of a father up to now?"

"He is teaching me things." I didn't want to get into it. "Haven't you heard of fasting?"

She stared at me for a long moment, her large eyes like two drills, then let it go. Perhaps she believed in my father a little bit. She brushed her hand over my head. "You still have to open your hair and wash it, wash your school uniform. Don't think I'm doing that for you."

The morning was easy, but by afternoon, there was nothing I wanted to do but sit and not move. I went over to the shade of the mango tree near Maama's garden, its thick green leaves a solid shade. It was not too far from the rubbish heap that was high, huge; Taata was supposed to have burnt it up last week. I couldn't ignore the mountain of yellow and white milk cartons, grey torn packets for posho flour, dark green-and-black curling wet banana peels, yellow-and-black ones too, some slimy orangey liquidy stuff, greyish fruit, torn bits of paper fluttering pink, blue and white, dust, old mattress stuffing of mildewed cotton, red sweet potato peels, hard brown cassava ones, mango leaves scattered all over like garnish, and on top of it all, fish bones that smelt as sweet as, as, what? As sharp as pineapple cutting your tongue pleasurably. I could only stare, smell and suffer.

This thin stray cat that was a dirty white all over, always hung around our neighbourhood, now crept up and over the rubbish heap. It jerked to a stop and turned to me, its red eyes sharp and unblinking. I had held this cat before when it was a scrawny slip of a kitten. It used to wander into our kitchen to steal scraps, and I had the job of chasing it away. But it would claw into the weaving of my mother's blue-and-green sisal mat and cling fast. I tugged at it by its thin neck,

81

feeling muscle and fur only, no bone, as it squealed and squirmed in my hands. Finally, its tiny claws tore out of the mat, and it hung limp in my hand. I would rush out and fling it away as forcefully and fiercely and as far away as I could, out into the garden, where it landed so gracefully, like water flung and forming a pattern in the air before landing. The kitten would shake itself and skip away, and I was always left jealous. It would always return.

Now grown, it dismissed me quickly, and continued its slow crawl over the refuse, bones under the thin patchy fur moving gracefully, menacingly. It found the fish bones, and picked and played with them with small teeth, dropping precious bits of whitish-grey skin and flesh. My fish. The wish to grab that small skeleton from the cat's claws was as sharp as the need to pee. Like when you have diarrhoea and you are running to the toilet, holding it, holding it. The smell of near rot intensified, wafts of it killing me, like moonflowers whose scent whispered at you at dusk, then disappeared with faint promises. The cat took its time cracking the soft bones. My stomach lurched loudly. Did it hear it? The cat shot its small head up and glared at me, its red eyes flaring for one long moment, tiny pieces of flesh hanging from its mouth. I could easily have shouted it away, thrown a stone at it, anything, if I had not seen a person in its eyes. I mean a demon. I swear. It snarled a laugh, tempting me, just like Jesus was tempted. I knew it. The cat gobbled up the rest, sending only more smells my way, then it crawled over and away from the heap, satisfied. But it didn't go away. I kept my eyes on it as it sat a little distance away from me and licked itself clean, long pink tongue working out and in quickly, like a darting flame. It yawned, showing me its tiny yellow fangs, pink eyes still leering, and there we sat, staring at each other: it, languid; I, mad and afraid.

Hunger crawled through my whole body, stomach, arms and legs, like how that cat had swarmed over the heap of refuse. But hunger made my mind stark and clear, emptied it of all but one idea: I would kill this cat, not shoot some silly bird. It was a demon that sensed the saint in me. My father's drunken murmurs of good and evil begun to make sense.

I told him so later that evening as we sat by our wall. His eyes widened and he looked at me strangely. Was he scared, or pleased? I couldn't tell.

"You? A cat?"

"Yes. It ate my fish."

My father just kept on staring at me.

"It isn't afraid of me. It thinks I am weak." Then I whispered, half-hoping he wouldn't hear. "That cat is a demon."

My father turned away from me, as if to hide a grin that had sprung out of his severe, squareish face. The smile turned into chuckles that came out in short painful spurts, and he held his chest as if to stop them, but couldn't. I had pleased him, I think. Now he was coughing, so I got up and rubbed his back over his frayed brown coat as he bent over, weak, but warm. He said I could eat that night.

My father said we used to get poison from snakes, but there were hardly any snakes left; they had all been killed or were hiding in the forest. So the next day we went up the main road to Auntie Sukuma's store. Everyone called her Auntie: who wouldn't want to be related to someone whose store had everything under the sun, including black sticky sweets that tasted of shoe polish mixed with bananas. They were from China. If I had a chance to move there, I would eat only sweets. Taata did not waste time with long greetings, like most people, but Auntie was used to this.

"Rat poison?"

"How are you, Namuli?" She looked only at me.

"I am fine, thank you, Auntie. Do you have any rat poison? We are suffering with too many rats." I was used to talking for my father.

She scanned her eyes over shelves upon shelves of blue soap, cartons of matchboxes, petroleum jelly, instant coffee, hot sauce, plastic cups, plates and jugs, and on and on. It would have taken a whole day to list all the things packed together on the shelves.

"I had it here somewhere, hmmm... but why don't you get a cat?"

"Do you want money or not?"

I cringed. Taata should have had a drink first before coming here. She turned and gave him a stern look. She was not scared of him. If I had a store like hers, I wouldn't have been either.

"Ah yes, I put it far up there just to be safe." She got a stool, moved to a dark crowded corner, climbed up, pulling her bulky frame up with effort, and got a jar from among the colourful packages it was squashed with. She clambered down, dusted it off with a rag, and peered at the label.

"Be careful with this, eh? This poison is very strong, it's not a joke."

"Who's laughing? We can read the instructions just as well as you. How much?"

"I was talking to Namuli. My dear, give it to your mother to use, okay? Don't touch it. Five thousand only."

I took the jar wrapped in a black plastic bag as my father searched his pockets. For some reason Maama gave him money. She was like me: we did what he wanted, eventually.

As we turned away, Auntie said, "*Kale*, Namuli, greet your mother, okay? Such a nice woman." She shook her head at my father, but he was already gone. I rushed to follow, pulling my skirt down over my knees.

Back home, my father got busy. We moved to our side of the compound, and using a stick, he mixed the thick poison paste with a little water on the cracked half of an old plate.

"Go get some of yesterday's supper."

My mother was not in the kitchen, thank God. I found some groundnut sauce and posho, which was now as hard as a brick. Taata broke it up into pieces, and mixed in the pink sauce and greyish poison. I was relieved, because I had thought I would have to kill the cat with my bare hands. This was going to be easy.

"Okay, don't touch it, you hear?"

I nodded, and he went indoors and began rummaging around in his old bags again. He came out of the house brandishing a decrepit looking bow and arrows. The bow's string was frayed and sagging, the bow worn smooth with age. The arrows were as long as my arm, with rusty looking metal pointed tips. *Me*, use those?

"Isn't the poison enough?" I tried.

"E-eh, Namuli, that's not killing, that's cheating. We're using it just to make it easier for you. But later, a gun, why not?" His eyes glinted, and he chuckled as if the demon had entered him too.

All I had to do was tell my mother so that I could get out of this. It was getting too much.

"Ah-ha, you want to run back to the skirts, I can tell. Go then." Of course I couldn't. I knelt in the dust next to him as he fidgeted with the small skin sack he had brought out the other day. His fingers trembled as he struggled to undo the strings tied around the top of the sack. I knew what he needed, and went off to get him his bottle. He took a swig, head leaning back, then sputtered and coughed. It didn't help right away; I still had to help him open the bag, pulling at the tight knots first with my fingers then with my teeth. "There you go," he muttered. "Use whatever you can." Again, he scraped the bottom of the sack and came out with whitish dust. "Now I remember," he said. "A rooster's crown, dried and crushed. He sprinkled it on the mash we had prepared for the cat. He continued, "This is not easy, not simple, but necessary, you understand? Can you be – you must be dedicated, slow, methodical, mechanical. Don't think too much. Act." I would. I would.

My mother knew how to choose the worst times to appear. "Taata, are you – what are you two playing at now?"

"Cat and kid," my father giggled, and took a sip of his drink.

"What?"

"Why ask when you won't understand?" He was busy tightening the bowstring.

"He – we are going to, um, practice hunting." I said.

"*Katonda wange*, Chalisi, when will you grow up?"

"Ee-h, you hear her. You think killing is a child's game? I am trying to show her what is real: death after life."

Her eyes turned a boiling red. "Rubbish. If you want to play, play with fire. What about that heap of rubbish you were supposed to burn? That's why cats are here all the time–"

"And I am trying to get rid of them. Fire? You want fire, yes, okay, we'll burn it. Don't worry. Just go. Go see Lidiya."

I hid a small grin behind my hand as Maama chewed her teeth and turned away. She knew by now that you could not reason with my father. She stalked off, her big hips saying back off as they rolled away like a cement-mixing machine. Her backside could say come hug, or I'm sick of you, or I could be your pillow. My father smiled, his lips curling over his scattered moustache.

We moved to the garden, not too far from the huge mango tree. Taata stood poised, one leg in front of the other, steady. He took aim, one eye almost closed, and in a blink, the arrow whizzed through the air and got stuck in the trunk. It sounded like a big fat bee racing past.

"Now you." He stood beside me, slightly bent, and held the bow in my hands, his fingers over my own. He stretched the string taut with me, aimed for me. My beating heart was soothed by his warm hands. "Steady, steady, pull, now... let go!" Out of my hands it flew, fast and sure, but then curved downwards and hit the ground just in front of the tree. "Not bad. Try again, pull harder, use more force." I did so again and again, wiping the sweat off my palms onto my dress, wiping my forehead with my hands. This was my favourite tree. I struck it on the fifth attempt, screamed and jumped high. Taata laughed. "See!?" The direct hit, aiming for something and getting it, my mind ably controlling my eyes, hands, the air, the bow and arrow, was power. A quick shot of pleasure swarmed through my arms and legs, and I found myself trembling. I had to do it again.

I picked up the scattered arrows and handed them to my father. We could not stop grinning. As I squatted beside him and watched, excited, he dipped the arrow tips into a thick mix of rat poison and a few drops of water, adding some muttered words into the mix. I swear I heard some Latin from the priest at church. The other words I didn't know, but yes, we needed God to help us with the demon.

To be frank, the exhilaration of could-I-hit-or-not was sharper now than the evil that had gleamed out of the cat, despite a dream I had the night before. The cat had come up to me, eyes glowing like hell, and rubbed its dirty grey damp fur against my legs, its fishy smell trying to suffocate me. I tried to pull it off but it clung to my legs tighter, whining, not snarling, as if it needed me, like a baby starved of milk, while I pulled and pulled at it. It would not let go, its body stretching long like thick slimy elastic. As it wailed, I begun moaning with it until finally, thankfully, my whimpers woke me up. Relief gushed through and out of me like sweat. I sat up in bed and vowed not to sleep again that night, but did.

But now, now the dream was mere shadow, as the bow and arrows became a potent extension of my arms. More than fear, I wanted to see if I could aim accurately again, and hit and hit and hit.

The cat had kept away while we were practicing, but now all was quiet. It slunk back to the rubbish heap, which was still nice and high and colourful with fresh refuse, the cracked plate of food and poison balanced on the top where I had placed it. A few flies that landed on it failed to fly off. My father had told me not to eat again to help me focus. "Sit in the sun and wait," he said, and I did, closer to the heap, its smell stinging my nostrils. My father sat a little way off under the shade of the mango tree, watching and waiting with me. My mother was not even a thought in my mind.

As the sun struck my forehead, and my father drank more spirit, he began his mutterings again. "Sacrifice. For my father's father's gods, a chicken was enough. A goat, maybe, a cow even. But what better sacrifice than a *man*? The Son of God, who is God also. What my father could have done, but many *many* times over. For the past, the present and the future, even for those not yet born. Yes, we must learn it too: sacrifice."

Taata's words became an incessant hum in my ears as the sun bore down. I watched the cat sniff at the plate then gobble up the food quickly. It licked its lips and face with that agile pink darting tongue, then sniffed around for more. I kept my eyes on it as it moved down the heap, heading towards me. It stopped abruptly and started coughing, its little white head jerking up and down. I had to act before it got away. A part of me coughed with it, a strange echo of the wails in my dream. Another part of me was also the cat, rising up slowly, body taut with resolve, all arms and shoulder and muscle and aim and stretching; all with the cat's sure grace. Tight, tight, I pulled and stretched the bowstring, hungry for the cat's narrow body, hungry not to miss.

With all my will I let the poisoned arrow go. Its swift zing was joined in the very same second by a devilish screech; and I felt it, I did, the sharp metal point plunging through soft fur and skin, the second of resistance, then the impossibility of it. My mind shot back to when my mother had passed a needle though fire then stabbed my ears lobes, one after the other, while I, all fright, felt my flesh from the inside, deeply. Now, as sweat fell into my eyes, I saw red bursting bright like a flower out of the grey. A bubbling flower that I had made.

The cat scrambled and slipped, desperately trying to crawl away; but I scrambled too, quickly, my mind sharp and clear. I aimed and shot again, and again felt that sweet sharp invasion of hard cold metal meeting, tearing and entering soft hot skin and flesh. I grabbed yet another poisoned arrow, but from somewhere faraway, heard my father shouting, "Stop!" I staggered back, and like the writhing cat, could not escape. I was its body, as the poison gained life as it took it, seeking veins and invading, racing quickly throughout the dirty little hot body. Now the body itself became thirsty for it, begged for it, just as after my fast I had drunk water so frantically I almost choked, and felt it flush so cold down my throat and spread, spread, even to the tips of my fingers and toes.

The cat had to stop writhing, and it did, slumping down dead. Still, blood moved out and over it, covering the once white skin with blotches of crimson. Its red eyes remained open. I had chased out its sleek and tawny grace, and now all I had was a limp grey thing. I would have to throw it on the rubbish heap, and I wanted to throw myself there too.

Instead, I turned away and ran to my father who, with his arms raised, filled the air with shouts of praise. He stopped long enough to give me a small precious sip of his almost empty bottle, for the very first time, then he went on hollering to the sun. What could I do but try to shout like him, even adding a dance on trembling legs, until I could dance and shout for real. I waved the bow and arrows over my head and screamed, "I did it! I did it!" My father was full of loud hallelujahs, so I danced for him. But he had not seen the cat's red eyes. Though they had stopped glowing, they were not defeated.

I swivelled round and round, my skirt flying, then threw the bow and arrows down as if in victory, not disgust. I can end a life, I Namuli. The dancing finally took hold.

My mother must have heard all the commotion and rushed out of the house. "Have you gone mad?" She shrieked like the dying cat, like me, only louder.

"I killed a cat! I killed–"

She came right up, and with all the weight of her wonderful body, shook me by the shoulders until I shut up. When she let go, I fell down, stunned. But finally, like the cat, I could let go, go limp. I did, and something warm oozed out of me, streamed down my leg. Blood? Pee. Warm, tangy pee. What had I done? Then came the tears, and I let them.

Mother continued to scream, her cries filling the air like pesky lake flies as she tried to put the up-side-down world straight again, tried to make us sane, but it was too late. My father tugged at me. "Come on, stop, you're too old for this now," but I turned away from him. He walked off, mumbling and grumbling. He was not going to stay and listen to my mother's cries and curses. He would have to get his own drink today.

My mother got quiet as Taata walked away. I knew what she wanted to do: pull me up, wipe my face with her wrapper, try and fold me back into her; but couldn't she see I now had claws like a cat? " Leave me, I'm okay, really," I said. I got up and moved away. I would wash myself, and go sit on my stool for a while. But I wanted to sit alone.

Doreen Baingana is a Ugandan who lives both there and in the United States. Her short story collection, *Tropical Fish: Stories out of Entebbe,* won the Commonwealth Prize for First Book, Africa Region, 2006, and was a finalist for the Hurston-Wright Prize for Debut Fiction, 2006. It was published after winning the Associated Writers and Writing Programs (AWP) Award in Short Fiction. She has been nominated twice for the Caine Prize for African Writing and has also won the Washington Independent Writers Fiction Prize. She teaches creative writing, works for Voice of America radio, and is a columnist for the magazine, *African Woman.*

The First Time I Said Fuck

Darrel Bristow-Bovey

I REMEMBER THE SUMMER of 1981, because that was the summer Wayne Houghton caught the snake. It was also the summer Beauty left. But mainly I remember the snake.

We lived in a pink, rented house on a green ridge over the sea. It was a double-storey house but we only had the ground floor – the Houghtons lived upstairs, Roy and Vi Houghton and their daughters who were older than me and played music loud until my father banged on the ceiling with his Malacca walking stick, and their son Wayne who was also older, about fourteen, and used to teach me swearwords. Mainly, he tried to get me to say fuck, but I wouldn't. I was afraid my mom would just have to look at me to know I'd done something wrong. But I did say shit a few times, which was something.

The black rubber tip of my father's walking stick left small round marks on the ceiling until after his second stroke. Then it became too much effort to lever himself up from his beige leatherette La-Z-Boy recliner, so he would just sit there with a large-print Louis L'Amour cowboy book open on his lap, glaring at the ceiling. After his second stroke he found it hard to walk and he sometimes forgot what he was saying when he was halfway through. Also he started calling every maid we had "Beauty".

My mom said the maid we had when I was born was called Beauty and that must have stuck in his head because after his second stroke he called Doris Beauty and then Patience Beauty and then Mavis Beauty, and then another maid we had whose real name I don't remember because she was not with us very long. Each time we had a new maid he called her Beauty. We got used to it, and the maids didn't seem to mind. My mom said, "At least he doesn't have to feel like he's at home all day with a stranger." She didn't say that to me, she said that to Aunty Vi from upstairs.

After the maid whose name I can't remember left, our next maid was much younger. She came and knocked on the door and asked if we needed a maid, which is what always happened the day after one left. Word went round. We did need a maid but my mother was nervous about young maids. Often they didn't know how to cook or iron properly, and sometimes they got pregnant. Young maids got pregnant more easily than old ones. That's what had happened to the maid whose name I can't remember.

"Can you cook?" my mother asked her, standing outside on the stoep.

She could, and she could iron and vacuum and she could speak English and she wasn't planning to get pregnant.

"Do you have a pass?" my mom asked.

We weren't supposed to hire her if she did not have a pass, because she would be living in the khaya in the back and she wasn't allowed to live there without a pass from the police. She lowered her eyes and mumbled something. "No pass?" said my mom.

She handed my mom a tatty piece of cardboard, all frayed and worn.

"It's expired," said my mom. "It needs to be renewed." The new maid nodded and looked down.

"What's your name?" my mom asked.

"Beauty," she said.

"Really?" my mom said, smiling as though she couldn't quite believe it. "Beauty?"

So Beauty was hired.

Later I asked: "Aren't maids *supposed* to have passes?"

"Yes," said my mom, "and you aren't *supposed* to leave the table until you've eaten all your peas." So then I kept quiet.

My mom was a teacher, and some of the other kids in my street had been in her class, which is why they sometimes used to beat me up. Also, because I was younger than them. I did not mind – it wasn't personal. If there had been someone younger than me, I would probably have beaten *him* up.

Wayne Houghton from upstairs was kind of like my friend, although not really. If the other kids weren't around and he had no-one else to play with and he was bored with beating me up, sometimes he'd get me to throw a tennis ball to him in the backyard while he practiced his batting, and when he hit the ball into the garden of number 28, I had to go fetch it.

The old man in number 28 didn't like us. If he found any of our tennis balls, he'd cut them up with garden shears or throw them over the side of the ridge, down into the dark, tangled bush. There must have been a million tennis balls there, or maybe a hundred million, because none of us would go looking for them down in the bush, not even Wayne Houghton. That was where the snakes lived.

The snakes. There are snakes all over the Bluff, in the bush and the flowerbeds, in ditches and hillsides and drainpipes, under banana trees. At night adders slid across the lawns; in the day we walked wide around the patches of long grass beside the road. Once a snake killed Purdey our cat and my mom buried her beneath the frangipani tree in the backyard, but Tyler de Klerk and Donald McManus dug her up and left her on the doorstep of number 28, which made the old man in number 28 like us even less.

We hated the snakes. Mr Mocke at school tried to tell us not to hate the snakes so much. "They were here before us," he said. "We're just living in their front yard." But how did that help? They may have been there first, but we were there now.

When we were bored we liked to argue about which is the most dangerous snake in the world. Some voted for the green mamba because it coiled around overhanging tree branches and bit you as you passed, and others the King Cobra because it's the biggest and its bite can kill an elephant, but we all knew it was the black mamba. None of us had seen one, but we knew black mamba venom is the most powerful – just one drop in the reservoir could kill the whole city, which was maybe what the terrorists were planning to do one day – and instead of sliding away like other snakes the black mamba will chase you and it's the fastest snake in the world. There was a Chappies' "Did You Know?" that said the black mamba was as fast as a racehorse, so even if you were on a racehorse, you couldn't get away from it.

At the time it didn't feel like we were scared of the snakes, because they were just always there, like the wet summer heat in Durban that made you sweat so your back and your forehead were never completely dry, but you never noticed it, because that's the way it always was. It's only later that you realise you were always afraid. Always. Even if it felt normal.

It was a few weeks after Beauty had started working for us, that hot summer, when Wayne Houghton came to my bedroom window with the cardboard box. It was quite a big box, like a TV might come in.

"Look here," said Wayne.

I climbed out through the window and he used a stick to open the top flap. It was dark inside, but Wayne whacked the side of the box with the stick and a corner of the darkness seemed to move. I jumped back and made a sound like: "Haah!"

Wayne laughed and hit the box again and I could hear the dry rustle of snake against cardboard. "How's that!" said Wayne, his eyes shining.

"Where'd you get it?"

"Under The House," said Wayne, and I shivered.

Under The House.

Under The House was a kind of crawl-space under the ground floor, laid out exactly like the house above. You went through a hole in the side and it was all sandy and pitch-black, and the walls from above extended down with gaps in the same places where the doors would be, so you had a dark, upside-down reflection of the house, so low you couldn't sit all the way up and it always smelled of dry and dust. You wriggled through on your belly with your torch, shining into the corners of each room to make sure there was nothing already there.

We weren't allowed to go Under The House in summer because snakes went in for the cool, living there under our feet, under where we walked and slept and took our baths, but we sometimes went anyway. Wayne buried things down there, especially his stack of *Scope* and *Giggles 'n Gags* magazines, which although you might encounter a snake is safer than hiding them under your mattress where your mother will find them.

Wayne hit the side of the box again.

"What kind is it?" I asked, stepping very slowly closer. It began to rear up, so Wayne used the stick to push it down again and closed the cardboard flap.

"It's a black mamba," said Wayne Houghton.

My chest suddenly got tight.

"A black mamba," I said in a soft voice.

I wanted to see it again, but I didn't want Wayne to pull the flap back. If it got out it could chase us, and even though Wayne Houghton wasn't faster than a racehorse, and he wasn't faster than a black mamba, he was faster than me.

"What are you going to do with it?" I asked.

"I'm keeping it," said Wayne Houghton.

"Why?"

"I'm starting a zoo. I'll charge people to come see it."

"What other animals will you get?"

"Dunno yet. Maybe a monkey." I didn't think anyone would pay to see monkeys. You could see them all over the place for free.

"You could get a hermit crab," I said.

We looked at the box a bit more. It didn't look like a cardboard box with a black mamba inside. It just looked like a cardboard box.

"You must keep it," said Wayne.

"What?"

"Keep it for me."

"Where?"

"In your room."

Normally I found it hard to disagree with Wayne Houghton because I was grateful he was talking to me at all, but he wanted me to keep a black mamba in my bedroom.

"No ways," I said.

"Come on," said Wayne, "you have to. My mom won't let me."

"Nor will mine."

"But if my mom finds it in my room, she'll tell my dad. At least your dad can't give you the belt. He's had a stroke."

He had a point. "Why not just keep it Under The House?" I tried.

"Can't," said Wayne. "If it's there someone can come steal it."

That was another point. I didn't like the thought of a black mamba in the hands of Donald McManus, say, or Tyler de Klerk.

"I'll charge twenty cents to see it," said Wayne, "and I'll give you three cents for every twenty cents I get. We'll be partners."

And that's what had me. Not the money, but the thought of being partners with Wayne Houghton. A partner – that was something. A partner was like a friend, sort of. Then Wayne Houghton said, "Come on, please, man," and gave me a Vulcan Nerve Pinch, which was really sore but you only give people you like Vulcan Nerve Pinches, so I had to say yes.

Wayne fetched his father's *braai* grid and I made sure my dad was asleep in his chair like usual in the afternoon, then we carried it through to my room. I felt it coiling and uncoiling in the box, the dry, waiting weight of it, and I swallowed hard to stop the fear.

I cleared the shoes out of my cupboard and replaced them with the box. We weighted down the braai grid over the top with a couple of Funk & Wagnall's Encyclopaedias. It was quite a big cupboard but we had to squash in the sides of the box a bit so the door would close.

We pondered the cupboard in silence. I tried to think of something else to say. "Okay," said Wayne after a while. "I'll check you tomorrow."

I didn't much feel like being in my room the rest of that afternoon. I did my homework in the lounge while my dad dozed and woke and dozed, and my mom was surprised when she came home. "Why are you working in here?" she said.

"I'm keeping dad company," I said, and she liked that.

We had supper in the lounge as usual. Once Beauty had cooked the food she could go off for the night and go eat her own supper in the khaya, and once she'd gone my mom said to my dad: "I spoke to Beauty about her boyfriend."

Even though my mom had told her she wasn't allowed to have a man in her room, at night we sometimes heard a man's voice and Vi Houghton said she'd seen a man leaving early one morning through the back gate.

My dad sort of nodded. At mealtimes he needed to concentrate on cutting his food and not spilling it off his fork. If my mother tried to help he'd snap, "I'm not a child", which didn't seem like a fair thing to say. I *was* a child, but I didn't need help cutting my food. I said that once and my mom glared at me for about a minute.

"She said she told him not to come here but he comes anyway."

"Mom," I said.

"What?"

"What do snakes eat?"

"What?"

"What do snakes eat?"

"It depends. Some eat eggs."

Eggs? I couldn't imagine a black mamba eating eggs. "What else?"

"I don't know," said my mom impatiently, although she probably would have known if she'd tried. She said to my dad: "I think he drinks."

"Some snakes eat chickens," said my dad. "Do you remember we had chickens once and a snake ate them? In the old house."

I did remember.

"I don't know what to do," said my mom. "I don't like him hanging around here. It's not safe."

"And mice," said my dad. "They eat mice. Remember when you were small we took you to the snake park and they fed them mice?"

I remembered that too, just. It was a long time ago but I remember crying about the mice. I was young then. That was before I had a mamba in my bedroom cupboard.

"Sometimes," said my mom, " I may as well just speak to myself."

I didn't sleep well that night. I didn't like lying there in the dark knowing there was a mamba in the room with me. I pushed a chair against the cupboard door to stop the latch popping open and I lay in bed and held my breath, listening for movement. It was a terrible feeling – something in the dark with me, something that hated me. I thought of all the snakes out there in the night, all around us, underneath us, watching us. If they wanted to, they could all come and kill us, any time they felt like it. I didn't know what stopped them.

I must have fallen asleep some time because next thing I knew I'd woken up. It was still night and I lay in bed with my heart racing, staring into the blackness with the feeling that something bad had happened.

Then I heard it again, the noise that had woken me. It was someone shouting from the back yard, a man's voice shouting in Zulu. I didn't know what he was saying but it was loud and then there was glass breaking and the Alsatian next door in number 28 started barking. Then I heard Beauty's voice, also in Zulu but in that voice when someone's trying to be quiet and telling someone else to be quiet, and then there was more shouting and a crash and then I heard Beauty crying.

There was a sudden triangle of light from my mom's bedroom, and the shouting and crying died down. My mom's light stayed on for a while but she wouldn't go out in the backyard in her nightie and my dad couldn't go so there wasn't much she could do, but the noise stopped and soon enough I was asleep again.

Next morning I ate my Coco Pops in the lounge and listened to my mom and Beauty talking in the kitchen. Beauty was crying again and I heard my mom saying, "Did he hit you?" and Beauty was saying sorry and asking my mom not to fire her and my mom was saying "It's all right, it's not your fault" and Beauty was crying some more and saying thank you and when she brought my dad his morning coffee she was still sniffing and wiping her eyes.

After school I hurried home. I'd just changed out of my uniform when I heard Wayne outside my window. Sean Reid was with him.

"Hey, did you hear that zot in the middle of the night?" said Wayne once they had climbed in. "My dad wanted to shoot him."

"I didn't know your dad had a gun."

Wayne nodded. "He lets me shoot it sometimes," he said, which even then I knew may or may not have been true, but he said it so casual you had to admire it. I hoped when I was fourteen I would be like Wayne Houghton.

Sean and Wayne took the box from the cupboard and removed the braai grid and we stood on the bed, just in case, while Wayne pulled back the flaps with a pair of long braai tongs. I'd been expecting Sean Reid to hand over his twenty cents, but Wayne said he wasn't a customer, this was a consultation. Sean knew about snakes because he'd once done a project on them in Miss Stirley's class. He had a book about snakes at home, with only a few holes in the pages where he'd cut out pictures for the project. Miss Stirley gave it a B+, which meant he was like a snake expert. Privately I still thought Sean should pay his twenty cents.

We peered into the box. It wasn't moving.

"It's dead," said Sean Reid.

"It's not," said Wayne and banged the side of the box with the tongs. The snake twisted and moved its head.

We studied it in silence.

"It's not very big," said Sean Reid after a while.

"It's big," said Wayne.

"Not so big," said Sean. "Black mambas are bigger than that."

"Are they?"

"Think so."

"It's a teenager," said Wayne firmly.

"Are you sure it's a mamba?" said Sean after a while. "It could be a... mole snake. Or a house snake."

"Of course! Just look at it."

"Mm."

Sean's book didn't have a chapter about the care of the snake so he didn't have many suggestions to offer. I was just thinking that we hadn't gotten our money's worth for this consultation when he said, "You must feed it, hey."

"Feed it what?"

"They eat mice," I said, and Sean and Wayne looked at me as if they'd forgotten I was there, even though we were all standing on my bed.

"Oh, is it?" said Sean Reid sarcastically, to let me know that he was the snake expert and he knew that mambas ate mice. I don't think Sean understood yet that I was Wayne's partner in the zoo, not him.

"Where do we get mice?" said Wayne.

"Pet shop," said Sean, beginning to earn his keep as snake consultant. "My brother gets his from the one up on Greystone Road."

"Does he have a snake?"

"No, he has mice."

"Your brother's a spaz," said Wayne Houghton, and Sean Reid gave him a look, but he didn't say anything, because it was true. Bruce Reid wasn't quite right in the head. He went to a special school in Montclare and he wasn't allowed to play with us, because once when he and Tyler de Klerk were playing in a tree in Tyler's yard, Bruce Reid pushed Tyler out and broke his arm, although if you ask me Tyler de Klerk probably had it coming, if I know Tyler de Klerk.

Our attention came back to the box, where the snake had stirred to raise itself up the high cardboard side. Its head emerged over the rim, its tongue flicking and the box wobbling a little with the movement. And at just that moment the door of my bedroom, which I had closed but not locked because I don't have a key, opened.

Beauty screamed when she saw the snake. Wayne pushed it back down into the box with the tongs, but she'd seen it, and she screamed.

It wasn't just one scream. When she ran out of breath she breathed in and did it over again. Sean Reid was out of the window before she'd even finished the first one. Wayne dropped the braai grid back on top of the box and followed him. They didn't want to be around if a grown-up should chance to come see what all the screaming was about.

"Beauty, sshhh, sshhh!" I tugged at her apron and took hold of her arm.

"Please! Sshhh!"

I pulled her by the arm from my room to the kitchen. She was making little strange, high-pitched noises.

"Sshhh," I pleaded. "Please sshhh!"

"Martin!" I hurried through to the lounge. My dad was awake and half out of his La-Z-Boy recliner, looking confused. He was trying to stand up.

"It's nothing, dad," I said.

"What's happening?"

"Nothing. Beauty saw a snake."

"Oh!" He looked relieved. He stopped struggling and sank back into the chair. It was commonly known that maids had a terrible fear of snakes. "They think it's the devil," he said.

"Oh."

"Remember when you were small we had that magazine with the picture of a snake, and... and..." he frowned as though he were trying to see something at the bottom of a pool of dirty water. "And... Beauty wouldn't come into the room until we turned it upside-down."

I nodded.

"Where is it?" he said. "Is it in the garden?"

"No," I said truthfully. "Outside the garden."

"Well," he said, closing his eyes. "They're more afraid of you than you are of them."

I hurried back to Beauty. She was outside, squeezing her hands together.

"Beauty," I said, "it's OK."

She shook her head.

"Please, Beauty," I said, "it's not there any more. Wayne took it away."

She shook her head again. "It's there," she said.

"It's not."

"*It's there!*"

"Okay, okay, it's there," I said, "but it's safe. It can't get out, I promise."

She just shook her head and backed away and started saying something very quickly in Zulu.

"Please, Beauty," I begged. "Please come back inside."

"No, I can't!" she sobbed.

"I'll make sure Wayne takes it away tomorrow – you don't have to go into my room today, I'll put the ironing away. Just please don't say anything to the madam. Please! Just for tonight."

Beauty didn't want to go back into the house with the snake still there but I kept on and kept on and finally she agreed, even though she was still trembling.

"Thank you, Beauty," I gasped, "thank you, thank you, thank you."

The rest of the afternoon, she wouldn't go near my room. Every time she passed the door she glared at it suspiciously, as though she expected to see the handle slowly turning from the inside. I was grateful for her fear – it made me feel more brave.

Wayne and Sean Reid came back later, when the coast was clear. Sean Reid was carrying a brown paper bag, all blown up with the neck twisted shut.

"Is it still there?" Wayne demanded.

"Of course," I said with wounded dignity. We were partners. I could be relied upon to carry my side of the deal.

Sean held up the bag. There was the dry scratch of claws on paper. "Let's feed it," he said.

I stared at the bag. It seemed to move a little.

"Mice," said Sean Reid. "They eat mice."

"I know they eat mice," I said. "*I* told *you* they eat mice."

"Shut up" said Sean Reid, and punched me on the bony part of the shoulder, in front, where it hurts, but not nearly as hard as he usually would. Being part snake-owner was beginning to pay social dividends already.

And then Wayne Houghton said, "Don't hit him," and both Sean Reid and I stared at him in amazement. I thought I was going to cry with the simple, hurting happiness of that moment. Wayne Houghton was defending *me*! And to Sean Reid! Right then, if Wayne Houghton had wanted to feed *me* to the snake, I wouldn't have objected.

We went to my room. Sean looked at the box and shook the paper bag expectantly.

"Should we put them in one by one? Or all in together and see which one it goes for first?"

This, it seemed to me, was what growing up was all about – to be standing with two almost friends, about to watch a snake kill some mice. I felt I was becoming a man. I felt: here is a time I can say fuck. I was about to, for no good reason, just to be able to say it, when–

"Hey," said Wayne. "Is that your old lady?"

I heard it too – the sound of a car door slamming. It was about the time of day when our moms would be coming home.

"I think it's yours," I said.

"I think it's yours."

"I think it's *yours*. Go check."

I had no choice. "Don't start without me."

I went out back to the garages. We'd both been right. Our moms had arrived home at the same time, and now they were standing speaking in low voices that told me they thought what they were saying was important, although in my experience, grown-ups never spoke about anything *actually* important, like, for instance, say, a black mamba in a box in your bedroom.

"I know, I heard them," Aunty Vi was saying.

"But what can I do?" said my mom. "She won't get rid of him. You know how they are. Even if he breaks her arm."

"It's not safe," said Aunty Vi. "Him around."

"It's not safe!"

"And you've given her warning."

"But if I fire her, then what? Then she goes and tells her friends when I'm not here."

"That's the problem with having a girl. She knows your routine."

"She knows my routine."

"Ja."

"You know?"

"I know."

"But it's a shame because she's good with him. And she cooks well."

"But you have to do something."

"I know."

I was right. Grown-ups never talk about anything important. As I stepped back inside, I heard the shouting coming from my room.

"Give them back! Give them back!"

It wasn't Sean Reid shouting, and it wasn't Wayne Houghton.

"Give them back! They're mine!"

I ran back. My dad was coming up from his sleep, woken by the shouting, his eyes unfocused, the skin around his mouth weak and grey. My bedroom door was open.

My room wasn't very big, it wasn't really big enough for even just one of me and one snake, but now there were three people in my room, and several mice, and one snake. Sean and Wayne were standing on my bed, and Sean was holding a mouse by its tail and dangling it over the cardboard box. *They started without me!* I thought, a hot prickling of disappointment.

But they were looking guilty, and looking as though they'd been caught, and it wasn't because of me. It was because of Bruce Reid, Sean's older brother who wasn't quite right in the head, who was standing there shouting at them, his eyes popping behind thick glasses, his face red, so red it was purple, so purple it was turning red again. There was foam in the corner of his mouth.

"They're mine! You can't steal them!"

"They're not your mice, Bruce! I got them from the pet shop," said Sean, but I'm not his brother, and even I didn't believe him.

"They're MINE!" shouted Bruce Reid again.

From behind, in the lounge, I could hear the squeak-creak of dad's chair coming upright.

"Martin? What's going on?"

"Go home, Bruce," said Sean, but his voice was weak and he took a step backward on the bed, still holding the mouse by the tail.

"Give it BACK!"

Bruce Reid lunged forward for the mouse, and the cardboard box was in the way. Bruce Reid didn't look in the box, he just knocked it over as he went for the mouse, his mouse, dangling from his brother's fingers.

The box.

He knocked it over, the –

The cardboard box.

The cardboard box with the –

He knocked it over.

You could feel it leaving the box, unwinding into the world. The air thickened, as though the room were suddenly squeezed smaller.

"Fuck!" shouted Wayne Houghton.

Sean Reid just screamed and dropped the mouse.

Bruce Reid jumped onto the bed and tackled Sean, knocking him over, thrashing and whaling at him with his fists. Sean was still screaming and it wasn't from the punches.

I jumped forward, trying to get onto the bed.

"Fuck!" shouted Wayne Houghton again.

I wanted to say fuck, I tried to say fuck, of all the times in which it would be acceptable to say fuck, this was probably top of the list, but I can't in honesty say I said fuck. I said, kind of, "Fuuuhhhh!" as I flew through the air and landed against the Reid brothers and clung to them as they screamed and whaled and thrashed. I didn't want to fall off, I didn't want to fall back down there on the bedroom-carpet floor, down there with the empty cardboard box and what had been inside.

"Fuck!

"Aaarrrgggh!"

"Fuuugggghhhh!"

"Martin?"

But my bed was small and narrow, without sufficient space for three small boys and one slightly bigger boy who wasn't quite right in the head, especially when two of them are wailing and thrashing and screaming, and the third is clinging to them, and the fourth is jumping from one foot to the other, trying to levitate to the window. Bruce had Sean in a headlock, and as he sat up to get the leverage to strangle him properly, Sean tried to buck him and they fell back toward me, and Wayne Houghton tripped over us all, and we all fell backward off the bed, we fell backward, and off, and down.

The snake was there but we didn't land on it. It was against the skirting board of the cupboard, half rising, and it was bigger than it looked in the box, it was bigger and thicker. It reared as we hit the carpet. A kind of shudder ran through it, a gathered tension, a preparation for release.

We lay there still with fear, a tangle of small white boy, and the snake swelled and filled and gathered, angry, and I knew, I knew, oh I knew I would die in that room with the blue Indian Ocean outside, in the wet, salt heat in that yellow summer in 1981.

And then she saved us. Beauty with a broom. She came through the door and she swung the broom, the wooden kind, heavy, she swung it and the snake whipped and she swung and as the snake bent and knotted and came back on itself, and died, its heavy tail lashed against us. I can feel it now, that moment of touch, that contact. But I don't dream about it any more, which is something.

Afterwards, when the snake had been taken away to be buried in the garden and the brothers Reid had gone home, pockets bulging with recaptured mice, and Wayne Houghton had slouched off upstairs, looking mildly disappointed at losing the star display in his zoo, then Beauty started shaking again and crying and saying things I couldn't understand but which I guessed were about snakes and how much she didn't like them.

My mother told her how well she'd done, and how brave she was, and as reward she could go off early and she wouldn't have to make supper that night. Beauty said thank you. Then my mom asked how the snake had come into the room and I was nervous but Beauty shrugged and shook her head. I said maybe through the window, or through a water pipe, although of course there aren't any water pipes in a bedroom. My mom looked at me for a long time and narrowed her eyes. She frowned and she said okay, then she went off to buy Kentucky Fried Chicken for dinner, since Beauty wouldn't be cooking. She was suspicious, though, which made me glad I hadn't said fuck, even when I thought I was going to be bitten by a black mamba. She always knew when I'd done something wrong.

I went to Beauty after my mom had left.

"Thank you, Beauty," I said. "For not telling her. About the, you know."

101

Beauty said, "No more snakes."

"No more snakes," I said.

Then she smiled – I can't remember if I'd seen her smile before. Maybe she had, but I can't remember – and she went to go get the washing in off the line.

And I suppose that was the end of it, really, the end of that summer of the snake, except for one thing, the next day, Saturday. I was reading a comic I'd read before, wondering if Wayne Houghton would still want to be almost friends with me, now that we were no longer partners in the animal-entertainment industry, when my father looked out of the window and said, "Huh. It's the police."

There were two policemen in a yellow van, wearing blue uniforms and blue hats and brown holsters and black guns. They came to the door and spoke with my mom in low voices, the three of them, which made me think they probably thought they were talking about something important. I was reading an Aquaman comic, the one where he thinks AquaGirl is dead, but she isn't, she's been captured in a fishing net by Spanish people and she's lost most of her memory and she can only remember some things but not all.

Then my mom went to call Beauty from the khaya.

When she came round the front to the stoep and saw the police, Beauty stopped, and she didn't want to walk toward them, but one of the policeman said she had to. So she did.

Then one of the policemen said, "Let me see your pass."

Beauty looked at my mom and said, "Madam!"

My mom shrugged and she had an unhappy look on her face and she held up her hands, like to say, "There's nothing I can do."

"This is just a random check," said the one policeman. "It's got nothing to do with the madam."

But Beauty wasn't looking at him.

"Did you call them, madam?" said Beauty. "Madam, why did you call them?" She didn't sound as though she was going to cry. She didn't sound angry. She sounded old.

"Hey!" said the second policeman. "Don't be cheeky!"

"I didn't call them, Beauty," said my mom. "They just arrived."

And I'm her son, and even I didn't believe her.

They looked at her pass, not for very long, and then they told her to get into the back of the van. And when she did, Beauty didn't look at my mom, and she didn't look at me either. She just sat in the back of the van and I could see the side of her face through the metal diamond-grille of the bars as they drove her away.

"Where are they taking her?" I asked my mom, and she said, "She'll be fine, they're just taking her to her homeland, where she comes from." And then she said, "she'll be fine" again, but it sounded like she was speaking more to herself than to me.

I was about to ask where her homeland was, but just then Wayne Houghton came round the corner, wearing his baggies. He said, "Hey. Wanna come to the beach with me and Sean?"

And I couldn't believe it. Wayne Houghton was inviting me along. I was still his almost friend. Maybe, in time, if I was cool enough, if I showed I could belong, I wouldn't just be his almost friend any more.

"Yes, please," I said. "I mean ... yes."

"Just one thing, though," said Wayne Houghton.

I waited.

"Can you say fuck yet?"

I blinked at him.

On the blue sea white oil tankers were passing, heading to the world, or coming in. There was the low moan of surf and the remembering cry of gulls and the slow silence of the Durban heat.

I looked back at the house, where my mom was standing on the shade of the stoep, still watching the police car drive away, even though it had already gone. My mom was wearing slacks and a red shirt and this was before her hair turned grey. I've tried, I'm trying, but I can't remember what Beauty looked like. I can't remember her face, or her hands, or even her smile, that one smile I remember that she smiled. My mom turned and walked back inside the house. Suddenly I felt grown-up, and I didn't know why, and it didn't feel the way I thought it would.

I looked back at Wayne Houghton.

"Fuck," I said.

Darrel Bristow-Bovey is a columnist, travel journalist and screenwriter, living in Johannesburg. He has published four books, which have been translated into five languages. His book for young readers, *SuperZero*, won the 2006 Sanlam Prize for Youth Literature. He was a finalist in the 2006 Caine Prize for African Literature and won the 2006 SA Film and Television Award for best writing for the television drama series *Hard Copy*.

An Elegy for Easterly

Petina Gappah

I

It was the children who first noticed that there was something different about the woman they called Martha Mupengo. Following her was one of the games they played, past the houses in Easterly Farm, houses of pole and mud, of thick black plastic sheeting for walls and clear plastic for windows, houses that erupted without City permission, unnumbered houses identified only by reference to the names of their occupants. They followed her past *Mai*James's house, *Mai*Toby's house, past the house occupied by Josephat's wife, and her husband Josephat when he was on leave from the mine, past the house of the newly arrived couple that no one really knew, all the way past the people waiting with plastic buckets to take water from Easterly's only tap.

'Where are you going, Martha Mupengo?' they sang.

She turned and showed them her teeth.

'May I have twenty cents,' she said, and lifted up her dress.

Giddy with delight, the children pointed at her nakedness. '*Hee, haana bhurugwa,*' they screeched, '*Hee,* Martha has no panties on, she has no panties on.'

However many times Martha Mupengo lifted her dress, they did not tire of it. As the dress fell back, it occurred to the children that there was something a little different, a little slow about her. It took a few seconds for Tobias, the sharp-eyed leader of Easterly's Under-Eights, to notice that the something different was the slight protrusion of the stomach above the thatch of dark hair.

'*Haa*, Martha Mupengo is swollen,' he shouted.

'What have you eaten, Martha Mupengo?'

The children took up the chorus. 'What have you eaten, Martha Mupengo?' They shouted as they followed her until she went to her house near the road in the far corner of Easterly. Superstition prevented them from entering. Tobias' chief rival Tawanda, a boy with four missing teeth and eyes as big as Tobias' ears were wide, threw a stick through the open doorway. Not to be outdone, Tobias picked up an empty baked beans can. He struck a metal rod against it, but even this clanging did not bring Martha out. After a few more failed stratagems, they moved on.

Their mouths and lungs took in the smoke-soaked smell of Easterly: smoke from outside cooking, smoke wafting in through the trees from the roadside where women roasted maize in the rainy season, smoke from burning grass three fields away, cigarette smoke. They kicked the empty can to each other until hunger and a sudden quarrel propelled Tobias to his family's house.

His mother *Mai*Toby sat at her sewing machine. Around her were the swirls of fabric, sky blue, magnolia, buttermilk and bolts of white stuffing for the duvets that she made to sell. Duvets finished and unfinished took up space. The small generator powering the sewing machine sent diesel fumes into the room. Tobias raised his voice to be heard above the machine.

'I am hungry.'

'I have not yet cooked, go and play.'

He sat in the doorway. He knew that attention was always given those who bore the new. Casting about for such newness, he remembered Martha. 'Martha's stomach is swollen,' he said.

'Mmmm?'

'Martha, she is ever so swollen.'

'*Ho nhai?*'

Desperate to get past that dismissal, he indicated with his arms and said again, 'Her stomach is this big.'

'*Hoo,*' his mother said without looking up.

One half of her mind was on the work before her, and the other half was on another matter: should she, right this minute, put elaborate candlewick on this duvet, or should she use that time to walk all the way to *Mai*James's to make a call to follow up on that ten million she was owed? *Mai*James operated a phone shop from her house. She walked her customers to a hillock at the end of the Farm and stood next to them as they telephoned. On the hillock, *Mai*James opened the two mobiles she had, and inserted one SIM card after the other to see which would get the best reception. Her phone was convenient, but there was this: *Mai*James was the source of the gossip at Easterly.

II

In her home, Martha slept.

Her name and memory, past and dreams, were lost in the foggy corners of her mind. She lived in the house and slept on the mattress on which a man called Titus Zunguza had killed first his woman, and then himself. The cries of Titus

Zunguza's woman were loud in the night. Help would have come, for the people of Easterly lived to avoid the police. But by the time that Godwills Mabhena who lived next to *Mai*James had crossed the distance that separated their house from the rest, by the time that he had roused a sufficient number of neighbours to enter, help had come too late. And when the police did come, it was the clear fact of the murder-suicide that kept the long arm of the law from reaching into every house.

Six months after the deaths, when blood still showed on the mattress, Martha claimed the house simply by moving in. As long as she remained within, Martha was left undisturbed. As the lone place of horror on Easterly, her house was left untouched; even the children acted out the terror of the murderous night from a distance.

They called her Martha because *Mai*James said that was exactly how her husband's niece Martha had looked in the last days when her illness had spread to her brain. 'That is how she looked,' *Mai*James said. 'Just like that, nothing in the face, just a smile, and nothing more.'

It was the children who called her *Mupengo, Mudunyaz,* and other variations on lunacy. The name Martha Mupengo stuck more than the others, becoming as much a part of her as the dresses, from flamboyantly coloured material, dresses bright with exotic flowers, poppies and roses and bluebells, dresses that had belonged to Titus Zunguza's woman and that hung on Martha's thin frame.

She was not one of the early arrivals to Easterly.

She did not come with those who came after the government cleaned the townships to make Harare pristine for the three-day visit of the Queen of England. All the women who walk alone at night are prostitutes, the government said – lock them up, lock them up, the Queen is coming. There are illegal structures in the townships they said – clean them up, clean them up. The townships are too full of people, they said, gather them up and put them in the places the Queen will not see, in Porta Farm, in Hatcliffe, in Dzivaresekwa Extension, in Easterly. Allow them temporary structures, for now, and promise them real walls and doors, windows and toilets. And so they hid away their poverty, put on plastic smiles and planted new flowers in the streets.

Long after the memories of the Queen's visit had faded, and the broken arms of the arrested women were healed, Easterly Farm took root. The first wave was followed by a second, and by another, and yet another. Martha did not come with the first wave, nor with the next, nor with the one after that. She just appeared, apparently from nowhere.

She did not speak beyond her request for twenty cents.

Tobias, Tawanda and the children thought this just another sign of madness, she was asking for something that you could not give. Senses, they thought, we have five senses and not twenty, until Tobias's father *Ba*Toby, the only adult who took the trouble to explain anything, told them that cents were an old type of money, coins of different colours. In the days before a loaf of bread cost half a million dollars, he said, one hundred cents made one dollar. He took down an old tin and said as he opened it, 'We used the coins as recently as 2000.'

'Six years ago, I remember,' said an older child. 'The five cent coin had a rabbit, the ten cents a baobab tree. The twenty had ... had ... umm, I know... Beit Bridge.'

'Birchenough Bridge,' said *Ba*Toby. 'Beitbridge is one word, and it is a town.'

'The fifty had the setting sun ...'

'Rising sun,' said *Ba*Toby.

'And the dollar coin had the Zimbabwe Ruins,' the child continued.

'Well done, good effort,' said *Ba*Toby. He spoke in the hearty tones of Mr Barwa, his history teacher from Form Three. He, too, would have liked to teach the wonders of Uthman-dan-Fodio's Caliphate of Sokoto and Tshaka's horseshoe battle formation, but providence in the shape of the premature arrival of Tobias had deposited him, grease under his nails, at the corner of Kaguvi Street and Robert Mugabe Road, where he repaired broken-down cars for a living.

As he showed them the coins, he remembered a joke he had heard that day. He repeated it to the children. 'Before the President was elected, the Zimbabwe Ruins were a prehistoric monument in Masvingo province. Now, the Zimbabwe Ruins extend to the whole country.' The children looked at him blankly, before running off to play, leaving him to laugh with his whole body shaking.

The children thus understood that Martha's memory was frozen at the time before they could remember, the time of once upon a time, of good times that their parents had known, of days when it was normal to have more than leftovers for breakfast, a time of filtered memories. 'We danced to records at Christmas,' *Ba*Toby was heard to say. 'We had reason to dance then, we had our Christmas bonuses.'

Like Martha's madness, the Christmas records and bonuses were added to the play of Easterly Farm. And it was Christmas at least once a week.

III

In the mornings, the men and women who worked in the city washed off their sleep smells. They washed from buckets of water that had to be heated in the winter and dressed in shirts and skirts ironed straight with coal irons. In their smart clothes, thumbing lifts at the side of the road, they looked like anyone else, from anywhere else.

The formal workers of Easterly Farm were a small number: the country had become a nation of traders. They were blessed to have four countries bordering them: *to the north*, Zambia, formerly one-Zambia-one-nation-one-robot-one-petrol-station, Zambia of the joke currency had become the stop of choice for scarce commodities: *to the east*, Mozambique, their almost colony, *kudanana kwevanhu veMozambiki neZimbabwe*, reliant on their solidarity pacts and friendship treaties, on their soldiers guarding the Beira Corridor; this Mozambique was now the place to withdraw the foreign money not available in their own country: *to the west*, Botswana, how they had laughed at Botswana with no building taller than thirteen storeys, the same Botswana that now said it was so full of Zimbabweans that it was erecting a fence along the border to electrify their dreams of three meals a day; and, *to the south*, cupping Africa in her hands of plenty, Ndaza, *ku*South, Joni, Jubheki, Wenera, South Africa.

They had become a nation of traders.

So it was that in the mornings, the women of the markets caught the mouth of the rooster. In Mbare Musika they loaded boxes of leaf vegetables, tomatoes and onions, sacks of potatoes, yellow bursts of spotted bananas. They took omnibuses to Mufakose, to Kuwadzana and Glen Norah to stand in stalls and coax customers.

'One million for two, five million for six, only half a million.'

'Nice bananas, nice tomatoes, buy some nice bananas.'

They sang out their wares as they walked the streets.

'*Mbambaira, muriwo, ma*tomato, onion, *ma*banana, *ma*orange.'

In the mornings, the men and boys went to Siyaso, the smoke-laced second-hand market where the expectation of profit defied the experience of breaking even. In this section, hubcaps, bolts, nuts, adapters, spanners. Over there, an entire floor given over to the mysterious bits, spiked and heavy, rusted and box-shaped, that give life to appliances. In the next, sink separators, plugs, cell-phone chargers. Under the bridge, cobblers making *manyatera* sandals out of disused tyres. The shoes were made to measure, 'Just put your foot here, *blaz*,' the sole of the shoe sketched out and cut out around the foot, a hammering of strips of old tyre onto the sole, and lo, fifteen-minute footwear. In Siyaso, it was not unknown for a man whose car had been relieved of its radio or hubcaps to buy them back from the man into whose hands they had fallen.

At a discount.

On the other side of Mbare, among the zhing-zhong products from China, the shiny clothes spelling out cheerful poverty, the glittery tank-tops and body-stockings imported in striped carrier bags from Dubai, among the Gucchii bags and Prader shoes, among the Louise Vilton bags, the boys of Mupedzanhamo competed to get the best customers.

'Sister, you look so smart. With this on you, you will be smarter still.'

'Leave my sister be, she was looking this way, this way sister.

'Sister, sister, this way.'

'This way, sister.'

'This way.'

'Sister.'

'My *si*.'

Thus they spent the day away from Easterly Farm, in the city, in the markets, in Siyaso. They passed the day at street corners selling belts with steel buckles, brightly coloured Afro-combs with mirrors on them, individual cigarettes smoked over a corner newspaper, boiled eggs with pinches of salt in brown paper. They passed on whispered rumours about the President's health.

'He tumbled off the stairs of a plane in Malaysia.'

'Yah, that is what happens to people who suffer from foot and mouth, people who talk too much and travel too much.'

At the end of the day, they packed up their wares until the next day. And they returned to Easterly Farm, smelling of heat and dust, to be greeted again by Martha Mupengo.

'May I have twenty cents,' she said, and lifted up her dress.

IV

Josephat's wife was the first of the adults to recognise Martha's condition for what it was. It was five years since she had assumed her new identity as Josephat's wife. She had tasted the sound on her tongue and liked it so much that she called herself nothing else. 'This is Josephat's wife,' she said when she spoke into the telephone on the hillock above the Farm. 'Hello, hello. It's Josephat's *wife*. Josephat's wife.'

'It is like she is the first woman in the entire world to be married,' *Mai*James said to *Mai*Toby.

'*Vatsva vetsambo*,' said *Mai*Toby. 'Give her another couple of years of marriage and she will be smiling on the other side of her face.'

Josephat's wife made the connection on the day that she walked back slowly into Easterly, careful not to dislodge the thick wad of cotton the nurses had placed between her legs. Like air seeping out of the wheels of a bus on the rocky road to Magunje, the joy was seeping out of the marriage. *Kusvodza*, they called it at the hospital, which put her in mind of *kusvedza*, slipping, sliding, and that is what was happening, the babies slipped and slid out in a mess of blood and flesh. She had moved to Easterly Farm to protect the unborn, fleeing from Mutoko where Josephat had brought her as a bride. After three miscarriages, she believed the tales of witchcraft that were whispered about Josephat's aunts on his father's side.

'They are eating my children,' she declared, when Josephat found her at his house at Hartley Mine near Chegutu. In the mine where Josephat had a two-roomed house, she stayed only six months. After another miscarriage, she remembered the whispers about the foreman's wife, and her friend Rebecca who kept the bottle-store.

'They are eating my children,' she said and moved to her aunt's house in Mbare. There she remained until the family was evicted and set up home in Easterly Farm. After another miscarriage, she said to her aunt, 'You are eating my children.'

Her aunt did not take this well. She had, after all, sympathised with Josephat's wife, even telling her of other people that she had not thought of who might also be eating her children. In the fight that followed, Josephat's wife lost a tooth and all the buttons of her dress. Fate prevented the further loss of buttons and teeth by killing the younger brother of the aunt's husband. By the simple expediency of throwing out the dead brother's widow and her young family out of their own house in Chitungwiza, the aunt and her husband acquired a new house, and Josephat's wife was left in Easterly.

In the evenings, she read from her Bible, her lips moving as she read the promises for the faithful. 'Is there any among you that is sick? Let him call for the elders of the Church; and let them pray over him, anointing him with oil in the name of the Lord. And the prayer of faith shall save the sick.'

From church to church she flitted, worshipping in township backrooms while drunken revellers roared outside, mosquitoes gorging on her blood in the open fields as she prayed among the white-clad, visiting prophets with shaven heads and hooked staffs who put their hands on her head and on her breasts. At the Sacred Church of the Anointed Lamb, at the Temple of God's Deliverance, at the Church of our Saviour of Glad Tidings, she cried out her need in the language of tongues. She chased a child as her fellow penitents chased salvation, chased a path out of penury, chased away the unbearable heaviness of loneliness, sought some kind of redemption. And if the Lord remained deaf, that was because she had not asked hard enough, prayed hard enough, she thought.

As she walked past *Mai*Toby's house to go on to her own, she remembered that *Mai*Toby had told her about a new church that prayed in the field near Sherwood Golf Course in Sentosa. 'You can't miss them,' *Mai*Toby had said. 'You go along Quendon, until you reach the Tokwe flats. They worship under a tree on which hangs a big square flag; it has a white cross on a red background.'

It meant taking three commuter omnibuses, Josephat's wife thought, and planned the journey in her mind. First, the omnibus to Mabvuku, then one to town. She would have to walk for fifteen or so minutes from Fourth Street to Leopold Takawira, take an omnibus to Avondale and walk for another forty-five minutes from there to Sentosa.

'I will rise at five,' she thought, 'and catch the mouth of the rooster.'

She remembered that she had not been able to reach her husband at the mine to tell him of yet another miscarriage. The trajectory of that thought directed her feet towards *Mai*James' house. It was then that she saw Martha. The woman did not need to lift her dress to reveal the full contours of pregnancy. Josephat's wife could only stare. The sight reached that part of her spirit that still remained to be crushed. She ran past Martha, they brushed shoulders, Martha staggered a little, but Josephat's wife moved on. 'May I have twenty cents,' Martha called out after her.

That night, Josephat's wife ate only her tears.

V

In her dreams, Josephat's wife turned to follow the sound of a crying child. At Hartley Mine, her husband Josephat eased himself out of the foreman's wife's friend Rebecca who kept the bottle store. He turned his mind to the increasing joylessness of his marriage bed. Before, his wife had opened all of herself to him, had taken all of him in, rising, rising, rising to meet him, before falling, falling, down with him.

Now it was only after prayers for a child that she lay back, her eye only on the outcome. 'It is a matter of course that we will have children,' Josephat had thought when they married. 'Boys, naturally. Two boys, and maybe a girl.'

Now, he no longer cared what came. All he wanted was to stop the pain. He eased himself out of Rebecca, lay back, and thought of his wife in Easterly.

VI

The winter of the birth of Martha's child was a winter of broken promises. The government promised that prices would go down and salaries up. Instead, the opposite happened. The opposition promised that there would be protests. Instead they bickered over who should hold three of the top six positions of leadership. From the skies fell *zvimvuramabwe*, hailstones of frozen heat that melted on the laughing tongues of Easterly's children. The children jabbed fingers at the corpses of the frogs petrified in the stream near the Farm. The water tap burst.

*Mai*James and *Ba*Toby argued over whether this winter was colder than the one in the last year but one of the war. *Mai*James spoke for the winter of the war, *Ba*Toby for present winter. 'You were no higher than Toby *uyu*,' *Mai*James said with no rancour. 'What can you possibly remember about that last winter but one?'

It was the government that settled the matter.

'Our satellite images indicate that a warm front is expected from the Eastern Highlands. The warm weather is expected to hold, so pack away those heaters and jerseys. And a very good night to you from your friendly meteorologist, Stan Mukasa. You are listening to *nhepfenyuro yenyu*, Radio Zimbabwe. Over to Nathaniel Moyo now, with *You and Your Farm*.'

This meant that *Ba*Toby was right. If the government said inflation would go down, it was sure to rise. If they said there was a bumper harvest, starvation would follow. 'If the government says the sky is blue, we should all look up to check,' said *Ba*Toby.

That winter brought talk of the threat of more evictions. There had been talk of evictions before, there was nothing new there. They brushed aside the talk and put more illegal firewood on their fires. Godwills Mabhena who lived next to *Mai*James burnt his best trousers.

VII

By the middle of that winter, all of Easterly knew that Martha was expecting a child. The men made ribald comments about where she could have found a man to do the deed. The women worked to convince themselves that it was a matter external to Easterly, to themselves, to their men. 'You know how she disappears for days on end sometimes,' said *Mai*Toby. 'And you know how wild some of those street-kids are.'

'Street-kids? Some of them are men.'

'My point exactly.'

'Should someone not do something, I don't know, call someone, maybe the police?' asked the female half of the couple whom nobody really knew.

'Yes, you are very right,' said *Mai*James. 'Someone should do something.'

'That woman acts like we are in the suburbs,' *Mai*James later said to *Mai*Toby. 'Police? Easterly? Ho-do!' They clapped hands together as they laughed.

'*Haiwa*, even if you call them, would they come? It took what, two days for them to come that time when Titus Zunguza ...'

'*Ndizvo*, they will not come if *we* have a problem, what about for Martha?'

113

'And even if they did, what then?'

The female half of the couple that no one really knew remembered that her brother's wife attended the same church as a woman who worked in social welfare. 'You mean Maggie,' her brother's wife said. 'Maggie moved *ku*South with her husband long back. I am sure by now her husband drives a really good car, *mbishi chaiyo.*'

She got the number of the social department from the directory. But the number she dialled was out of service, and after three more attempts, she gave it up. 'There is time enough to do something,' she thought.

And when the children ran around Martha and laughed, 'Go and play somewhere else,' *Mai*Toby scolded them. 'Did your mothers not teach you to respect your elders? And as for you, *wemazinzeve,*' she turned to Tobias. 'Come and wash yourself.'

The winter of Martha's baby was the winter of Josephat's leave from the mine.

It was the last winter of all.

VIII

On the night that Martha gave birth, Josephat's wife walked to Easterly from a praying field near Mabvuku. She did not notice the residents gathered in clusters around their homes. Only when she walked past Martha's did the sounds of Easterly reach her. Was that a moan, she wondered. Yes, that sounded like a cry of pain. Without thinking, acting on instinct, she walk-ran into Martha's house. Through the light of the moon through the plastic sheeting, she saw Martha, naked on her mattress, the head of her baby between her legs.

'I'll get help,' Josephat's wife said. 'I'll get help.'

She made for the door. Another moan stopped her and she turned back. She knelt by the mattress and looked between Martha's legs. 'Twenty cents,' Martha said and fainted.

Josephat's wife dug into the still woman and grabbed a shoulder. Her hand slipped. She cried tears of frustration. Again, she dug, she pulled, she eased the baby out. Martha's blood flowed onto the mattress. 'Tie the cord,' she said out loud and tied it.

She looked around for something to cut the cord. There was nothing in sight, the baby almost slipped from her hands. Through a film of tears she chewed on Martha's flesh, closing her mind to the taste of blood, she chewed and tugged on the cord until the baby was free. She wiped the blood from her mouth with the back of her hand. The baby cried, she held it to her chest, and felt an answering rise in her breasts. She sobbed out laughter. Her heart loud in her chest, she cast her eyes around and took up the first thing she saw, a poppy-covered dress, and wrapped the baby in it.

In her house she heated water and wiped the baby clean. She dressed it in the clothes of all the children who had slipped from her. She put baby to breast and he sucked on air until both fell asleep. This was the vision that met Josephat when he returned after midnight. 'Whose child is that?'

'God has given me this child,' she said.

In the half-light Josephat saw his wife's face and his stomach turned to water. 'I will go to the police,' he said. 'You cannot snatch a child and expect me to do nothing.'

His wife clutched the baby closer. 'This is God's will. We cannot let Martha look after it. How can we let her look after a child?'

'What are you talking about, who is Martha?'

'Martha Mupengo, I left her in her house, she gave birth to it. She can't look after it, this is God's ...'

Josephat did not hear the rest of what she said as he blundered out of the room. It could not be; it could not be. A great fear seized him. He counted, calculated and found it was just as he thought. Along this road had he walked, ten months before. He had arrived home, and found his wife not there. 'She has gone to an all night prayer-session,' a neighbour said.

A wave of anger and repulsion washed over him. He had only this and the next night before he was to go back. 'A wasted journey,' he thought.

He had gone on to the beer garden in Mabvuku. The smell of his wife was in the blankets when he returned. The hunger for a woman came over him. He left the house to urinate and relieved himself against the wall through the pain of his erection. A movement to the right caught his eye. He saw the shape of a woman. His mind turned immediately to thoughts of sorcery. He lit a cigarette and in the flare of the match saw the mad woman his wife had told him was called Martha. 'May I have twenty cents,' she said, and lifted her up dress.

The need for a woman came over him again. He almost staggered beneath its force. He followed her inside, grappled her to the ground, forced himself on her, failed to control himself, let himself go, and in that moment came to himself. 'Forgive me,' he said, 'forgive me.'

He could not look at her, did not look at her until she said, 'May I have twenty cents.' He looked at her smiling face with horror; he fell over his trousers and backwards into the door. He pulled up his trousers as he ran and did not stop running until he reached his own house. 'It is not me,' he said again and again. 'This is not me,' he said.

His hand shook out a cigarette to light. There was a smell of burning filter, he had lit the wrong end. He wished to leave the earth, he wished to leave his own skin. He bargained with God, he bargained with the spirits on both his mother's and his father's sides. He bargained with himself. He would touch no woman other than his wife. He would not leave her, even if she never bore him a child. And even as he later gave in to Rebecca, to Juliet, and the others, he told himself that these others meant nothing at all.

IX

Josephat found Martha lying on the floor on her back. He raised her left arm, it fell back. The thought of flight shut out everything else from his mind. In a second he considered all possibilities. He covered her body with a blanket, and left the house. As he walked, snatches of conversation reached his ears from the group gathered around *Ba*Toby. For the first time he realised that Easterly was still up, unusually so, it was well after midnight and yet here were people gathered around in knots in the moonlight. Heart in mouth, he moved close, he had to know, had anyone seen, what had they seen.

The Babel of voices was interlaced with incredulity and fear.

'They were at Union Avenue today, they took all the wares.'

'They just threw everything in the back of the lorries.'

'Didn't care what they broke. Just threw everything.'

'In Mufakose it was the same, they destroyed everything.'

'Siyaso is gone, Mupedzanhamo too.'

'Union Avenue flea market.'

'*Kwese neku*Africa Unity, it is all cleared.'

'Even *kuma*suburbs, they attacked Chisipite market.'

'My cousin-brother said they will come for the houses next.'

'They would not dare.'

'*Hanzi* there are bulldozers at Porta Farm as we speak.'

'If they can destroy Siyaso ...'

'But they can't destroy Siyaso.'

'That is not possible,' said *Ba*Toby, 'I will not believe it.'

'I was there,' Godwills Mabhena said. 'I was there.'

'You men, the only thing you know is to talk and talk,' *Mai*James said. 'Where are you when action is required? Where were you when they took down Siyaso? *Nyararazvako.*' The last word of comfort was directed to the crying child on her hip. His mother was one of three women arrested in Mufakose, two for attempting to take their clothes off in protest, the third, the child's mother, for clinging to her box of produce even as a truncheon came down, again, again, on her bleeding knuckles. The child sniffled into *Mai*James's bosom.

'I will not believe it,' *Ba*Toby said again.

X

In his house, and without talking, Josephat took down a navy blue suitcase and threw clothes into it. His wife held the baby in a tender lock and crooned a lullaby that Josephat's own mother had sung to him.

'Your child will not be consoled, sister.'

'We are leaving,' he said.

'She cries for her mother, gone away.'

'We have to pack and leave.'

'Gone away, to Chidyamupunga.'

'The bulldozers are coming.'

'Chidyamupunga, cucumbers are rotting.'

'We have to leave now.'

'Cucumbers are rotting beyond Mungezi.'

'Ellen, please.'

She looked up at him. He swallowed. Her smile in the half-light put him in mind of Martha. 'We have to leave,' he said. He picked up an armful of baby clothes. He held them in his hands for a moment, then stuffed them into the suitcase and closed it.

'It is time to go,' he said. As they walked, to Josephat's mind came the words of his mother's lullaby.

'Cucumbers are rotting beyond Mungezi.
Beyond Mungezi there is a big white knife,
A big white knife to cut good meat,
To cut good meat dried on a dry bare rock ...'

They stole out of Easterly Farm and into the dawn.

When the morning rose over Easterly, not even the children noticed Martha's absence. They were running around and away from the bulldozers. It was only when Josephat and his wife had almost reached Chegutu that the bulldozers, having razed the entire line of houses from *Mai*James to *Ba*Toby, having crushed beneath them the house from which Josephat and his wife had fled, and having razed that of the new couple that no-one really knew, finally lumbered towards Martha's house in the corner and exposed her body, stiff in death, her child's afterbirth wedged between her legs.

Petina Gappah is a Zimbabwean writer. Her short fiction has appeared or is forthcoming in literary journals and anthologies in Germany, Nigeria, South Africa, Switzerland, the United States and Zimbabwe. She lives in Geneva where she works as a lawyer.

Root Gold

Shalini Gidoomal

AS MILESA 'OGOMBO' KUNGWU placed his highly polished shoe onto the 14th step of his new *mvuli* staircase in the posh Nairobi suburb of Gigiri on that Monday morning, he was sure he felt a shudder run through the building. He paused, turned to Tesai, who was, as always, a few steps behind him.

"Did you feel that?" he asked as he moved his other foot forward, towards the 15th step.

There was no time for a reply.

With a sharp crack, the staircase let go of the wall of the house. Ponderously – it was, after all, large and lumbering still – it began to make its way earthward. As it split into smaller sections – a railing here, a wooden step there, ugly steel supports clanging everywhere – it gathered speed, component parts landing on the burnished mahogany floor of the front hallway. Bits of intricately carved banister settled into a haphazard pile with blocks of cement, twisted struts and remnants of stairs. All were encased in a hazy uprising of dust.

Kungwu's back met with this mess when he headed downward. He floated for a moment, then his body sounded a dull thud as he landed on top of the debris. Above him, a section of balustrade wobbled, then followed. It was a weighty chunk, hand carved with primitive reliefs by makonde artisans, who had yet to be paid for their work. Destabilised by the crashing staircase, it too left its place on the first floor, and dived downward, finishing its trajectory by landing firmly on top of Kungwu's groin.

He would have let out a howl at this point. The wood after all was exceedingly heavy, and it caused his pelvis to crack and splinter into tiny little shards, stimulating a thousand nerve endings to jangle underneath his skin. But Kungwu's breath had effectively been knocked out of him, and he managed instead only a small, strangled squeak of air.

From Tesai there was no sound. Poised just behind Kungwu at the moment of collapse, a decorative spike of banister had impaled itself through him, and into the ground when the staircase fell. As the dust began to settle, Kungwu was able to clearly see the entry wound just above Tesai's belly button. A touch of gut had been forced out of his body and was lying by his side, gently peppered with the grey of powdered concrete. It was clear that he was irrefutably dead. And Kungwu was alone in this very large house. Trapped.

He tried to curse Tesai – who in fact was responsible for overseeing the construction of this home-to-be. But he couldn't. He still had no air in his lungs. Instead he lay there, lips open, lungs full of cement dust, grabbing for oxygen. His pupils dilated as he watched a sliver of steel strut swing above him, attached to the first floor balcony by a slim rod – the equivalent of a single thread. It moved slowly to and fro, teasing him, threatening to dislodge and mess with his head, in the same way that the other chunk of masonry had reconfigured the lower half of his torso.

'Get up get up,' his mind pushed, urged, cajoled. But his body refused.

For the first time in a decade, Kungwu felt truly powerless.

* * *

"Heh. That wabenzi is throwing parties already for that stuff," said Ameru as he flicked through the pages of the society section of the *Daily Nation*. A badly printed photo of Kungwu, smartly suited, arm outstretched, a handful of gnarled roots laying on his palm smiled out at him. Below the photo was a sycophantic list of Kungwu's successes. Trader. Businessman. Road-builder. And now, Ogombo entrepreneur.

Ameru flicked his gaze to the bottom of the story, irritated. There, a separate box-out at the end of the page summarized the result of the contentious demonstration he'd led the year before. And reminded that the outcome from the commission of enquiry was due any day.

"They've focused on us in this section. The protest. Do you think they'll want to come here to talk about it again?" Ameru passed the well-thumbed much-shared newspaper over to his wife, who had just returned from her early morning foray to collect old maize cobs and stray grass for cooking. She'd taken to walking the mile through the plantation just before dawn to avoid being harassed by the guards.

"Tch! What difference will it make if those thugs come around again? I mean how much more can they do?" Sana gestured around the emptiness of their small hut. Only a haze of cloying sweetness invaded the space, settling in the back of her throat. She coughed. She hated the dust that the hot dry wind blew over from the plantation. The air was stifling. She still wasn't used to it, this change in the weather. She took the newspaper outside. Only a year ago, she could have sat under the sprawling mango tree to read it. Now her small stool perched on parched earth, looking out at the hard fractured permanent fissures that surrounded their home.

Their dreams had drained down these cracks only a year ago. When they lost their goats. Their pig. Their donkey.

The bigger animals went first – it was just too hard to find fodder to feed them. Sana had been quietly relieved when it came to the donkey. Ameru insisted she tend to it each morning, and she hated the smell of the thing, the feel of its bristly hair, the resentful way it yanked back its ears and puckered its nostrils at her arrival. As the search for grass took more and more of her day, her resentment grew larger. The animal got thinner. Ameru took it to trading centre just a little too late. Its pronounced ribs meant that even with ferocious bargaining it only fetched half its value. He made the same mistake with the pig.

They meant to keep the goats. But Sana lost those early one morning, nine months ago while taking them to graze near the stream in the half cleared forest.

"*Eh Wewe.* Stop," ordered one of the *askaris* as he appeared from a thicket of yet-to-be-cut trees. He planted himself in front of her, and pushed her roughly on her shoulder, "*Lete nyama.*" He gestured to the goats. "You are trespassing with your animals here." The skin of his face stretched into a leer. She looked away, down at the ground. He bent forward, dropped his face to hers, breathed towards her mouth as he spoke.

"We can arrest you. Or your goats. You choose." His teeth shone yellow in the sun as he straightened. Waited.

As they led the animals away, occasionally clobbering them with their *rungus*, Sana wept a mute rage. Later that evening, as she and Ameru sat outside their house, the rich smell of *choma'd* meat, spiced with laughter, filtered up on the wind from the plantation.

Roast Goat.

She has not tasted meat since that day.

Instead their diet has shrunk, diminished. In the half-light of early morning, Sana creeps along the new plantation fence, hunting for entrance. Collecting material for cooking has become a major hazard, an obsession, now that logs, twigs and grasses are just a memory on that land.

"Eat," she instructs, placing the monotonous serving of boiled vegetables and a dollop of ugali on a plate in front of Ameru. He stares. He is much thinner too, now that they can only manage this one meal a day.

Late at night on the last Sunday of each month, Ameru goes with Sana through the plantation in search of wood to burn. From habit, they skirt the low-built *mbati* dormitories of the labour lines, even though they know the guards, along with the workers, are occupied tonight. As they steal silently past, they hear the rows of grunting men humping their monthly treat of women, shipped in by Kungwu from a few villages further north. Even there he turns a small profit, paying the women fifty bob for the night, and charging the workers double that, automatically deducting it from their salary.

When they reach the far end of the valley, they find twigs, broken stems, small shards of splintered tree trunk. Together the pair collect, gather and bundle sufficient wood to build a fire big enough for Sana to cook their monthly ration of beans.

* * *

Pinioned, Kungwu stared upward. He noticed the sliver of strut above him had stopped its pendulum swing and was resting, straight as a spear above his head. Of its own accord, his breath returned in one quick flabby gasp and he sucked in hard, compensating for what felt like hours of no air. The house made small sighs, wheezed a little, knocked a bit, but was otherwise silent. A gentle soft light that spoke of teatime filtered through the rough wood-framed window to the side of the room. Mahogany. 180 years old. Kungwu automatically inventoried the timber he'd used to make this new house. The fruits of his forest, he liked to tell visitors.

He remembered the leaflets he had found, pinned to hundreds of trees when he had first gone to inspect the land. They read; *'If you imagine the history of the world as one month you have been here for about a minute. About an eighth of a second ago you began to industrialise. In no more than a nano-second – from the 1970s onward – you ate 30 per cent of all the natural resources at your disposal. Don't add us to your statistic. SAVE KARURA FOREST FROM DESTRUCTION.'*

He had laughed as he grabbed and tore down a handful of fluttering signs attached to fig and prunus, grevillea and the occasional shrub bush. They floated pink and yellow to the ground, like useless confetti at the wrong celebration.

That had been the starting point of this venture. Just after he first met Tesai. They had been summoned to the sombre waiting room near the back entrance to State House. The room – all plush red velvet walls and heavy chairs with monstrous, dark carved backs – was, to Kungwu, the testing ground for any ambitious businessman. He carried his customary brown leather briefcase embossed with his initials. A gold-plated combination lock firmly sealed the heavy paper contents. It still surprised him sometimes that such small flimsy notes could weigh so much when placed together. He felt a kinship to them, a fierce pride and an overwhelming attachment. Late at night he'd open his safe to shuffle the stacks of notes bound with rubber bands, sometimes piling them high into little towers. To Kungwu they were everything. His life was dedicated to growing, gathering and gleaning as many as possible.

Tesai sat next to him, narrow shoulders rounded, lost in the chair. The sharp comb marks swept his thinning black hair back off his face, showing hints of pinkish scalp. A light film of sweat layered his forehead and a long finger worried the plastic strap of his Nakumatt carrier bag. Kungwu swung a disinterested glance at him. Some lawyer type he distantly remembered. Not a big player.

Tesai was summoned first, went in through the imposing black door in the corner, stayed four and a half minutes and returned, bagless. His shoulders adopted a more pronounced stoop as he headed for the exit. A lock of hair had lost its mooring and trailed over his eye, but he didn't bother to move it, scuffling out of the oppressive waiting room. Kungwu was next. He entered, got ten minutes' talk time, and came out having hand-shaken on the five-square-mile radius of Karura Forest conveniently sited behind the sprawling UNEP complex. In his mind he began sketching plans for flats, maybe a shopping complex, possibly an elaborate children's playground, and live music to attract Nairobi's aimless élite on the weekend.

They met again a month later, this time at an *Investors Today* conference, where Kungwu gave the keynote speech. A collection of chalk-pin-striped suits ponderously sat around a U-shaped table, pontificating over Powerpoint spreadsheets, and passing round the latest versions of their glossy embossed business cards during the tea break. In the early evening as they sat at the bar doing the real work of carving up more economic pie, Tesai approached Kungwu and extended a pale brown arm.

"Delighted to meet you in different circumstances. Drink?"

"Double Black Label and diet coke"

Tesai nodded to the waiter, and ordered.

"I'm sure you know that land you acquired was to be mine, sir," he began. "I even have the title deed issued to me for it. That last meeting was supposed to be finalisation of this deal. You should consider an equitable split. One that's profitable for both."

Kungwu sipped his drink, glanced briefly up at Tesai.

"No." he said.

Tesai reached into his pocket, fingered the small knobbly root and palming it in his hand, showed it to Kungwu, He turned his narrow shoulders away from the bustle of the bar, hunching them forward, creating a conspiracy around the two of them.

"Ogombo," he whispered, so quiet that Kungwu was forced to lean forward, belly resting on his thighs, to hear him. "Or *mondia whytei* to use its Latin name. An elusive natural-born viagra, found as climbing vines in selected forests in the east Africa region. It fetches a good $2,000 a kilo on the international market. The Chinese, Russians, Nigerians are all keen buyers."

Tesai folded his palm, closing fingers over the ivory coloured root. He carefully slid it back into his pocket.

"I refer to it as Root Gold." He smiled. "Easy to plant, now that we have done the research to determine ideal soil conditions. Relatively fast growth. Low investment. High return." He racketed out his words.

"It even has an additional side benefit – it cures gonorrhea. If used fresh of course. A few days after cutting it loses all potency and becomes just a veg – still good for you – lots of zinc, iron and calcium. Forget maize, or cane, or coffee. Or these new-fangled carbon credits and emission-reduction investments. Or the standing value of timber. None of it compares what can be earned from planting Ogombo."

Tesai paused.

"My High-Up friends love it. Naturally I give some to them on successful completion of business negotiations. Sometimes they ask for women to accompany it. I try to oblige."

He stood up to leave, the chunk of Ogombo, a small bulge in his suit pocket.

Kungwu motioned him back down. "Let's talk more," he said and he turned to the waiter to order another round of drinks. Tesai sat down. He surreptitiously wiped his moist palms on the armrest of the sofa, took a breath, and got ready to do business.

* * *

Without the forest, Ameru no longer has timber to trade. Instead he sits outside their house, his hair stained on one side by the ochre dust as he rests his lolling head against the wall, staring at the newly erected fence around the plantation. He reads, whenever someone visits from the trading centre and hands him down a newspaper. He eats. His only activity is to obsessively patch the holes and cracks that appear in the walls of their house, slapping on thick handfuls of damp mud, patting, smoothing, filling the gaps. Sana lets him do it. There is no way to bake bricks, to make proper repairs anyway. Not a log or tree is available to use in the kilns that trotted out thousands of clay bricks each week, just a short year ago.

Their price has tripled at the trading centre. And Ameru and Sana can no longer afford them.

* * *

The light through the window told of pale moon. It bleached Tesai's corpse, which had begun to smell. Kungwu's groin had assumed a life of its own, throbbing, pushing against the balustrade that covered it. Any small movement intensified his feeling of discomfort, of desperate impatience. A restless fly landed on the end of his nose, walking delicately up the bridge, investigating. He snapped it away with his hand. It returned, insistent. He waved his arms in angry frustration and understood the origin for the cliché, seeing stars. They swam in front of his eyes as the pain rippled through his hips, his frozen back. His lips were swollen, as though they too had been punched by falling debris. His tongue filmed with dust found little when he ran it round the edge of his mouth, seeking moisture. There was none in that region. The back of his trousers, however, were damp, soiled by the steady leaching of pee some hours earlier. It had been sweet relief at first to let go, allow the warmth to infiltrate his nethers. It reminded him that he was still alive beneath this hunk of wood. But as it cooled down, it became just another irritant. His thigh itched. His bottom itched. Yet he couldn't reach either, and didn't dare shuffle his position to scratch. How many hours has it been now? He couldn't calculate. Where's the search party? Surely someone's missed him? He thought of his wife. Of how she used to swing her long legs over the sofa arm when she watched cookery programmes on DSTV. How he could no longer spread those same long legs in their giant four-poster at night.

She had left him three months ago, sweeping their children and several bulging suitcases into her new red Landcruiser. He could see the small cold sore at the top corner of her lip, the first visible sign of the dose of herpes that he first acquired – and then gave to her. He reckoned he caught it from test-driving one of the women he offered to his workers. A wave of frustration swept over him at the reminder that there was no-one waiting for him.

"Jesus balls," he screeched to the empty house, feeling the word gargle at the back of his throat.

For a month Kungwu refused to attend social functions, furious at the loss of face caused by her departure. She had rented a small two bed flat in 5th Avenue Parklands and dispatched the landlord to collect the six-month rent cheque upfront from Kungwu. Determined to get her back by his side, he decided to starve her into acquiescence. He refused to pay school fees or any stipend for living. He cancelled her credit cards and requisitioned the snappy red Landcruiser. All the while he instructed Tesai to supervise the construction of the new house – the one she'd planned and dreamed and designed. The one he would line and face and hang and panel with every conceivable hardwood taken from the forest. The one he lay in now.

He closed his eyes and wished for the oblivion of sleep. Anything to change this relentless monotony of waiting. At least at home in insomniac moments – a common occurrence with his wife and family gone – he could summon Tesai to the house, even at two or three in the morning. Tesai always came. He listened as Kungwu issued instructions and peppered him with accusations, voice slurred, whisky glass in hand. "Crop this area!" "Why hasn't that gate been fixed?" "I see the growers came over the wrong weighbridge yesterday – I'll use your share of funds to pay the weight differentials if it happens again."

Occasionally, Kungwu chomped some Ogombo and ordered Tesai to bring a girl or two to the house, but that had to stop after a near fatal heart attack during one particularly energetic session with his favourites. Stress-related high blood pressure, the doctor told him. Not too much excitement allowed. It scared Kungwu enough for him to give up such strenuous cavorting. Instead the reality channel on DSTV became the background to solitary drinking sessions punctuated by the occasional foray onto the internet to play poker. At which he mostly lost money. Aggravated, he'd renew his early morning assault on Tesai, speed dialling his number on his mobile, snapping out questions at the sound of his sleepy voice. "How long does it take for this stuff to mature? There's only money going out. When does it come in?"

Kungwu could feel the lump of leather wallet in his back pocket, the wads of cash he habitually carried, pressing into his buttock as he lay there. But with his wife gone, and Tesai's prone body beside him, it could hardly rescue him now. He let out a long, wavering, frustrated, enraged wail.

* * *

When Ameru first caught the rumours flying around about the plans for his forest home, he burst into action. Wobbling his bicycle down bumpy forest paths, he went from village to village enticing, and inciting all to come out in protest.

"These trees are our soldiers," he repeated in each place he visited, paraphrasing a speech he'd recently heard from Wangari Maathai. "A soldier's job is to protect their territory from invasion. That Kungwu is creeping in, cutting our soldiers, to take our land for himself. We must fight. We must stop him."

"Join me," he urged, "We'll take placards onto Uhuru Highway, wave them at the motorists trapped in traffic on the way to the city." Many agreed to follow him. Some to break the monotony of their day, others for novelty, and even a few for his cause.

As expected, the traffic had built predictably up to its rush-hour three-lane congestion. Cars competed with honking *matatus* as they inched their way into the day. Hawkers slid in between the vehicles holding up magazines, sun visors, clothes hangers, bandanas, TV aerials, pushing goods through open windows in their exhortation to passengers to buy.

Leading the straggle of demonstrators through the morass of cars, Ameru took to the central reservation. He carried his petition, carefully penned on a large white double thick sheet of paper, and passed hawker-like, from motorist to motorist asking them to sign;

"Shocking. That Kungwu *makora*? Bring me a pen."

"*Enda*, idiot – what do I care about your forest?"

"Sorry but I don't give out name and address, even for good causes."

"You want to hamper development? What's so important about these trees anyway?"

"*Ati*, where will I get my charcoal for cooking if we don't cut trees."

"Stop what you're doing. Do you have a permit for this gathering?"

Ameru looked up. It was then that he noticed the tanks moving in from a slip road by the roundabout; the array of police, *rungu*'d, riot-attired, polished boots, moving steadily towards them. He saw the stopped traffic ahead, the space created for the army to move forward. Like a lumbering elephant about to squash a flea, the column advanced on the small group who'd been waving their flimsy banners, as the cars crawled by. He glanced behind him, watched as his supporters began backing away before turning to run. As if that was the signal, the first tear-gas canister flew overhead, smoking into the air. Just before his eyes cluttered up with their own water, Ameru spied his neighbour's son; a new recruit to the forces. His gaze held a mixture of apology and malice as he raised his police issue *rungu*. It was the first of many blows to land on Ameru over the next hour.

Nearby, a photographer snapped, clicked and whirred, capturing the blur of action.

The shot that was used on the front page of the next day's *Nation* newspaper showed a truncheon laying waste to the side of Ameru's cheek. In the background Sana was crying. Behind her a tank had swallowed a woman, leaving only a white scuffed-heeled shoe as she disappeared under its tracks.

'Collateral damage' is how the Chief of Police, Pangani division, described the unfortunate deaths that occurred as they cleared the demonstrators. Assigned the task of investigation of this 'unfortunate incident' he had often heard that expression used by the American press spokesmen in their TV briefings on military action in Iraq. He liked the professional ring of those words and decided they were appropriate to this situation. He inserted them into his statement, following it with a regular rant about thugs and gangsters destablising our precious nation. He added a final section about how these criminals hid out in forests plotting and planning their attacks on innocent civilians. About the need to hunt them down with no mercy.

The day after, the paper carried an inside, page three snap of Ameru's head, swollen to twice its size. Next to it, an editorial seethed about the donation of public land to private individuals. As Tesai fielded calls from journalists, politicians and businessmen, Kungwu opened his safe, heaped little stacks of notes into different piles and listed their respective destinations. Ministry of Lands, News Editor, City Council, Nema. Reaching for his briefcase, he ordered Tesai to mobilise the bulldozers, quick.

Sana had rested Ameru's head on a gunnysack stuffed with soft grass. Now the size of an overblown balloon, the side of his forehead was split open, as if the skin could no longer hold in the contents of his inflamed brain. She pressed a compress of infused tamarind leaves to the wounds and spooned a bitter distillation of marula fruit into his half-open mouth. Some slid down his throat but most crept out the side of his lips, dribbling down his chin as he slept on in their small house. She enlisted help from the local herbalist to prepare new potions, and each day as Sana pressed leaves and bark and sometimes soft red earth to his scalp, the bumps began to subside, like a leaking football sighing out air.

On the day that Ameru's head returned to its usual size, the carnage began.

And so did Sana's nightmares.

She hears the rumbling first. Then, as she looks out the window, the bulky form of a yellow bulldozer menaces past. A green lorry follows, disgorging a platoon of workers who swarm through the forest, spreading out to the left and right. Within minutes, the buzz of incipient chainsaws begins. One, then two, then tens of machines fill the air with a constant thrum, like a million bees speaking in tongues at an evangelical church convention.

As Sana watches from her small kitchen window, trees crash and fall around her. The large mvuli *that protects the small outhouse where they store tools, the huge fig used for shade, the sturdy deep green avocado, releasing its pulpy green fruit in great big splats as it falls to earth.*

She runs outside, heart full of protest when she sees her precious mango tree tilting at an awkward angle, teetering on the edge of its sliced-through trunk. Sana spins her head to search for her husband and sees him, rungu *in hand, reaching out to grab one of the many men with a chainsaw. She sees them yank his head back as a pair of yellow-gloved arms encircles his chest and holds him from behind. He doesn't have time to wail, shout or choke, before the buzz of a saw turns towards him. As Sana screams she wakes up, shaking.*

* * *

Each day Tesai stalked through the forest checking, counting, as the trees were felled. He measured and calculated, staked, and raked, cleared acres and created rows of turned earth, ready for planting.

Each day Kungwu sat in his office, stroking his soft belly with his pudgy hands as he clicked and moved his mouse, tapped his keyboard, prepared forecasts and spreadsheets, plotted graphs and road maps of profits to come.

Each night, the chainsaws resurfaced in Sana's head and she woke screaming, searching for comfort from her husband.

But he was gone.

As soon as the bulldozers fell silent, Ameru entered the plantation. Clouds of mosquitoes rose from their damp resting ground in the leaves of the vines, diving towards him as he moved through the rows of staked Ogombo. He did not bother to brush them off. Late at night, he walked, by feel and blunder rather than sight, in this ever-shifting setting, searching for memories. He found the spot by the little stream where he used to retreat when his arguments with Sana made him hot with rage; where he trailed his fingers through the cool, soft water. But now this channel no longer existed – chased away by the plantation, shunted and directed into a small cement holding pond. He visited the stately fig, leaned against its dramatic trunk, but it too changed shape, becoming a collection of logs, stacked and ready to feed into one of Kungwu's many factory furnaces.

As the tree mass shrank and the open spaces relentlessly took over, Ameru's evangelical zeal for salvaging some livelihood evaporated like rainwater hitting hot bare earth. He walked less, slowing each night, stumbling in the ravaged forest. As the last few trees groaned to the ground and the fence grew to encircle the plantation, the hopelessness of his situation filtered into his bashed-up brain. And he came to a stop.

Ameru lay flat on his back on the cracked dirt outside his house, looking straight at the sky. He held his breath, watching the stars glimmer above him, tracing their familiar patterns in the blue-black night. For a moment, as he stared upward, he could ignore the decimated landscape around him, the vacuum caused by the vanished woodland, the claustrophobic panic that rose inside him as each tree fell. Staring into the night, he let his lips widen into a smile.

Meanwhile, less than a mile away, Kungwu's jaw also stretched sideways, amplifying into a grimace, as he sought to squirm away from the grip of the weighty wooden balustrade, that only a short while ago had stood witness to

Ameru's nightly wanderings in the forest. His dusty shoes waved to one side, then the other as he squeezed his chest, braced and fought to drag himself out of his cell. But sandwiched firmly between mvuli and mahogany, Kungwu's efforts to escape collapsed in the firecracker of hurt generated by his attempt to release his ambushed groin. He lay there panting, still pinned on his back, held by the cadavers of the forest. With hope pressed out of him, Kungwu felt hollow inside, empty to the core, like a rotten tree stump. As his mouth dripped downwards, he closed his eyes, and fought the urge to cry.

Shalini Gidoomal is a freelance journalist, writer, businesswoman and inveterate traveller, born, and currently living, in Nairobi. She has worked extensively on various UK and international magazines and newspapers, including *The Independent, News of the World, FHM, GQ* and *Architectural Digest*. She profiled five Northern Irish photographers for the book *Parallel Realities,* and has worked locally for *The Standard* and *Camerapix*.

The Emperor's New Clothes: A Bedtime Story for Children of all Ages Living in Democracies

Farhad A K Sulliman Khoyratty

To Amal Sewtohul, wode peng you, wode da ge

Finding Paradise

No one is absolutely certain where Paradise is.

Try this. Look for the Continent that doesn't know it is the richest in the world, head south and turn abruptly. You are there. Can you see it? Perfect nature; multicultural harmony; *demos cratos*; model of development for its continent; more or less evenly spread affluence.

A small island shimmering like gold, as golden as all that glistens...

The writer Mark II called the island Paradise, and he is a difficult father to have. From the other side of the Ocean, San Pedro, the mother, left a similarly heavy heritage, calling it idyllic. How to live up to such perfection? Many a child bearing such a heavy burden will end up going to the other extreme for an identity – perhaps a certain devotional attachment to "Unity in Mediocrity".

2037: Goldtooth has served as a Minister during the last forty governments, regardless of the party in power. The crucial point at which to choose your party carefully is just before elections. He has done so consistently by an irreproachable instinct, a good ear on the ground but also thanks to a good number of men with a good ear on the right doors and to women with the right gymnastics in the wrong beds. He has been miraculously capable of prescience, and he always wins the jackpot, the right political party combination that will win – he *knows*, the way many in Paradise *know* who will win an election ahead of time. Goldtooth is ever a winner, with the right touch for the wheel of fortune of Paradise politics. When referring to his exceptional political longevity in a country that changes governments as often as it can, Paradise Islanders call Goldtooth the Emperor, a name that makes him beam imperially. Perhaps the name also refers to certain other attributes...

Goldtooth's endless re-election, some say, makes *vox populi vox dei* more like an empty mantra in a dead language. They fail to understand how it simplifies election. No matter who the people choose, the same remain in power. This is part of an effort to simplify both the political system and the electoral process. It is an effort *in favour of* the grateful people of Paradise. To further simplify things, political parties and their names are no indication of anything. All parties are neither right, nor left: they drive straight down the middle of the road hoping nobody will hit them. So vote according to your favourite colour – so much simpler – and prettier.

Goldtooth is Minister of Paper Clips, Pins & Related Affairs. The Ministry of Paper Clips, Pins & Related Affairs was instituted in the middle of the Economic Depression 2012. Its motto "Waste not, want not", its main aim was to reduce expenditure across Paradise by minding small waste, such as of paper clips and pins which, it assured, would raise the economy out of the quagmire. Indeed, under Goldtooth's guidance the Ministry has led to savings of the order of US\$ 1 million no less almost every year. When founded, it was hailed as an unprecedented innovation. Experts from all over the world arrived to learn from the experience. The Ministry of Paper Clips, Pins & Related Affairs costs, on average, US\$ 100 million a year to run.

Goldtooth changes mistresses as often as he changes governments but stays with the one wife as surely as he will stick to his one Ministry of Paper Clips, Pins & Related Affairs. His wife, Pallida, is a face with no body – she is a long-faced, pale-faced, sad-faced matron, who uses oil-paint on her face to draw expressions. She wanes next to Goldtooth as he sits sunnily in the patriarch's chair. Next to Goldtooth are the two pineapples of his eyes, his son and his daughter – Silver and Bronze. Silver stands sulkily, hands in pockets; Bronze has a long thin hand on her father's shoulder that speaks of almost wifely ownership and looks at the world with the haughty eyes of the truly insecure – she knows that as a daughter she does not matter in her family, but also that she is the best son his father will never have. A regal family picture.

As surely as married people will frantically seek friends for and as distraction, bad luck craves company. In May of this year 2037, the Island of Paradise is facing double trouble. On the one hand global warming is causing the rise of sea-level, and the whole island is about to drown. On the other, and perhaps as a result of the rise of the waters, the island of Paradise is encountering a serious outbreak of ethnic blindness.

In 2037, there are no glaciers left, except, evidently, the new ice shelves of the Sahara and across the Eastern Sahel, the new stopovers for cool dudes and dudettes, testing the new Hand-ski, also known as Upside Down Ski, where your miniature ski is tied to your hands as you scream your way down ice-dunes. Meanwhile, most of the lowlands of Paradise Island are submerged. It happens none too gradually. But there is no time for the past, no time for any long-term future either, just a hardcore present. Walls are erected to save at least the highlands, where those who matter live, with expertise from the Netherlands – Paradise Island *can* afford such solutions. So it is business as usual.

Ethnic blindness (*myopia generis*) was first diagnosed in the United States in 2020. The disease attacks one without as much as a Ni hao, a Jambo, a Salamalekum or a Howdy mate – no clear prognosis is available, but a disturbing friendliness to identifiably dangerous others is often noted in the weeks preceding the onset of the disease. Isolation is recommended as soon as it is diagnosed. One night you go to bed, in full possession of your faculty of ethnic consciousness. You can see clearly who to trust, who not to, good and evil, family values, diplomacy. Overnight, it attacks your retina, debilitating retinal sensibility and inhibiting the normal spontaneous dilation of your pupils. It mostly disables the nerve ends that send colour signals to your brain. At first you are unable to recognise physical differences but during the late stages of the disease, your sense of hearing and smell are also affected and you are unable to recognise accents and – more debilitating still – to *smell* difference, so essential to survival. The only good news – and there is one, fortunately – is that ethnic blindness is not very contagious – how it is caught, however, is mostly sporadic and unpredictable.

Although the popular view in Paradise that ethnic blindness was introduced by immigrants is absolutely discounted by scientists it continues to persist, side-by-side with conspiracy theories about government. Paradise hospitals are at a loss over how to deal with this strange new ailment, as are hospitals elsewhere. To ward off both the rising waters and ethnic blindness however, the good men and women of all communities gather together regularly to sing to their various gods, to burn at the stake the weak, promiscuous women, immigrants, homosexuals and drug-addicts and also to partake of fizzy drinks and homemade sandwiches.

* * *

Golden Opportunities

Goldtooth's son, Silver, is reading for a degree in Legal Medicine with specialisation in Medical Law, every mother-in-law's dream of a degree, at the Expensive University. He is following a new family tradition. It is his father's old university.

As a boy, Silver once played at wearing his father's University tie. And while Pallida, his mother, rushed to wriggle the tie from Silver's neck, Goldtooth was beaming with pride. Goldtooth announced to the six-year old cinematically: "Someday, my son, you will be an Expensive graduate too!" Just then, the little boy had suddenly thrown up on the precious tie, mistaking tie and bib. Goldtooth had reminded his son of the incident before he left for University. "Son!" he declaimed grandly, "You owe your dear father something – a new tie. At your graduation, you will have to pay back your debt thus – I will ask for a new tie from Expensive." This time they both cried, holding each other – this time Silver did not throw up.

Goldtooth has made good through a determination not be like his own father, whom he judged to be an unambitious loser and a dreamer. His father had been totally unschooled. The memory of his father chased him like a mad dog throughout his existence, so he could never rest on his laurels, but he could and did win the race of life.

The motto of the Expensive University is: "Felix sine culpa" and it teaches sons and daughters of the great how to be great, how to win always.

Silver has a silver spoon in his mouth and he carries the metallic taste through his University days. The father awaits the son's return, degree in hand, waiting to congratulate him for his effort by offering him an effortless, well-paid job.

At University, Silver is unable to see the pain of less fortunate foreign migrants, those with no hope behind and none ahead, those sent out to send back money to feed wife, husband, children, mothers, fathers, uncles, aunts, nephews, nieces and other dependents, those who cannot afford to return, who live in small boxes, hold on to each other desperately. Silver never sees any of this. What he sees of the Outsideland is coolforeigners, easywomen, and greatplans. Retrospectively, most of Silver's memory of University is of a drunken and smoken blur. Such is the greatness of the Expensive University that his intellectual obscurity will last a lifetime, hardly affected by certain calls of the grassroots in everyday life. In short, he is to remain essentially innocent of knowledge until his actual return to Paradise. There he will be trained into a very particular brand of pragmatism.

From his University in the Outside, Silver is waxing lyrical to his pater:

"I was lost in a small country
Found myself in a big country
Yet I need to return to the narrow Inside
To make sense of what I learnt in the wide Outside."

Meanwhile, Goldtooth is rather desperate for the Boy to start waxing practical.

This is urgent – Silver is his only boy and somehow he senses that now the boy may have to become a man pretty soon. He will need to understand and engage with power-play in Paradise – that the Republic is going bananas may not be such a bad thing after all.

* * *

Plato's Republic and a Recipe for Disaster

Power has a phallic shape. And courting it has nothing platonic about it. More like courting disaster.

The Paradise banana is small and flavoursome. It, and not the apple, is the national fruit of the Republic of Paradise.

There is a major battle in the country over how best to prepare the Republic's small delicious bananas, the banana republic as they are called after the French habit of reversing adjectives and nouns. Some argue they are best picked half-ripe, sliced julienne, quickly seized in and sealed with sesame seed oil and prepared with fish and a dollop of tamarind, a sprinkle of small dried shrimp, thickened with shrimp paste and a little curry powder. Others feel the banana is best selected ripe, chopped roughly, tossed in butter, with muscovado sugar, vanilla, cinnamon, folded into condensed milk and crushed none too smoothly with a fork, spooned into a crumbly biscuit casing, covered with flour lattices brushed with egg and syrup and baked until golden.

Anyone suggesting one can have both, one as main course with plain rice, and the second as dessert, or that the debate is useless, runs the risk of being scoffed at universally. If anything, the laughter this may occasion may end up uniting everyone in mirth, which is quite a feat.

While this debate is raging, the water-level is rising steadily, threatening to engulf the land with its intense debaters.

Whereas Goldtooth styles himself one of the fathers of the Nation, fork-tongued Paradise Islanders call him the Storytelling Father. They say that he is a master of storytelling, tells the people tall tales, and what he wants them to hear, then sends them to sleep, numbing their vigilance. What kind of father...?

* * *

Golden Calf

When Silver returns to Paradise Island, he is immediately weighed down by high hopes. Not of course before he is treated, like a Prodigal son, to the fatted calf.

Goldtooth is swimming in money, in a pool emptied of water then filled with gold coins of which the straightforward Minister's salary is only a tiny drop. The rest of the pool comes from supernatural sources – pots mysteriously appearing at the foot of rainbows, afreets pointing clammy fingers at buried treasure, dehins summoning demonic apparitions with the smell of fresh baby's blood, and a present from Minisprins guarding your house and family, standing over five metres tall, or the fabled accursed treasure of the corsairs revealed by a one-legged apparition.

Goldtooth sits his son down a mere week after his return and explains how dire the situation is, what with the rise of the waters in the country and the outbreak of ethnic blindness, and delineates his responsibilities as well. Silver is most attentive to his father, who explains frankly to his son how, while the son will have to struggle to extend the Dynasty, he isn't exactly starting with nothing. Besides the pool of money, people respect Goldtooth in Paradise.

"Sow your oats wild, get all the fun you will. I myself am no saint, you know..."

Pause for a masculine guffaw to share.

"Ho! Ho! Ho! Ho! Ho! Ho!"

"But do not fall into this business of love. It will only weaken you and thwart your plans for the future..."

The father continues:

"Marriage for you will need to be based on strategy alone."

"Is that why you married Mom? Was it Grandpa's money?"

"There are things that you are too young to understand, son. I myself didn't comprehend the ways of the world until much later in life."

Goldtooth stops to look into nothingness for a while, an effort to look wise. His gaze then returns to Silver.

"Your other grandfather, my father, is a bad example – he was a weak man, dominated by his emotions. Where would we be if I had followed him? You carry his blood in your veins and success, my son, is a constant struggle between one side of you and another, a struggle between what you are and what you could have been. Under no circumstances let the mask down. Never let go."

"Thanks, Dad!" Silver is feeling like a little boy.

"One final secret, son. Whenever you feel weak. Whenever you feel like you are in danger of too much sympathy with the people of the Republic, think of them as sperm from lesser men."

"Yuck, Dad!"

"You got it, son!"

Goldtooth explains to his son further how ethnic blindness is eroding the Republic's morale.

The appointment of Ministers in Paradise is a purely ethnic game – they are appointed solely on an ethnic basis. In turn, the Minister is expected to 'pay back' by giving priority to those of his/her community. Over the passing years he had done more than his fair bit. He had procured for so many of his community jobs, taxi and market patents, promotions, priority on hospital lists, inside information about government tenders, trips abroad on invented missions, exemptions, religious licences, fake addresses for schools, import and export licences, and so on. Indeed, why is a person appointed Minister in the first instance if it isn't for serving his group? In what way is communalism worse than patriotism? Isn't it a virtue to serve your kind?

Such an Elysian picture is being spoilt by the outbreak of ethnic blindness, for Paradise Islanders are becoming incapable of recognising their kind, electing them, and offering them particular advantages. It is a most dire state of things. To make matters worse, as the waters rise and threaten to cover the entire Paradise Island, some people's concerns are moving away from divisions, and focusing on the collective and the pragmatic. Fortunately, most are still very ethnic conscious. There is hope yet for Silver.

Goldtooth signifies to his son that he will get him to meet members of his current party the very next day.

Silver is very excited. This is the University he has been waiting for – the University of experience, the University of real life, in the shape of his father. That night is a blessed night, a night of perfect understanding between father and son. Both Gold and Silver sleep contentedly under the same roof, under the same stars. That night, consistently, the sea around Paradise gains an extra two centimetres over land.

But all is not well for long in the Gold household. Silver doesn't know that he will fall in love yet. The girl he will love bears a strange name. The girl's name spells Trouble, with a capital "T". This is because she was an unwanted child, born to a society hostess. Need one add that Trouble belongs to a different ethnic group?

* * *

Chemistry and Biology

Silver meets with Trouble for the first time three months after his father's warning. It is at a party at the Mahmoods.

Mahmood the Patriot is Goldtooth's friend. He is called the patriot because he has married four wives, four houries, one from each of the main communities of Paradise. Mahmood the Patriot is not just a patriot, he is an egalitarian at heart – for he mistreats each of his wives equally. It may be hard to understand why Paradise Islanders call him a patriot, except perhaps in that he is optimising local human resources and quite clearly practises an anti-discrimination policy.

Mahmood Jr. is Mahmood the Patriot's son. Objecting to his father's polygamy, he has a wife and three mistresses, each from a main community.

As soon as they are introduced, right away, Silver is deep into Trouble.

What causes love? Is there a formula?

Sometimes there is. Here, it is Mahmood Sr. who plays the unwitting and unlikely (he looks more like Father Christmas) Cupid.

Mahmood spots Silver and Trouble in deep animated conversation through most of the evening. So he swoops in to intercept with the fabled grace of a warthog.

"Silver, my son, can I talk to you? I mean, privately?"

"Of course, sir."

"You know, Trouble is my wife's cousin."

Which wife's cousin, now? "Aah! Yes, sir!"

Trouble is still within earshot. So, Silver suggests to Mahmood that they take a walk.

"Trouble isn't the kind of girl you ought to be with – you are a politician. If you want fun, there's plenty of girls out there. Don't blush, boy. Just remember that."

Now Silver is a matchmaker's dream come true, so there is no dearth of marriage proposals coming his way. But, such a specific warning cannot but make Trouble that much more interesting to Silver than girls he has a passing interest in. Such is, often, the formula for love.

So, while Mahmood is thinking how Goldtooth owes him one, Silver is getting suitably intrigued by Trouble and is thinking how he must keep any eventual relationship a secret from everyone.

"Also, she is from another ethnic group."

The cheek of it – Mahmood of all people!

By the end of the night, Silver is determined. This is the woman for him.

The relationship develops naturally. Two young souls in love. Certainly, it isn't easy for a politician, and an eligible bachelor at that, to hide from the paparazzi. Yet, all that hiding and ducking, jumping into bushes is part of the spice that keeps their curry hot.

It is a year later, and they are still together.

One day, lying in the grass after some hot lovemaking in a clearing in the woods, feeling like the only people on Earth, like Adam and Eve, they wonder about the future:

"You will leave me once you're Minister, won't you?"

"Stop that nonsense!" He kisses her to stop her nonsense. "Not until you are old and wrinkly. Yet, even then, I'll reconsider!"

He giggles and buries his head between her breasts and forgets it all as he drifts into deep sleep. Her eyes are open, watching the flowers fall from the trees above.

With his father, Silver is behaving perfectly. He is frequenting the right people and has followed his father's footsteps in his current political party.

* * *

Double Trouble in Paradise

It is bound to happen on the small island of Paradise: people gossip all the time – all to do with boredom. Also, on a small island is a concentration of susceptibilities, petty envy and back-biting. Despite the waters rising.

One day, Bronze, Silver's sister, finding out about Silver and Trouble's relationship, decides to disturb the couple's Eden bliss. She bides her time and watches the couple's movements silently. This is much cleaner than planting things, for instance. A couple of weeks later she is thus able to find an exposed heel where best to sting. For, Trouble's flatmate is into the occasional dope although she herself has given up, indeed, ironically, to refrain from creating problems for Silver.

One sibilant phone-call later, Trouble is picked up by the police with her flatmate. Trouble is very distressed but Silver promises to do the right thing for her.

That night, a very nervous Silver decides it is time to inform his father of Trouble's existence before any of it splashes onto the whole family.

He is taken aback when Goldtooth informs him that he already knows. More so when he declares he has no objections to the ethnic difference.

"Do you think I will allow my boy to go out with a girl unsupervised? I even met with Trouble's mother. We both agree some fun will do both of you a lot of good..."

"So, you have me followed?"

"Learn, my boy, learn! It is better to be informed than not to be."

"!"

"This is all a learning curve."

"The fact is: I love Trouble!"

"Ah! Love! Been there myself many times! It will pass. See how easy things become when you toe the line – one phone-call and Trouble is off the hook."

He makes the phone call.

"See, my boy, you must admire this country. Things are so simple here. Make sure you don't get involved with Trouble again. It might be better."

He agrees not to seek Trouble again.

When informed about the decision, over the phone, by Silver, she tells him she was expecting this.

"Huh!" she says to Silver, "When it comes to love and politics, we seem ready to follow Daddy's footsteps, don't we?"

Elections come and go. As sure as clockwork, Goldtooth's elected party is elected. As sure as clockwork, he becomes Minister of Paper Clips, Pins & Related Affairs. But this time, his son, Silver, becomes Minister of Wood & Other Inedible Stuff, admittedly a lesser ministry than the Ministry of Paper Clips, Pins & Related Affairs, carrying a smaller budget, but what a solid start! Few moments in the lives of few men can match Goldtooth's pride as he welcomes his only son into the Most August Parliament (so-called since Parliamentarians only work the one month at most).

One evening many months later, after a prolonged session of dinner and boozing, Silver decides to sleep it out at Goldtooth's bungalow.

As he walks in, first Silver finds half-eaten Chinese takeaway boxes on the table. Intrigued, he walks into the sitting-room. Suddenly, Silver catches sight of Goldtooth whispering sweet-and-sour nothings to some lady tarted up and varnished like a Peking duck (whole, sliced – Item 96). The tip of her panty-hosed foot is stroking his socked ankle, for some rather elaborate footwear love. Sadly, they aren't wearing much more than footwear.

The varnished rouged lady is truly lipstuck and lipstruck to be caught thus by Goldtooth's son. Silver can only point and point a finger at this, the Emperor, one of the Fathers of the Nation, thus caught, with no clothes on.

"Et tu, Pater? And to your own sperm?"

For the painted lady, undressed to the nines, is no less than Trouble.

* * *

Paradise Lost

Outside, the waters are rising in gurgles and with a flushing sound; Paradise Island is being covered steadily, relentlessly. The Islanders are up a certain creek without a paddle, so they use their hands instead.

Farhad A K Sulliman Khoyratty was born in 1972, and lectures at the University of Mauritius. Awarded more than twenty academic titles, prizes and fellowships, he also won the HSBC/SA PEN Literary Award 2005 (2nd), the Mauritius Ministry of Arts and Culture Short-Story Writing Competition (1st) and the Prix du Jeune Ecrivain Francophone. His publications range from literature to philosophy, from gastronomy to geopolitics to cinema.

1985
(When memoirs fail)

Charles A Matathia

THE TIME IS ABOUT now. If I had a watch I would have told you the time down to the last second, but I do not have one. Neither do I know what day of the week it is. It could be Monday, Thursday, Sunday... who cares? There is a calendar on the wall. I am staring at it but it is of no help. The calendar is stuck to December 1985.

1985. Was that the year the government truck rolled into our settlement with blankets, soap and vials of antibiotics? All those things that we didn't need because all we cared for was some food. Maybe that wasn't the year. Maybe 1985 was the year my mother bought a can of Ambi skin-lightening cream from the *duka* and got a free calendar; a calendar that she could use as a countdown to what they refer to today as before (hydrocortisone bleach) and after photos.

December 1985 is such a long time ago and I was a little boy back then. There isn't much I can remember. I am told that after they brought in all those unnecessary goodies, the chief, being the government's representative, asked them to bring what we had use for: food. The next day a caravan of government Land Rovers crawled into the settlement laden with yellow maize.

Yellow maize? No one had seen yellow maize before. The village *doctor* took a few grains and threw them on his holy skins. "This is bizarre," he yelled. He grabbed a whole sack and disappeared with it into the eerie depths of his hut. The whole village stood outside bated breath twisting their famished expressions. My mother swatted a plethora of gnats off my emaciated body nonchalantly, or so she tells me in retrospect. Those are the times for which I wish this was Ethiopia and a celebrated photojournalist had swept the scene with his bionic arm bringing the video camera to bear on my sallow face and freeze framing my moment of deprivation.

That would have made me famous, right? Made me the poster child for Africa's

143

biggest exports: hunger, pestilence, disease. All the global newspapers would have had my visage plastered beneath their screaming headlines: Do they know it is Christmas? Two decades later, that photojournalist would still be selling rights to my image to other one-armed or one-manned Save Africa Crusades: Bono, Angelina Jolie... even Nesson May-ndila would have autographed those photos as true replicas of his impoverished childhood in Umkhontoland.

* * *

"1985! So many harvests gone by," My mother rumbles. So many harvests or the lack of them, I say to myself. I throw another log into the fire and sparks fly up into every nook and crevice of a kitchen that has been dark since the lamp ran out of paraffin. For one moment I imagine the cockroaches biding their time in there, rattled, and I can even hear some rats scampering to safety. But my grandmother, sitting, half lying in her usual corner doesn't flinch. Tens of sparks cling tenaciously to her dress, an ancient calico dress that my grandfather bought her on their wedding day back in the *magineti* years. A thing she has refused to shed these last eight years that grandfather has been dead. A rag that out-stinks both the goat in the inner corner of the kitchen and the pig outside. The pig that the butcher boy has refused to come collect even as he continues to roam from one village pig sty to the next, hands in pockets and nose in the air speaking only in shoulder shrugs: "Always bigger pigs to fry on the next ridge!"

I watch in fascination as the sparks cut through grandmother's dress making contact with her skin. In all this darkness I can see more sparks lunge through the flimsy membrane of cloth finding their target, and scarring grandmother's ancient skin. I imagine them wiling their smouldering wiles in folds of withered skin and assume that when enough of them are gathered, I will be able to smell the sickly sweet aroma of singed flesh. Does burning human flesh smell like *nyama choma*?

The insane thing is that grandmother doesn't flinch. Even as those sparks keep hugging her obscenely close, mingling with the dry edges of her breasts and crawling into her thighs, she shows no feeling. It all makes me worry about that disease that mother says grandmother has. The one-sider disease that has killed all sensation on the left side of her body. I do not know why everyone says it has killed her left side because as far as I know, and I have jabbed her sides with a thorn to prove it, even her right side has no feelings.

I remember the day I set out to test how much feeling grandmother had on her right side. I had come in from grazing the cows and I was thoroughly upset. For a long time, me and the other boys had had to walk further and further away from the village in search of pasture. That plant that the forestry officer and the smile smiley *mzungus* in the big cars had planted near our homes had killed all our pasture. We had come to call the plant *mathenge* and we were afraid of it because every time a goat got entangled in it, the plant would stab at it with its gangly thorns and the goat would get paralyzed on one side like grandmother. Some of the boys even said that their goats had gone blind after being pricked by *mathenge* thorns. Grandmother was blind too. Sometimes I thought she had crawled into a *mathenge* bush in search of a toilet and paid the price.

I stabbed grandmother on her right side with a *mathenge* thorn. Nothing happened. She just sat there as paralysed on her left side, and her right too it seemed to me, as ever. I stabbed her again, a little lower this time and something finally happened. A thin fluid the colour of blood-stained puss began to dribble out of her, slowly at first and then like sour milk through a rip in the goatskin gourd, the fluid rushed out. I had just jabbed her on the exact spot where my mother had pricked giving the last insulin injection.

I do not know what happened to grandmother after that. Honestly. I sneaked out of the smoke filled kitchen and made for my mud and wattle lean-to next door. I was convinced that the old woman was going to die on my watch. So I packed the two yellow shirts and the khaki shorts that were part of my school uniform, the old green sweater that grandfather had retired into my possession and a pair of stone-wash jeans, the sum total of my wardrobe, into a tin box and made for the city.

* * *

The old woman didn't die. Yes, thank God for small mercies. So here she is sitting right where I left her and still wearing the same expression – a vacant expression.

I came back home yesterday. I walked right up to her mumbling that I was sorry for what I did to her that day.

"Hello." I said

Mother was in the kitchen too. She shook her head sadly, "She cannot hear you *baba*. Her hearing is gone."

I shed a woeful tear. By the owner of *Nyaga* I did. And even now I shed another because I really want to talk to grandmother. I want to ask *cucu* where she was in 1985. I want to ask, but grandmother cannot hear me. I shed a tear because she sits in the same place, after all these years, and wears the same expression. The only thing changed is that she is now deaf.

"Where was *cucu* in December 1985?" I ask mother. Mother's face crinkles into

145

a smile. This is probably the only time I can remember seeing mother smile. Isn't it surprising how pretty she is?

Too bad the smile doesn't wipe out all the harsh scars that tattoo her face; her trophy haul from numerous *chang'aa* den brawls. But it sure does tone them down.

"*Cucu* saw us through that heavy time," Mother whispers as she caresses grandmother with an admiring glance. "Those were difficult times *baba*. Most of the time I was out there trying to keep all these hoodlums off my *chang'aa* stills. Can you imagine those buttocks coming to steal my grain? Bad devils these villagers. Before, they used to steal the alcohol which wasn't too bad a thing because they came when the liquor was cooked and I had sold most of it and added water to the rest. But the grain... *shidwe!* How can someone steal fermenting grain? *Alafu*, if they steal my grain, how do they think I will make the alcohol, the alcohol that feeds my family?"

Mother went quiet for a while squinting into the dancing shadows. Saliva seemed to be dribbling from the corner of her mouth. When she sighed and blew her nose, I knew that she was crying. The past is too painful to remember.

I know how painful the past is in remembrance. These last fifteen years I have spent them battling my past. My past. A past that lives in utter contrast with my present. A past whose ubiquitous struggles are continuously rivalled by my innumerable successes today.

"Why do you ask all these things *baba*?" Mama tears through my train of thought.

"Because I want to know," I respond matter-of-factly.

"But all these years *baba*, where have you been? For fifteen years I have worried my heart out. I didn't know where to look for you. I gave you up for dead. Frankly. Maybe I should have had more faith in the owner of *Nyaga*... but surely, I just came home one day and you weren't there. And the next day and the next... Why did you go... where did you go...?"

I do not respond.

My mother squints deeper into the shadows. I pick up another log and throw it into the fire. Yellow flames lunge at us, sparks make a beeline for grandmother as always and the shadows dance to the drone of our uneasy silence.

I step outside and light a cigarette.

* * *

Outside. The aggravating buzz of the cricket; the receding croak-croak of a frog; the starry night; the screeching of nocturnal predators; the discordant notes of *Baba* Mwai's drunken return home; the animal howls of *Mama* Mwai as *Baba* Mwai's misshapen boot connects with her distended belly again. Fifteen years later, nothing has changed. The village seems as though stuck in an interminable vortex of time. Like grandmother, the village doesn't seem to have seen better days.

I can see a red light blinking attentively from inside my shirt pocket. I reach into my pocket, pull out the Dictaphone and press the record switch to turn off the light. The recorder is off but the night-noises play on. What is there to record though, I wonder, as I slip the recorder back into the pocket: the eerie night sounds of a poverty-haunted village?

I take a deep drag on my cigarette and flick the stub onto the roof of the mud and wattle lean-to. The lean-to that was once my bedroom; a home to all my worldly possessions until that day fifteen years ago.

Today five hens and one proud cock call that lean-to home. What about me? I have no home here. I am dead to this family, this village, and they are dead to me. Whatever I mean to them now that I have reappeared I cannot tell; but all I know is that to me, they are mere characters in my next book.

My grandmother sitting, half-lying in the same spot is nothing but fodder for an angst-filled story. A poverty-struck mother, a human vegetable for a grandmother, a homecoming – what better formula for a best selling memoir?

What will the reader think about me stabbing my grandmother with a *mathenge* thorn? I wonder. That I was a sociopath? And now that I am returned home, will they think that it is redemption I seek? That I wanted to say sorry to grandmother because I really am?

How can I make the reader understand that all I meant to do was to massage my grandmother into filling the gaps in my past? That all I wanted was background information on how we survived the drought? That all I needed were snippets about life in an impoverished village? All I want is sound bites, colour, turns of the phrase; the subtle nuances that add texture and depth to a good story.

But readers will be readers. Since my first book: *Time and Place – Rock Art of the Bango Tribesman*, I have received thousands of letters from readers who thought that I should make my characters less evil. Readers who have been raised on the literature of: Good triumphs over Evil. Readers who want to own my story. Too bad I cannot make them understand that I wrote it my way.

You see, my memoirs are all done now. The story of my life as told by me. The story of a self-made man. The only thing missing is my impoverished childhood and of that I mean to write tonight.

It is hard to make the reader understand that I didn't run off because I thought grandmother would die. That I ran off because I knew a better life existed out there in the city. But look at me now, can't you see that to be true? Would I have published three Bestsellers looking after blind goats and an equally blind grandmother in the village?

This to me is not a homecoming. I am only here to get background information. I see myself as nothing more than that photographer who brought us the image of a vulture set to pounce on the starving child. I do not want to make history fair, I just want to record it. Objectively and as it happened.

I turn my Dictaphone on again and brace myself for that kitchen with its billows of smoke, a tearful and aging mother and a death-defying grandmother. From a mercenary corner of my mind a middle finger thrusts itself towards the reader screaming: love me or hate me, but I have my final chapter.

* * *

"You still want to talk about that bad time?" mother moans.

"It is important to me, it is part of who I am, who we are as a family." I respond not quite believing it myself.

"These nice clothes, and all these many questions you have son, why can't you tell me first what it is you have been doing in that place with many lights?"

This woman is annoying, I think to myself. Why can't she just tell me what I want to know? I start to get the feeling that she is looking for a way to ask me for help: money. These village folks are so predictable. They all think money grows on streetlights. But if this woman had any sense, she would realise that my business is story-telling. I listen to people's stories and retell them for others to read. That is why I have these good clothes and these many questions. But how can I make her understand the work that I do? That her answers pay me?

"Listen mother, I am a writer..."

"Oh, okay *baba*, so what do you write?"

"I write about 1985." I retort but she is too blind to see sarcasm even if it were a noose around her neck. She is just a villager anyway and villagers think that the only work in the world is that which makes your muscles ache, your brow sweat and your armpits stink.

"But why 1985, why not '84... wasn't that the year of the big drought?"

"It has nothing to do with the drought," I shout. "I love to set my scenes and I saw that calendar on the wall, you see? And it is stuck to 1985. I can barely remember 1985 or earlier, so 1985 looked like a nice place to begin.

Nothing fancy, mother. I just want to hear some stories about my early life!"

Of course I do not mention that the only stories I want to hear are the dark ones. The ones that will make the reader sigh: "Oh, this man has done well by himself."

If mother doesn't have any particularly dark stories I just might have to make them up. But really she had better have some and soon because I really do not intend to clog my pores with wood smoke. I am a city boy now, you see?

"I am writing a book mother," I explain. "A book about me."

"*Haiya*, a book about you... why would anyone want to read a book about you, are you a big man now my son?"

"It is not only big men who write books mother. People read stories about all kinds of people. Even you, if you could tell me your story, I could write a book about you."

"*Ai*, about me? *Si* then you let me tell you a story about me and then you write it. I know I cannot read much but you can read it out to me when you are done."

"But mother, the book I am writing is not about you, it is about me."

"Yes, but I am your mother so what is a book about you without me? Or have you become too important that you forget the woman that gave birth to you?"

"I do not forget mother, but maybe some stories are more important than others. Besides you will be part of this story..."

"*Woi Woi Woi*... so my story is not important?" Mother interjects.

This is getting mighty annoying. I cannot just sit here and watch an entire chapter slip through my fingers. Not after having it all figured out: *1985*. Neat and to the point. Catchy.

What is a writer to do now? I guess I will have to fabricate it. Making things up is what I have always done. That is what I did in my first book. There is no tribe called Bango, of course, but if there was I am sure its people wouldn't have managed to be as interesting as I made them up to be in that book. And that's the thing: the best stories are the fake ones.

I step out into the noisome night.

The red light continues to blink attentively from inside my shirt pocket. I reach in and turn the Dictaphone off.

Charles A Matathia is a social thinker and reluctant writer. He was born in semi-rural Kenya in 1979 and still lives there. If this story is not true, then it is his first published work of fiction.

Postcards

Tinashe Mushakavanhu

from Carmarthen, Wales

THIS PLACE SUCKS MAN. I mean yes, it is better than home, but it has its own issues. So many things have struck me since I made the great trek. I live in a small market town in the south-west of Wales. Believe it or not, the only black face I am used to seeing everyday when I wake up is mine. I am getting used to the curious stares. I am the odd one out everywhere I go. I am different. There is always baggage that comes with that, this feeling that you're constantly on display, being judged and stereotyped and never knowing quite how people feel about you. Sometimes I just want to bolt, disappear.

The shift in the weather from dry summers to the cold has been unbearable. It's a complete contrast from the always bright and scorching Zimbabwean sun. What you call *cold* in Harare is what they call warm here. See, I am more worried about the weather than, say, food and clothes because unlike home these are things one can easily afford.

Perhaps I should start from the beginning. At the airport. We disembarked from the South African Airways Boeing 707 and walked to the immigration desk. We had to produce our passports. My Zimbabwean-ness crawled in my skin. I didn't want to be the latest deportation statistic.

The official sitting behind the desk, a small purse of a mouth set in a cake face, looked at me with a stern uncompromising expression. I passed my green passport to him. Cake Face scrutinized the authenticity of the visa stamp inside it. He asked so many questions. I answered them. Cake Face was not done yet. 'What are you going to study?' I responded curtly this time. 'A Masters in Creative Writing.' He gave me a what-is-that look. I didn't expect him to understand. My family had failed to understand. My friends didn't either. He flipped through the pages of my passport, a scene that reminded me of my young days when my father used to turn over and over my dismal report cards while contemplating the harshest punishment. *Thud, thud, thud.* Deportation was creeping in my way, I thought. Was fate going to deny me access into this land of plenty and opportunity? Were my ancestors going to forsake me? Now. Fifteen minutes. Cake Face stamped my passport. *6 September 2004.* The passage was not clear yet. He sent me back through the same entrance for a medical check-up. I wasn't alone. Two other people were in front of me in the queue; a young woman from Swaziland. The other I could not tell where she came from. She sat too far from me to see her passport. We had to fill in some forms. No tests were done. Phew! I returned the filled form and was referred from one desk to another and finally cleared through. I smiled my toothpaste advert smile. I was there at last.

I looked round me with the proud face of a Commander-in-Chief ready to inspect the guard of honour. There were people everywhere, chattering boxes excitedly singing. There is a new kind of coming and going in the world these days. Heathrow Airport was overcrowded. It had the face of a re-branded *United Nations.* Here you meet and see people from all countries of the world – Eritrea, Mongolia, Bangladesh, Latvia, Thailand. Everywhere. My nose pinched with stuffed air. I knew I had finally arrived at that little spot on the atlas. I followed through the sign-posted instructions on the walls to collect my suitcase. A catalogue of black and white faces rushed past me. Sooner or later, I was going to find out what it really meant to be black and different.

I thought this place had all the answers to rest my heart upon. But it seems to me now that who you are is always determined by where you are. The bigotries of this place weigh on me sometimes. I have met condescension in the eyes of bank clerks and shop attendants and malign intent in store detectives trailing me along as I follow the maze of shelves to pick my groceries. No. Fact. Perhaps it's just the cynical me with a jaundiced perception of this place

Man, I thought this place was supposed to be full of endless opportunities but they always narrow down to petty, greasy kitchen jobs, till operators, waiters. You probably know the Form 4A girls, Precious Nhema, Maggie Sachiti, Liz Muti, I heard kuti they are all 'whoring' here as bum-cleaners (nurse care-workers) in London. White shit, black shit, it's all the same – stinking and disgusting. See, I can't stand my own thoughts. My mind has this woeful capacity for the tarnished view. This is not home.

from Harare, Zimbabwe

I thought hell was this damned place. Is that place so bad as well? Why do you have to think about being black? That is who you are, man. Just focus on your studies. Make them see the real you. Make them colour blind. I know nostalgia does that sometimes. You imagine things. And what made you go to that place of all places? What is that town again? Kamativi. I thought Unit K was London. Is that place really a Lowdown?

Things are terribly bad this end.

Harare is not the same without you. The guys ask about you, you know the type of thing, what happened to your friend, the one you always walked around with, the one with the thick spectacles, the one who carried books everywhere he went, the one who wrote poetry, the one we used to call Dickens. People remember you, man, they really do miss you.

I finally broke up with Juliana. To imagine she was cheating me. I am really beaten about it and still trying to get over the affair. She is now married to this insurance guy, Modify. You probably know him. The dark skinned chap with missing front teeth who lives in Tsuro Street. Of course she made a choice. She is already pregnant.

Tapiwa, Solo and Munyaradzi have all gone away too. I don't know how I am managing without all of you guys. And remember *kwa*Mereki *hakuchina*. No more Saturday braai. No more hang-outs. The place was razed to the ground during Operation Clean Up. You probably won't recognize Harare anymore. It's now an entirely new place. Harare is now being run by Nigerian and Chinese nationals. They own the place, man. Harare is tired. People are leaving this wretched land in droves. I should probably go somewhere too but I do not have the travel documents. I do not have the heart to cross the swelling waters of the Limpopo. I can't swim and yet it is my only way out, my key to freedom, to escape from this prison of a country. Everyday I get closer to that step.

Do you remember the times we used to sit and dream of one of us becoming the next state president? And how he would appoint the rest of us as cabinet ministers? Come to think of it, there is no difference between *our* government and *their* government. It's all buddy politics – who knows who. What does it take to effect real change? I wonder.

I must confess I am terribly miserable. That is why sometimes I need friends like you around me. Friends like you give me something I lack, something like optimism. Friends who make me think everything is going to be all right with the world as long as we live. It may seem childish to want to depend on friends, but is it really?

from Carmarthen, Wales

Here, it's different. Everyone is a tortoise living in his shell. People keep their distance. Your business is nobody's business. I know in Harare you are never yourself. There is always someone to talk to. I really do miss home – its colour and texture and characters.

You probably think I am exaggerating my situation and that I am the weepy kind and not grateful to the gods. You see, it is impossible to live in a different place and be a realist, especially when you are looking at people with different habits from yours and seeing things you had never seen before. You look and notice everything. You get so overwhelmed by contrast and colour, by every minute details – accents, eyes, skin colour and every damn little thing.

(I can't believe you gave up on Juliana just like that. Man, that chick was your right kind of woman. And how did she end up with that insurance guy, I mean honestly, I always thought that guy had no balls. He is the last person I expected to have taken Juliana from you).

Just to think I have been away for a year and half. It's like I have been away a lifetime. It is incredible how in a short space of time things have changed in Harare. So far, I haven't experienced any power cuts here, there is no water rationing, traffic lights work most times, fuel from bloody Iraq flows endlessly, and sometimes it seems there are as many cars as there are people.

Public transport is timetabled, not in the haphazard Harare way. Buses follow a schedule. Trains do the same. I know back home some buses never run at all. There is no fuel. The Freedom Train never arrives on time because of the intermittent electric power outages. And the planes are too often diverted from their normal routes to carry the president and his wife.

This is a weird place. There are Christians. And then there are professed heathens, atheists and pagans. I came across a poster advertising a pagan meeting. They had one remarkable condition for acceptance: *prospective members should not believe in the existence of God*. This is frightening but true. I have passed empty churches on Sunday. There is an old Baptist Church (building) that's been turned into a popular pub. Outside it still looks like a church, inside it's a totally different world. They live. They have everything.

Most people here live their lives by following their hearts. I have met several eccentric individuals. What is baffling is their ignorance. For them, the world begins and ends in Europe, and/or America, if they are privileged enough to travel that direction. There is no Africa in their curriculum. There is no Africa in their imagination. Africa is one big country. There is no difference between Zimbabweans and Nigerians and Kenyans and Tunisians. We are just the same. I was approached the other day in restaurant by an elderly man. He wanted to know which part of Africa I came from. I told him. Zimbabwe. "O-oh! Rhodesia you mean?", the old man asked as a matter of fact. Yes, that's right. There are some people who still live in the past, whose minds are still tuned backwards: those who refuse to accept the present in its context.

Tell me, what news is coming out of home? What is happening? Do you see change on the horizon? What are people doing about what is going on? Tell me other interesting bits too. Who is marrying who? Who has died? Anything.

from Harare, Zimbabwe

Events are moving so fast that I can't keep up with them. I am fighting demons as I write. This place has become so unbearable. What would you do if you are stuck in one place and everyday is the same and nothing you do matters? Everybody in Mufakose is a PhD. The whole township is now full of PhDs. We pass our days sitting at the footbridge in Mukonde Street, on the *stoeps* at Mhishi Shopping Centre, at Defe's tuck-shop, at the OK bus-terminus, everywhere. We are all Permanent Home Developers and yet the ideal life should be about going to work and getting home and going to work again.

Remember Reuben Mawoko, the prefect everyone disliked in high school. He is now the new MP for our constituency. He rebuked me one day when I tried to ask for his sympathies. He told me rather scornfully that the problem with me is that I am not patriotic as if patriotic is some kind of food to sate my appetite. I never attend ruling party meetings. I never join campaign rallies *because I hate the hypocrisy of the exercise*. I am never up to date with party subscriptions *because I am always broke to the bone*. And yet I have the habit of turning up for all party functions with food and drink. Yes, I drink as much free beer as I can and talk as loud as I can and pick quarrels with the party leaders who grow fat on donor consignments meant for us, the povo.

Look, now there is also this political party and that party and a faction of that party and that party, and people just don't care anymore. We are fed up. The trouble is that everything has become awful. Newspapers scream hell all the time: ZESA to plunge country into darkness. Harare goes without water. Fuel shortages to persist. Mealie-meal in short supply. Price of bread goes up. Maybe I am going to pieces.

Even MPs from the opposition party seem to have adopted the lazy habit of sleeping through deliberations in parliament. What happened to Promises: if we persevere, change will come: *rambai makashinga tirikuchinja maitiro?* Promises! We are a living mockery of those slogans. It's just like a game of draughts, they are playing us. But we don't bother anymore; we escape by building private forts around ourselves. To think kuti everyone in Mufakose now has a dura-wall around their yards. People have become indifferent. When you look into their eyes, you see a sort of emptiness, as if all the life has been sucked out of them and all that remains are husks. Maybe I am just imagining things.

And worse, the president's endless trips abroad churn me with nausea as if the act of vomiting itself would deliver me from the unceasing torment of *hate, hate, hate*. It is 'unchristian' to hate but I can't help it. Sometimes I wonder why and how the world was made like it is. I know. It makes me want to throw away all the decent beliefs about God.

Stay put *ku*Unit K *ikoko*, things do not promise to be better here. They are no longer issuing out passports *ufunge* as they are embarrassed with the way we are all going away. It's like a child running out of the house naked with scalding marks exposing the secreted abuse that haunts it. This place has reached the bottom hole that has no bottom. It is all grey.

Ps. I will probably tell you what happened with Juliana next time. I am pretty emotional at the moment, lolling in the groove of depression. I am stressed, man. It's all this business of having to find work, of survival. Also, the passing of each day is a reminder that I am growing older. Outta!

from Carmarthen, Wales

I probably sound naïve sometimes. See, the insistence with which solitude insinuates itself into my everyday life is enough to leave me doubting my own mind. Sometimes I wonder if I am making up the sly expressions of the bank clerks or the patronizing tones of shop attendants. It is loneliness.

There is more to Carmarthen.

I do not hate this place. It just gets under my skin sometimes. Yes, the landscape is beautiful. Miles and miles of total green – hills sprawling into one another, patterned with winding roads. Carmarthen town is very small. I don't need a map to walk around the place. It reminds me of Harare, where everyone knows where they are going.

I met a girl, a Canadian girl. The only friend I have. Perhaps, she too, is homesick and understands better what I am going through. Her name is Leonah. Nothing serious is going on between us. We are just friends. I know it's hard to believe. People in Carmarthen do not see it that way either. The other day we walked into this pub and I remember a haunted hush greeted us, conversations stopped and eyes pierced through my soul with a kind of reproach that said *motherfucker you are now growing too big for your head*. White guys don't like it when you get along with one of their girls. Of course we stayed, had one drink each, and walked out. I expected a group of them to follow us and beat the blackness out of my skin. They didn't bother. No bleach can do that. Michael Jackson failed the test.

I remember three young white girls, probably in their late teens, walking towards me and standing just behind me in the pub. Perhaps I was the first black person they had ever seen outside TV. Perhaps. These girls started caressing the mop of my black *mufushwa* hair and pulling its coils straight as if to test its tensile strength. I turned to look at them and they all walked away giggling. No, it was no fun to be an exhibit.

I can't even make faces or even smile to small babies in their push-chairs. They scream as if they have seen the Devil himself. The mothers apologise, 'Sorry, it's just that he has never seen black skin before.' I walk away, smiling, and say to myself, as long they can feel my presence.

Sometimes when I am walking in the streets and lanes, I just start laughing loud and long. (My degree of madness is now becoming more apparent.) There is no mirth in the sounds. People hurry past me afraid to meet my eyes for fear I am a drunkard who is mad/paranoid/delusional. At least I know I have one thing they will never have. My mother tongue. I have a language they don't have. I can speak and write and dream in their language, but here Shona is mine, and mine alone. I want to call out and say to them, *Murikunditarisirei? Munonyatsondiziva here? Mutupo wangu munouziva here? Ndati murikunditarisireiko? Siyanai neni mhani!*

I am writing still. My novel is coming out soon, *Outside Inside.* I can't wait to send you a copy.

from Harare, Zimbabwe

Now you are talking. So you got yourself a white girlfriend? How serious is it? Hey come on, don't tell me the friend theory, we all know what it means, man. At least, you have found someone to share your burdens with. Please, send a photo with both of you. Please, please?

Nothing promises to be good here.

No rains. Another drought looming?

Shades of a dark horizon cover our land.

Hope is elusive and yet not impossible.

There is talk about presidential elections being pushed two years forwards. And they have started beating up people. Our leaders know how to subdue our withering spirits. Imagine the terror of walking through the streets of Harare milling with youth militia clad in plain army green uniforms. The Green Bombers. You never know when they might descend on you with their black military boots and baton sticks. They are doing a good job in creating fear. We are now a nation of fear.

There are now all these kinds of social sanctions imposed. No gatherings of any sort. Four is a crowd. Waving is *almost* a crime, for lo and behold, the opposition party emblem is an open palm. We are reaching a point where we would have to seek permission to have weddings and funerals. It's affecting those of us who do not work. We cannot sit at the footbridge in Mukonde Street.

It's difficult to think straight. It's even risky to write letters because everything has just turned cockeyed and sour. They might get intercepted and the next thing plain clothed police officers might come and take me for a brief visit to Marimba Police Station. The post is not safe anymore. There's now all these kinds of censorship. I don't know what is happening to this bill that will enable the government to read the whole country's emails. Yes, no private communication please. They don't trust you *ma*Diaspora. *Hanzi* you are selling your souls to Tony Blair. Yes, they are dis-owning you, *hanzi* you don't belong here anymore. And it seems you don't belong there either. What happens to you then?

What I hate is this inner restlessness, this fear of the unknown, this fear of not knowing what will happen to me, this anxiety of waiting for something that may never happen or come.

Perhaps one day soon we will meet, be together, and grow old together as before. Perhaps. Remember friends meet to part and part to meet. So long!

Ps. You see, I think I am coping well without Juliana. I am happy for her, I suppose, though it was a sad end to our beautiful love story. Man, the thing is, it is different to tell a girl you love her and have nothing else to give her. I only had love to give. The insurance guy has bread and butter. She chose the most enriching diet. Can I begrudge her that?

from Carmarthen, Wales

Life goes on man. Let's not worry ourselves to death. Let's make the best of ourselves with the time we have. Sad about Juliana. It is not her, I think. It could just be Harare's corrupt sensibilities.

It's difficult to pretend that everything is going alright. At the slightest opportunity people ask me the same questions. What brought you here? Is Africa a desert? Do the women walk naked? Is your father a polygamist? They ask as if they learnt these questions the first day they were born. I have come to accept interrogation as their form of greeting. But aren't we all like that? We call strangers names too. Everyone is something else depending on where they are.

The odd times I meet black faces on the streets of Carmarthen, there is always an element of recognition and/or an element of labelling each other. We speak with our eyes. Where do you come from? Where are you living? What are you doing? Questions we never answer. We are all coloured with prejudices. Nigerians are conmen and thieves. Zimbabweans are hungry and desperate. Somalis and Ethiopians are refugees.

I hate the pity I get. Some people *shame shame* me. Some accuse me of being a chicken, a coward, for running away. At first, I hoped that coming to a different country would ease away the tension, the confusion of living in Harare. I was escaping from the demons of the place – violence, food shortages, unemployment, endless queues, incessant power cuts, water rationing.

I don't wish to stay here forever and at the same time I don't want to come back to the tyranny and poverty. My stay here is not indefinite. My visa expires in six months. Thinking of coming back home terrifies me and yet I just can't stop thinking about it. I keep wondering how things are going to turn out. Nothing promises to be better. I can see it is going to be a long time before any good news comes from home.

But my memories of home have not gone away. They come back to me every day even stronger. What we think is what we are and what we are is what we think. Perhaps...

memories are stubborn stains
etched on my face

memories are scars
that run deep in my bosom

memories are stitches
that keep me together
whole

Tinashe Mushakavanhu is a young Zimbabwean writer. His short stories have been published in six anthologies in America, South Africa, Wales and Zimbabwe. He is a former participant of the Crossing Borders Project run by the British Council and Lancaster University and African Literature Programme Coordinator for the Hay-on-Wye Festival.

Once Upon a Time

Millicent Muthoni

I stick out my neck and squint my eyes until the four yellow stripes come into focus. That says Captain. My back towards the noonstruck waiters behind, I swivel my bar stool to the right so that I watch him walk straight at me from the newly painted 'Arrivals'. I wonder how it feels to Arrive. From some better place beyond. Like all the other times, there is a thump in my stomach, and then ripples that spread down to my thighs. Such longing! They are always a spectacle, these uniforms. They never betray the numerous time zones they have crossed. He straightens the lapels and pushes back his darks into his cropped head. I sit at attention. The Tusker malt has made my head hot and airy.

How would it be? Me behind him, my travelled suitcase, white stickers on black, trailing after my uniform and eucalyptus legs. Two duty-free bagfuls of Dolce and Gabbana, Marks and Spencer and Black Opal in the other hand. We'd talk again about the London Eye and the Thai Buddha and the Palm Jumeira – like we were ants, and the world was a plate of leftover food we have all to ourselves.

* * *

Sophia lived for end-month. She would go to the airport, sit at The Bar, and offer exactly half of her three thousand (excuse me sir stroke madam we have a fabulous promotion on socks and toothbrushes) shillings salary in homage to crew, travellers and her itching wanderlust.

She flagged down a waiter for her change and handing him the thirty shillings, popped off her high seat. She could never make enough money to take her through the month anyway, so she had long stopped guilting herself into budgeting. Having and lacking had ceased to be different. Everything to her was like walking a plateau. She cupped her hands to her ears as she walked out, trying to silence the persistent wheeze of a taxiing plane. She closed her eyes and thought how that drone meant that some people were lucky enough to escape. Why not her? She got into an EasyRider and rode back to her *ugalisukuma* life, the one she despised.

Ugalisukuma was served yet again the day Sophia returned home from the university. The most annoying thing was that her mother knew she was bringing a friend along, and yet did not prepare a more welcoming meal like rice and chicken or chapatti and *ndengu*. Her friend Ciku had accommodated Sophia in campus after she had dropped out, sort of.

"Kwani you never unpack?" Ciku had asked when she found Sophia organizing her hand luggage one evening. She said that Sophia lived in transit – not even her toothbrush left the tiny suitcase that summed up her belongings. Every evening Sophia pulled out her suitcase from under the bed. Starting with the envelope of documents, she flipped through the passport, her impressive secondary school certificate which was not as impressive as her primary school certificate and the newspaper cutting of the top 100 students the year she sat her KCPE. She was in position 68, highlighted with a green felt pen. Then there were numerous certificates she had won in the debating club and the one she had received for inventing a Chemistry board game for the inter-school Science Congress. As part of the ritual, she'd then unfold and fold her clothes, starting with the pleated blue sundress her mother had handed down to her, then the pair of jeans that had been too small for Sara, then the two skirt suits, one red and one green, that she had asked her cousin to send her from Britain, her all-red underwear...

"Try and find a job." Sara was always careful in casting her suggestions to Sophia.

"Using what qualification? O Levels? Ha!"

Frugal as Sophia was she knew that Ciku's student loan was strained by the extra twenty-two shillings for her two meals at the campus mess every day. Plus the toothpaste got used up faster. And the roll of tissue. And the bottle of Love body lotion. And at home, her siblings expected her to give them pocket money.

Sophia often slept into the afternoon and woke up to flip through batches of newspaper back-copies she had collected from the friendly college librarian. A Dubai hotel seeking Kenyan staff, a beaming face with the caption, *My Name is Conrad Oluoch; I won the Green Card. You can too,* Study-in-Australia scholarships, a low-cost airline seeking cabin crew... she applied for them all.

She also posted an application in response to an ad for a sales and marketing job with a 'respected company' which did not seem to require any respected papers. That is how she ended up on Tom Mboya street, waylaying passersby with her assorted wares.

"Excuse me sir stroke madam we have a fabulous promotion on socks and toothbrushes, will you try some?"

She made not more than three thousand shillings in commission either because she, an A student, could not bring herself to buzz up and down like a desperate bee or because men usually stopped not to listen but to mark their territory. It was her sweet face with large cow-eyes, wet and sad, and her gutsy legs that interested them. She avoided Kenyatta Avenue most, because that is where her former classmates in Law School ducked into cafés to discuss cases.

The campus psychiatrist finally wrote Sophia off with a prescription. "Manic depression." He had pronounced from under his breath on her first visit.

"Recite the alphabet for me please..." She clammed up like a mimosa leaf. She may have taken to sitting all afternoon at the grand staircase outside the library in bathroom slippers, an afro comb in knotty short hair and worn kikhoi shorts, but she was not mad, or mentally challenged, or depressed. She was an A student. The only reason she was here was procedure. Getting the psychiatrist on her side was the only way to switch to the newly introduced International Relations course.

"Young lady, what do I do with you? You are like hyacinth... all gropy but with no roots. In which department do you intend to sow trouble this time? Eh?" That was the worst visit, when he finally gave her bullets for drugs and administered an indefinite break from school.

Her file indicated that she had switched a year ago from Law. She was now waist deep in the muck of an Urban Planning degree. There they made model blocks with *ushindi* soap all semester, all night, with obscene *muugithi* lyrics blasting from students' stereos in the studio. Not her idea of a profession. Before that, she had given Law a year's shot. She left when she got her second consecutive D in criminal law, even after being the only student who typed her work. D for Defeated.

She had never trusted 'our universities' anyway. They dealt in mediocrity, she said. She saw herself in a world where roads stretched faster, like they did when she was a child, in Japan. She knew that her father said to her, "You, my little girl, have a bright past, like your father. Hold on to it." She had been born in Japan, just after her mum hooked the man whose star was shooting beyond the borders; Ambassador Mweru. The son of a colonial chief, his was a long friendship with the President. When President Kenyatta died, the politically orphaned Mweru family tumbled back to the coffee farms of Maragwa, bringing with them an obnoxious five-year-old girl. She became popular in the village, teaching both teachers and pupils in school how to pronounce English.

* * *

It is now noon. The plane from Entebbe has touched down. It was delayed so I had to sit longer at The Bar. The security officer sidled up to me and called me aside, his walkie-

talkie interrupting our conversation. He said he had on several occasions seen me sit at The Bar, and then go away. He asked what my business at the airport is and I told him my boyfriend is a Captain, and that in fact I think that's his plane landing, excuse me, and I walked off. Can't he tell apart a woman of the world from a prostitute? I'm at the 'Arrivals' with my suitcase. It is empty, but not for long. One day I will walk in this same place, and doors will fling open. I know it just as I know that people think I'm mad. Passengers are now streaming on to the Arrivals bay. I don't see him. I'm looking around and feigning a frustrated face just in case these security guards think me the kind that hides explosive contraptions in the suitcase. One has to be careful at the airport. The bay is now empty save for two disappointed tour guides in khaki uniform with lowered placards. As I turn for the exit, someone taps me from behind, and there, here, is Ciku, smiling as if to say "I think you need help." I did not know that she had followed me.

* * *

Sophia had warned Ciku that her mother was unlike all normal mothers, but Ciku still insisted on going home with Sophia. She did not expect anything – no chicken soup beaten with tomatoes to welcome visitors, no flowered seat covers to conceal the gaping wounds in the yellow sponge and no shirt to cover the breast milk stains on her camisole.

Ciku sat through this gripe every day. Sophia hated her mother for being weak, so weak that she could not stand up for her family when her father married another woman. Plus she had a well-rehearsed case of chronic hypochondria. Recently, she was bedridden with a toothache that seemed undecided between the upper left jaw and the lower right one. Sophia's greatest fear was that she would one day like her mother be left in the crevices of life.

So Ciku did not wonder why Sophia's mother was watching Nigerians do *juju* in her living room at midday, on the 14-inch Toshiba TV powered by an Oxide battery, her legs sprawled over a bowl of half-eaten bananas on the floor. Sara had noticed that the barbed wire that lashed across the wooden X in the gate was coming off. There were rotting avocados on the lonely garage space next to the old Mercedes with grey ringworms all over it; a paintjob gone wrong. Through the grass, one could pick out a hint of concrete on the path that led to the house and past the avocado tree to the farm.

The sitting room was large and had two arms, one leading to the kitchen and dining room, and the other to the sleeping quarters. There were different colours and sizes of sofas aging badly and arranged in a crescent to allow for the only action in the room; the red television on a stool lined with newspaper.

"You are still resting?" Sophia greeted her mother.

"We are still resting." The mother stretched a listless hand to greet them as Sophia introduced Ciku.

"Don't you have *Chacha* Loan? Go to the centre and bring a packet of milk for your friend's tea."

"Toto has missed you. You did not bring him a schoolbag?"

That evening, as they were eating and before Sophia finally told them that she had dropped out of college, her mother had reeled out all their Japan home videos from twenty-one years ago for Ciku to watch. Commentating, she came alive and lost her skippy eyes.

"That was me outside the public bath. *Hee*! We would enter naked I tell you."

"There is that dress Sophia wears. I can't believe I could fit into it! Look..." She jiggled her loose upper arm "I can't!"

"There is queen," she would say as three-year-old Sophia beat the house-help's head with a pan or smeared black shoe-polish on the sofa Sara was seated on. The stain was there, only faded with age.

"She was never number two!"

Sara watched and listened and saw. This family had frozen at the point of descent.

The psychiatrist was glad to see Sophia. She was a very refreshing patient. Though she was just as deflated by the campus experience as most of the other students who came, she did not put her life in his hands. He wasn't even sure that she was taking her pills. Once she had broken down and cried, and then just as he placed his hand on her shoulder, she had dried her tears, blown her nose hard and said, "End of commercial break."

She said the pills were causing her to eat and sleep too much and he told her that's precisely what the break from school was for. She suggested that he get rid of his beard and his thick windscreen spectacles and wear jeans because that would make him look accessible. 'Social solubility', she called it.

He had wondered why most students seemed to take his prescriptions and leave his advice. With Sophia, they talked about the mother she despised, the father she longed for and her roommate who was too agreeable. They discussed her disappointing university education and her obsession with the word *abroad* which she dropped into every chat. He thought she needed to settle somewhere, learn to stay.

"Get yourself a boyfriend. You need a man to count the strands of your hair and show you River Tana and Mount Kenya in the palm of your hand."

Sophia had not bet on the psychiatrist's poetry. She was not given to the sentimental, but what he said sounded like something she needed.

"I have a boyfriend now," she said

"Does he know about this... what you are going through? I mean, do you ever let go and let yourself look stupid?" He leaned back, and scribbled something on a paper.

"Look stupid? Oh yes. Every end-month." She spilled it. "I see him every end-month."

"Good." He said handing her the piece of paper. "Call this number. This young man is travelled and intelligent and has a lot of free time. He might even ask you to help him move house this weekend. You never know..."

Ciku asked Sophia if her relationship with the psychiatrist was still the doctor-patient kind. She worried that the psychiatrist kept popping up in their conversations as 'doc'. Sophia, she said, had been using the man as an emotional crutch, which was not appropriate, especially now that she was so vulnerable.

"He's like a father to me!" Sophia fished out the telephone number from her pocket.

"See. He gave me this. It's the number of my new boyfriend." She smiled as she reached for the phone.

"You are sure that's not his number... the psychiatrist's?" Sara asked. They both laughed at the thought. Ciku teased as Sophia shushed her, her finger on her lips.

"Hallo... my name is Sophia... may I interest you in a promotion we have on furniture... you are just moving house?... we have beds, seats and wardrobes... yes... aammh... leather, wrought iron and wood... our showroom is on Tom Mboya Street... yes... at the Business centre... when can I expect you?... tomorrow... 10 o'clock... call me when you get there... I'll be waiting... Thank you."

That was too easy, she thought as they burst into laughter.

"His name is Oyugi."

Ciku shook Sophia's hand in admiration. She could never imagine herself, a girl, making the first move on a man.

"How do you do that?"

"I just don't want to be a signpost like my mother; sitting by the roadside and cheering others running past."

Sophia went about her business, scanning around for a man who looked travelled and intelligent. She took as premonition the psychiatrist's words "you never know". So she wore her red suit from abroad and had Ciku bring out her eyes with smoky shadows. Her nails were shocked with red polish. She had forgotten how beautiful her hands were. The stilts on her feet were Sara's. Sophia had never bought a pair of high shoes. A black bag with socks and toothbrushes hung on her shoulder.

"Excuse me sir stroke madam we have a fabulous promotion on socks and toothbrushes, will you try some?"

The sun attacked and the street rushed. A man whose shoes were caked with dust bought a new pair of socks, leaned against the display window and put them on. A student promised to pick three pairs on his way from school and called her *gacungwa*, a ripe orange. It was only ten o'clock and Sophia had witnessed a fight between *matatu* touts and another between hawkers and the council *askaris*. The Asian man with the clothes shop was asking the book vendor to get his Jackie Collins and Good News Bible rubbish out of his entrance.

* * *

It's the shaven head with the silver lined darks that I see first, then the broad shoulders that sit on a lanky but graceful frame. I squint my eyes and feel the fear mixed with anticipation. His hands are prominently veined, and his legs form a slight bow. Even in a T-shirt and cargo pants, he looks travelled and intelligent. He takes out his phone and dials. I do not pick up. He walks past me to the door of the Business Centre and steps back to read the signage. He is about to dial again when I approach.

"Sophia," I say.

"I know you from somewhere," his head is tilted and he's smiling, his eyes stuck on mine.

"You never know... Captain," I say.

* * *

Millicent Muthoni trained as an architect at the University of Nairobi. She is a columnist with *The Standard*. She went through the Crossing Borders creative writing program and has written two plays, staged at the Kenya National Theatre. She has had her work read on the BBC world service.

Then, Now and Tomorrow

Glaydah Namukasa

Then

"Take her anywhere. Drop her by a church door, a hospital gate; by the fence of a nursing home... just take her away from me and my daughter."

A LOUD RUSTLE CUT through the noise of the wind. I paused and listened. Someone was making their way through the *bisagazi* grass towards me.

"Lule!" No mistake, it was Madam Jalia's voice.

"Madam!" I responded.

She surged towards me, with the grass and weeds slapping all over her body.

"Lule, come with me now!" she stared at me, her large eyes focused on my forehead. She had no eye-shadow, no lipstick and she had no eyebrows! The lips were bunched, pink perhaps, but not blood-red as they always were.

In the nine months of working as Madam Jalia's *shamba* boy, I had learnt that every one called her Madam because that's what she wanted to be called. That she was an outstanding woman who deserved an outstanding title. She owned three cars, four shambas, thirty heads of cattle, and a two-storeyed house with a stone fence. The first thing I had learnt from Rosa, the housekeeper, was that if Madam Jalia had no makeup on her face, then something was either wrong, or about to go wrong. When she made an order, that order had to be obeyed without hesitation.

I followed Madam Jalia, all the time dodging the grass and weed that swung back after she had past. She smelt like *kawunyira*, and I loved it because for once I was spared the sting of her usual perfume 'Shanel no.5' which always made my stomach protest whenever she was near me. But the housekeeper preferred 'Shanel no.5' and she said it was 'the most refreshing fragrance' that had ever entered her thirty-five-year-old nostrils.

Madam Jalia had parked her one-week-old Starlet at the edge of the field. She never said anything as we drove home, with me in the back seat and my gaze on

169

the nape of her neck. Her braids were tied in a ponytail, so I had a clear view of the folds round her neck. The housekeeper said they were rare marks of beauty and anyone who had them was considered a princess.

Madam Jalia lived in 'half London', a place two miles away from Entebbe town. It had been named 'half London' because only rich people with houses as big as palaces lived there. The gatekeeper was quick to open the gate, as he does always when Madam Jalia hoots. Madam Jalia drove directly into the garage. I had three minutes to go to my quarters and change, she told me. Home was quiet, as usual. The housekeeper had gone to the market to do the week's shopping. Madam Jalia had taken her only child, Sophia, away nine months ago. There was only the gatekeeper, who rarely went anywhere.

Three minutes found me seated right back in the Starlet. I had changed into my best; a red T-shirt and grey trousers I had bought especially to wear for the Christmas mass, which was three days ahead. Just as I was clipping the seatbelt into place, Madam Jalia emerged from the inner door that connected to the corridor inside the house. She had something in her arms, wrapped in white baby clothes. She opened the back door and handed it to me. I gaped.

It was a tiny sleeping baby: more like a sleeping kitten. I sat immobile, with the baby in my trembling arms. Anyone in my situation would have asked Madam Jalia what was going on, but I could not. I was a *shamba* boy, who was obliged to obey, to answer, not to ask questions. I saw the tinted window rolled up before we drove out of the garage, out of the gate, to the tarmac road and headed towards *Kikubamutwe*, a surburb known for grooming pick-pockets. We drove through the suburb towards the long strip of eucalyptus that finally opened up to the main road. The car came to a stop a few metres from the main road.

Now I was holding the baby to my chest in the manner one holds a short, heavy log. Madam Jalia began, "Do you remember what happened to my daughter nine months ago?"

"Yes I remember, madam."

It had happened on my first day at work. Madam Jalia had taken me to show me around her *shambas*. We were walking around the field where I was to collect grass for her cattle. She was showing me which contours to cross or not to cross, when we heard a scream. 'Sophia!' Madam Jalia said. 'That sounds like my daughter's voice.' She dashed forward. I followed her, passed her, and I headed in the direction of the scream. I was only in time to see a figure I understood so well. It was a beggar, whom I had met sitting outside Madam Jalia's fence the first day I came to look for a job. And then I saw a girl; she lay sprawled amidst the grass. Her skirt was above her waist, her legs apart, her inner thighs soiled with blood. The right side of her face was swollen. Her school shirt had been torn and I could see her small breasts.

"You remember that I paid for your silence."

Madam's voice was a welcome interruption of the memory of that day. "I have kept silent, madam." That day, when I told Madam Jalia that it was the beggar who had raped Sophia, Madam Jalia made it clear to me that we had to keep the rape a secret. She said she would not follow up the case because it would discolour her reputation. 'Silence, Lule, silence!' she had said. From that day, Madam Jalia told me I was her special servant.

"Do you know the reason why I took Sophia away?"

"You took her to... to a school in Nairobi."

"I took her away because she was pregnant."

"You said you had taken her to study in Nairobi."

"I lied. I had to take her away because she was pregnant! There, in your arms, is Sophia's one-day-old daughter."

It was enough that I had known about the rape, and that had been heavy enough a secret to keep from the housekeeper, gatekeeper, and the rest of the people. Why was Madam Jalia giving me such terrible information? I looked down at the baby, choking on the question I was dying to ask Madam.

"My daughter is yet to turn fourteen," she continued. "She cannot be a mother. And I am just thirty: I cannot be a grandmother." She reached towards me and slipped a small wad of money into my shirt pocket. "Take her anywhere. Drop her by a church door, a hospital gate; by the fence of a nursing home... just take her away from me and my daughter."

The sound of the receding Starlet drained all the energy from my body. I sat down right in the middle of the junction. Why was it me who was seated in the middle of the junction, holding this baby on my lap? What was I supposed to do? The baby wriggled under the wrappings, making faces; bunching the small lips then sticking out a tiny pink tongue, flaring the small nostrils. The kitten eyes fluttered but did not open. The baby went back to sleep, and I smiled.

A trailer rattled by announcing its bulky presence, hooting as if it meant to scare the rest of the cars off the road. But there were no other cars. This part of the main road was a sharp corner. But the trailer did not only announce itself; it awakened my mind and I got an answer to one of the questions: I was going to take the baby to my parents.

That evening found me in Biligi, my home village, where the day was dictated by the farmers' activities. They were cockcrow risers who were in their gardens at six a.m, on the way back home at midday, back to the gardens for the evening cultivation at five p.m, and back once again, at home, at seven p.m. Mother was seated outside the kitchen, legs stretched in front of her: she was peeling tiny stems of cassava.

"Maama," I said. The baby opened its mouth and gave out a small cry.

"Bikira Maria Nyabo!" The piece of cassava in Mother's palms dropped on her lap.

"Ha, ha! Word reached me in the garden that my son had come driving in a car." It was my father. He halted in his steps and stared at the baby in my arms.

"I wasn't driving," I said. "That was a hired car." My words stayed hanging in the air.

"Is that a baby?" Father asked.

"The baby isn't mine but... the woman put this responsibility on me."

"The woman?"

"Yes, she abandoned this baby at my door... and left–"

"You went to the city to work. You are supposed to bring back home money, not trouble!"

Relying on a lie was like chewing with a loose tooth. Right where we were standing, I decided to tell them, "My employer, Madam Jalia is the grandmother of this baby. Madam Jalia's only child, Sophia, is the mother of this baby. Sophia was raped by a beggar nine months ago and got pregnant. Madam Jalia kept everything a secret, and now, she has told me to take the baby anywhere..."

Now

Twenty-five years....

Time has added twenty-five years to my age and made me forty-five. Time has added twenty-five years to Madam Jalia's age and made her fifty-five. Time has added twenty-five years to Sophia's age and made her thirty-nine.

I have lived within Madam Jalia's home. Days and nights have not been long enough, and life has slipped by like a lizard flitting across a grass thatch. My mind has played over and over the lie that I was made to plaster on Sophia's brain, "The baby died in your womb, so they had to operate on you to save your own life." Words, sharp as the machete I once possessed as a *shamba* boy. How was I to know they would chop up Sophia's heart? I was just the special servant, and I was just playing the obedient *shamba* boy that I was supposed to be. But the weight of regret for having succumbed to Madam Jalia's control has weighed down my heart.

Sophia's life stalled when she learnt from Madam Jalia that she could not see her baby because the baby was already dead and buried. Since then, her mind started deteriorating. Madam Jalia took her from one psychiatric hospital to another, one country to another, one psychiatric consultant to another, but Sophia's mind could not be restored. She stopped thinking. She stopped talking. Her teenage and twenties followed the direction of wind.

I am seated in Madam Jalia's living room, waiting for her to come back from a business meeting. I spend my days nursing Sophia; I have to make sure each meal prepared contains Irish potatoes or yams, fish or beans, her favourite food. She has a television in her room, which she doesn't watch, except when I am with her to explain what is going on. She doesn't eat if I am not seated with her. And she doesn't talk if it's not I talking to her. She is so attached to me. Sometimes I get to think that somewhere in Sophia's head there is a voice that tells her about my relationship with the baby she gave birth to.

Twenty-five years ago, when Sophia first showed signs of mental instability, she talked to everyone, talked every time, and talked anywhere: words which only she could understand. But as time went by, day by day, night by night, her words ebbed like a fire in the savannah grassland, leaving fragments of charred grass. My job officially changed from *shamba* boy to Sophia's 'nurse.' My salary was highly increased from fifty thousand shillings a month to five hundred thousand a month. I remained silent about all that had happened. Silence brought up 'the baby' whom my mother named Yatuwa [God gave us], silence educated Yatuwa in first-class boarding schools. Silence bought me acres of land in the village. Silence opened me a bank account, and silence deposited money in that account every month!

Madam Jalia's entry into the sitting room grabs me by surprise. I swing my legs off the small table on which I propped them, and sit up. "You are back early," I say.

She slumps into the sofa opposite me and covers her face with her palms.

My heart sinks. Is Madam Jalia drawing back into her usual attacks of guilt? Whenever she gets like that, she lies on her back and stares at whatever is above her, tears just flowing down the sides of her temples, lips parted, face systematically arranged in self-blame and regret. At times she sits, like now, face in her palms, silent; tears falling drop by drop on her lap. She never stirs once in such a state, and whenever it happens in my presence, I excuse myself slowly till she comes out of her fit. But I do not excuse myself now because definitely, Madam Jalia is not having a fit. She is upset by something I am yet to learn.

"The young psychiatrist. That female doctor!" She seems not to see me. "The young psychiatrist," she repeats.

She turns to look at me. I realize that her bleached face has taken on a different look: her eyeballs roll in their sockets, as if searching for a suitable place to focus. The lines on her face, which rebelled against whichever bleaching chemicals she uses, are well pronounced as evidence for her fifty-five years. But I know age isn't the issue. Each day that Madam Jalia lives multiplies the weight of the guilt she harbours in her heart; guilt, which I, too, share an equal portion of.

"What about the young doctor?" I ask.

"It was something about her. Every word she said, every action she took– " Madam Jalia rises off her seat and stands still, eyes rolled up, mouth agape; she's poised like someone trying to conjure a mystic scene in her mind. "– It was something about her! The way she was staring at me without blinking, asking one question after another and wanting me to explain more about Sophia, Nodding her head, and then writing down on the chart... the way she talked, with that low and calm voice. Her generous smile. I saw something in her that I can't explain."

My heart vibrates in dread of the threatening possibility that Madam Jalia saw or even talked to Yatuwa. How can it be that they have met? Madam Jalia had gone for a meeting in Entebbe. Yatuwa currently lives in Butabika, fifty miles away from Entebbe. She is doing what she calls psychiatric internship at Butabika Hospital.

For twenty five years we have shared a common secret with Madam Jalia, but I have never found it in my power to open my heart, my mind, and my mouth, to tell her about Yatuwa. I told her I had gone to a certain hospital posing as a young father who had taken his baby for immunization. "I didn't get the name of the hospital, Madam, but I know it took the taxi two hours to get there," I said to her when I returned after taking the baby to my parents.

"I left the meeting early and went to the clinic to see my doctor. There I met a group of young doctors from Butabika hospital; they are doing some research. She was among them."

Sweat collects on my forehead and in a while it drenches my whole face. I use the back of my hand to wipe it off, but my endeavours are in vain.

Madam Jalia adjusts position; she leans against the back of the seat. "Well, that young doctor reminded me of my early years. When I got pregnant with Sophia, I was seventeen. The pregnancy belonged to my high school classmate, but I trapped this high ranking government official I was seeing, and told him he was responsible. I needed money. Much money!"

This is the time I realize that much as we lived in the same house for many years, we never knew each other at all. We never talked about the past, just as we never talked about the future. We lived in the present, with only one reason for living, never to let it be known that Sophia's baby was alive somewhere. Many times we disagreed with each other, especially when I wanted to visit my parents, and she tried to stop me. No matter the different situations, we kept the secrets intact. I want to ask her more about Sophia's father but I let the impulse pass. "So you told the young doctor about Sophia," I say instead.

"And she was so touched. I could tell she is good with the mental cases. But...

Why? Why does she make me feel...?"

I stare at Madam Jalia as if I am looking for signs to confirm that the young doctor is her blood grandchild. But as I look at her, I notice that her bleach-resisting face is only knotted with the usual warped lines of regret and guilt; lines definitely similar to those on my own face.

"I have asked her to come and see my daughter."

"That's impossible!" I say, but I know my words are not sharp enough to cut through her decision. I wonder if perhaps it's high time I retransformed into the shamba boy who never disagreed. At the same time, the urge to protect Yatuwa's identity is so strong that I decide to sharpen my words; the only weapon I can use. I say, "There are so many experienced psychiatric doctors we've consulted–"

"The way I feel, she will bring a change to Sophia's life. Don't ask me how because I don't know. I just feel it."

"Sophia won't talk to anyone. You know that."

"But she listens to you. You can convince her!"

"I know she won't–"

"Lule, try or else I will just bring the doctor anyway." She has the same steady gaze she had twenty-five years ago, that day she found me in the field, and ordered me to follow her immediately. The stare is clear enough to make me realize that I can never sharpen a weapon against her armour.

I leave the sitting room without uttering another word to Madam Jalia. I am that obedient *shamba* boy once again, but now I am not following her. I am climbing up the stairs, to the upper corridor, dragging my feet on the padded, pink carpet, my head bent low, arms dangling under my shoulders. But how will I stand aside and let Yatuwa enter this house? Yatuwa, the bean plant that my parents and I watered till it was plant enough to absorb its own water from the ground, is destined to meet her mother in circumstances more tangled than a spider web.

Sophia's room is closed as always. No one except me enters her chamber. Inside, she is seated cross-legged in the middle of the room, calm and relaxed like a flamingo on water. This is how she sits when she is in withdrawal. Sophia's bouts of withdrawal occur almost as often as Madam Jalia's fits of guilt. She sits, or lies down on her bed, or even stands in the middle of her room, quiet, her staring eyes focused in front of her. She never stirs even when touched.

I close the door, and take my position on a chair at the foot of her bed; I sit waiting. Sophia has a doll which she named Elena. The doll has a crib beside her bed. In the first five years of her mental instability, I made an observation about Sophia. She would fold whatever was foldable, into a figure of a baby, and then carry whatever it was to her chest in a manner a mother carries a breastfeeding child. And so I bought her the doll to act as a child. Sophia's life is centred on the doll, which she calls her own child. Like a six-year-old, she sits, taking her time to comb the doll's hair and changing its dresses.

The doll is laid on Sophia's bed, naked. Its clothes are all scattered on the bed. Sophia's room is always neat; we clean it together. She makes her own bed, wipes the table where we sit while eating, and then she mops the bathroom. All I do is dust the windows, and sometimes, I redo what she has finished, especially when her mind is very unstable. In such a situation she makes her bed, and then crumples the bedcover, or pulls out all her clothes from the wardrobe and throws them on the floor. Despite the twenty- five years of nursing her, I still have gaps in my understanding of her behaviour. The doctors Madam Jalia has so far consulted have diagnosed Sophia as a deranged woman but I say Sophia is just mentally unstable. Sometimes she talks, or stares, or tosses the doll from the crib to her bed, sits for long hours without saying a word; and at other times she seems sane: alert, aware, thoughtful.

I keep my eyes on the doll, which is occupying the place Yatuwa would have taken twenty-five years ago. Yatuwa, what will she do when she finds out that the patient she has to see is actually her mother? Will she ever forgive the three people: my aged father and mother, and me, who have kept her in such dreadful deceit? Kept her away from her mother, away from her grandmother: away from her blood relatives. She will denounce us, that is if she is lenient. Perhaps she will have us killed, thrown over a cliff down onto jagged edges of rocks. Or perhaps she will say "I forgive you, Uncle Lule. I forgive you grandmother. I forgive you, grandfather." And then I have Madam Jalia to think of: how she will react when she realizes the *shamba* boy should never have been trusted perhaps...

Sophia returns. She blinks and blinks, turns her head side by side as if looking for someone she can't see. Slowly, she struggles back to her feet, delicately falling on her knees, planting her forearms on the floor, then rising on all fours like my mother, Yatuwa's grandmother, back in Buligi. She sees me seated on the chair but she ignores my presence. I watch as she walks towards her bed, reaches out for the doll and places her gently into the crib. She starts on the doll's clothes, neatly folding one by one into a pile. I join her. We work silently.

"Thank you very much." Her voice is a little softer than it is usually.

"You are welcome," I say. She walks to the crib and gets out the doll. She sits on her bed, rocking it. "Elena is naked," I say to her.

She jerks off the bed and hurries to the wardrobe. "My daughter shouldn't be naked. She shouldn't." She slips the dress over the doll's head then holds it tight to her chest.

"I have to protect her always!" she says. "And when she turns thirteen, I will never at any time leave her alone, not even a second! We will sleep together, wake up together, eat and bathe together... I will never leave her alone. My Elena. I am dreading her thirteenth birthday, and I hope she never turns thirteen!"

The finality of Sophia's words is etched in the dilated eyes. Her voice, which was previously soft, is now heavy with what I can refer to as righteous anger. Sophia has never forgotten her thirteenth birthday: the day she went in the field like a deer prancing into a trap where an arrow would pierce its heart. I remember that day and my heart sinks. We never found out how Sophia ended up in the field. And that baboon of a beggar who raped her, I never saw him again.

As I look at Sophia, a mentally unstable beauty, I feel happy that I have devoted my care to her, loved her, and taken care of her daughter. This feeling makes me comfortable. Right now she needs me because her anger is refreshed. The bouts of anger are rare, compared to withdrawal. Much as withdrawal happens almost every day, anger happens at least once in a week. Unlike with the withdrawal, where I always leave her alone, with anger, I calm her down by saying something good about the doll.

"I want to carry Elena," I say.

She turns immediately and carefully hands the doll to me. The doll helps me have my way with Sophia. When she refuses to eat, I tell her she has to eat because she needs strength in order to be able to protect Elena. If she refuses to go to sleep, I tuck Elena in her bed and tell her Elena cannot sleep alone.

"There is someone I told about Elena. She's dying to see her." My words bounce right back to me. Sophia is still, the anger in her eyes has been replaced by despair. After a long silence, she speaks, "I will watch over her every day."

"We will watch over her together," I say. "Elena is really precious, that's why someone wants to see her."

Silence again. When I turn to look at her, her face has lit up; lips have parted to expose her white teeth. She is smiling: a wide smile, which only those with Madam Jalia's blood possess. This smile so alive and real; is it good or bad omen?

"Who is it that wants to see Elena?" she asks.

"A young woman."

"A young woman," she repeats. Her face is bright as a warm sunny morning.

"She is good, that young woman, isn't she?" she is still smiling.

"She is very good and kind. She will love Elena and you."

"When will you bring her to see Elena and me?"

"Tomorrow."

Tomorrow...

177

Glaydah Namukasa, Ugandan, is a midwife/writer, a member of FEMRITE, formerly on Crossing Borders. Her novel *The Deadly Ambition* (Mallory Publications UK February 2006) won the Michael and Marylee Fairbanks Fellowship for the Bread Loaf Writer's conference USA. *The Voice of a Dream* (Macmillan UK September 2006), a young adult novel, won the Macmillan Writers' Prize for Africa, senior category. Short stories include *Dreams Dreams and Dreams*. She has also published in anthologies in Uganda and UK. Poems: *That place* (FEMRITE) and *Yet hope survives*. Shortlisted for the Ken Saro-Wiwa's Legacy anthology 2005.

Rejoice

Elizabeth Pienaar

I

THEY HAD WAITED FOR so long, what else could they call her, except Rejoice? Gabriel walked around like he'd been crowned king of the world. After eight years of marriage in which there was no child, not even a miscarriage, after eight years of watching siblings and in-laws surrounded by ever more laughing children, after consulting *sangomas* and so much praying, at last, there was Rejoice. It was simple. Lindi, his wife, came down from Hwange to stay with him – only a month or so, and then she had to go back, he needed her to care for his aged mother. And nine months later – Rejoice. He told me then: "I am a lucky man."

But Rejoice was only six months old and he was telling me, "Marina, I am going to die." His work had gone to hell. There were always weeds he didn't see, seeds he forgot to plant, leaves he just didn't sweep. He complained constantly of being tired.

"What's going on Gabriel?"

"Someone is jealous of me. Someone has put a very strong curse."

Gabriel had been working for Mark and myself for twelve years, all the years really, since he was an open-faced young kid, coming to Johannesburg to be with his other brothers and sisters. After about the fourth sad tale of being cleaned out, in his curtained-off segment of room in Alex township, I'd relented. There was a whole wing of rooms in the back of our rambling property, slowly filling with junk. He'd scrubbed them and painted them out and put flowers into the vases I'd chucked and made it his house. He was fastidious, fussy actually, and close to his family and terribly earnest.

I knew him well enough not to doubt him.

Still, standing next to me, six foot and built like a boxer – he did, in fact, work out daily using two enormous weights which he kept outside his door – it was hard not to sound incredulous. "Oh for God's sake Gab, you're as strong as six oxen, what do you mean you're going to die?"

He didn't drop his eye, and I stood staring back at him, hand on hip. But he knew I would not laugh like the other woman he works for. I don't laugh at sangomas and I don't mock the psychics or raki healers or exorcists either. He told me again, "Someone has cursed me."

I stared until my eyes lost focus, switched focus as you must if it is the other worlds you want to see: a sludgy grey mist clung to him, thickening slowly. But then I shook my head, my focus, back to the mundane world. I felt dizzy, so I sat down on the little stone wall near the avocado tree. "Why, Gab?"

He shrugged. Again: "Someone is jealous of me. It is my house. It's too big."

I've seen the photographs: everything we pulled out in the renovation he put back into a new house – all the old steel windows and french doors, my old kitchen units along with the sink and the stove and the carpets and the solid steel bath I didn't want to give away, even the basins. Both the toilets broke when we tried to chop them out. Mark said "Bad luck." But I went and got him a new one. Everything went onto the truck.

Even his bricks. Mark's great mate Malcolm runs a demolition company. Mark drives me mad with all the 'treasures' Malcolm brings and dumps here. "So can Malcolm bring us something useful for once?" I'd asked, "Gab's going to need bricks." Mark remained impassive. "Well?"

Mark shook his head. "You know Marina – you spoil Gabriel rotten." Mark bent down to kiss me. "I'll see what he can do," he said over the jangle of car and house keys.

And so, just before last Christmas when he was nearly ready to go, Mark called Gabriel. "Gab, have you got enough bricks?"

"No," he said, "I've got no bricks."

Mark was standing at the kitchen door, running his hand through his thick blond hair, screwing his eyes up against the sun. "So can you get a truck to come on Saturday?" He nodded his head for Gabriel to follow him and they went round to the front garden, to the gate we don't use. There, Mark had one of Malcolm's tipper trucks, way too big to get in the gate, idling, spewing fumes into the early morning air. They'd dropped the back and side panels down, and I could see a mountain of cleaned, used bricks. "Hey Gab," said Mark as I came up behind them, "You can unpack them here until Saturday, but no longer. You know what Marina will say if they stay any longer." What would Marina say? Same thing I always say when Mark unloads the 'finds' that Malcolm brings, when Gabriel's stuff piles up behind the workshop: *Keep the scrapyard at Malcolm's, my house is not a goddam public dump.* I glared up at Mark. He grinned and squeezed my shoulders.

"Happy now, Marina?" He loped past me back to the house.

Gabriel unpacked every single brick himself, even though the four guys sitting on top of the truck were supposed to help him. Instead, they folded their arms and watched him, stony-faced. Malcolm's driver is a Zulu man. He doesn't like Gabriel. David took me on once, we were chatting as his team off-loaded. I said I was sorry Gabriel wasn't there to help them. David scowled and said "You should give his job to one of us."

"Isn't he almost one of you?" I meant to jest. "You have a common ancestor, Zulu, Matabele?"

He sneered and said there was a good reason Mzilikazi ran away to Zimbabwe, and they should have stayed there. "That one," he stood, his big chest too close to me, "Uh uh, that one is a Lindela boy."

But it was only last Christmas, that Gabriel could unload 8,000 bricks without stopping, that Gabriel was still strong.

So now he has the biggest house in his village and a good wife and, at last, a baby and yet something is badly wrong. Next to me Gabriel is sweating. He says, "I'm no longer strong."

I stand up. "Ok," I say. "So what do you want to do about it?"

"Nothing I can do about it. I am going to die."

"What about Rejoice?"

"I will go home before I die. To see Rejoice."

"You can't just give in to this." I suppose I'm shouting, "You have so much ahead of you. You have Rejoice..." It sounds lame. I want to give him a lecture on taking responsibility for making his world, on the power of his own belief... but his eyes are dull. And I see it once more – a sludge of greyness falling over him like a cloak. So I sit down again "Have you been to a sangoma?"

"The curse is too strong."

"Try another one."

"I don't know another one."

"Ask Zama." Zama has worked in the house for longer than Gabriel's been around. "Just fix it Gabriel. You must know *you* can. You have power, you know, your own life-force." He's staring at me blankly. "You have to believe you can fix this thing," I try again. "Listen Gabriel, if someone cursed you, you can send it right back to them. You can fight it."

He just puts his head in his big hands.

I go, this time, around the corner into the kitchen courtyard. But I feel an uneasy tingle down the spine. I want to turn around yet again, because I need to see the physical body to be sure, be sure of this second sighting that sometimes comes to me – I have such a clear picture in my head of the grey mist sucking itself into him, squeezing every organ and cell of his body until there is nothing left.

There's something malign sitting over him. And he's accepting it, accepting his helplessness. If there is to be any help at all to be had, it must come from outside himself. How can I convince him it can be otherwise? What's magic anyway except the manipulation of energy? Send a curse? *I* know I can deflect it. I can send it right back. He could do this too. He has the gift. I am sure of it.

I can do things. I protect our property, for instance, I wrap the whole place in white light. In the midst of a crime wave, nobody unsavoury has ventured onto our land; and we've been here eight years. It was years ago, that I discovered Gabriel could also see things. We were discussing a burglary across the road. Gabriel said he knew why we never had trouble here, it was 'the light that was all around the house.' I was astonished. When George, the leader of the Circle, came to bind the house with Celtic runes on all the doors and windows, Gabriel followed him around. "I see the thing he's making," Gabriel said, "It's like a shining spider-web all around this house." I was thrilled. Another time Zama was telling us people were terrified of Hermes, my white Alsatian. Everyone thought he was somehow supernatural, more than a dog. Now Gabriel speaks softly but clearly. He said, "Like the other white dogs at night." So *he* could see them. You might call them astral guardians. They're a pack of white wolves who roam the garden. They were called to battle a malevolent presence I could not uproot. Gabriel understands more than most people on these matters. And yet, he doesn't know – or he doesn't want to know – that he has power too. But I'll never stop trying, to nurture this gift he has.

Almost everyone who came to this house felt that malevolent presence; and heard the feet walking in the passage, or shuffling around the living room. But it had seemed to rest behind the big green chair in the lounge. On Mondays, Gabriel helped Zama to move the furniture. Instinctively, he would never go near that corner of the lounge. I had to get George to come, finally, two years ago, to get rid of that presence. It was a truly vicious creature, lashing out and spitting, fighting all the way. But it fell down at last; and we banished it, out of the house, off our land, sent away forever to a dark limbo where it can never escape. It left George reeling, passed out flat on the ground.

When George exorcised the house he also went to Gabriel's rooms. I know something happened there. Gabriel looked stricken. His hands were shaking – and he was Gabriel back then, I mean he flung a bag of cement over his shoulder like it was a beach towel. He wanted to know from me exactly what George was – a sangoma? Could he see what was going to happen in the future? Gabriel was terribly afraid.

And he doesn't look very different now, from that day with George, as he comes around the courtyard wall. His eyes are wide and staring. "Marina," he says, "The time when George came to this house, I will tell you what he told me. He said, *be careful, I see a dark hand closing over you*. But then I was busy with my house and Rejoice. I forgot for a while, to be afraid. So," he's holding on to the wall, "His magic is strong, Marina."

"I can help you." I say.

"Your magic is strong, too, Marina. But nothing can help me." He turned and walked heavily away.

Since he told me about the curse, he and Zama have been to two different sangomas. And been away all day too, I might add. Never mind the housework, my garden is really suffering – every day there are more things he does not do. All the flowers in the front garden are dying now. The compost hasn't been turned once, certainly not watered, for weeks. The summer bulbs must come up soon, to be put away for winter. I ask him every day how he is, but I can see it is never better. Every day he will say, "I feel weak." Every day, "I am tired." He seems to sleep as soon as it gets dark and doesn't emerge till the sun is high.

And now he's started coughing. It's getting more persistent very quickly and I can't leave it although he says nothing. I get him a cough mixture. It makes no difference. "Did you take the medicine?" I ask.

"All gone," he says.

So I tell him to go to the hospital. I tell him every day. And he doesn't. It's only when I lose my temper that *he* tells me, "The hospital is full of people like Malcolm's driver, only more dangerous. If I go and they see I do not have an ID book..."

I'm losing patience with this whole thing. "They won't turn you away."

He looks at the ground miserably. "You are right Marina, they will not turn me away. They will give me an injection instead, they will say it is to fix me but I know it will be full of poison. This is what happens to any one of us who is not from here, everyone knows this."

"I insist you get that cough seen to. Gabriel, didn't you hear anything I said? You're *not* helpless, you know." And then, slowly surfacing, there it is: "Anyway, I need to know if that thing is catchy. Now the hospital will cost nothing except another day of my time."

Gabriel shakes his head; resolutely. I know he won't budge. "I think, perhaps I was not ever a lucky man, Marina. I am thinking for a long, long time some ancestor has been working against me. Because, why else should my sister Priscilla, and my brother Thursday, get their ID books, but not me. I'm thinking how many

183

people in Home Affairs I give money to but still, there's always a problem for me. Everyone else can buy their ID from Home Affairs. But not me. So I must always keep my cell phone in airtime and walk carefully."

"Look at it another way, Gabriel. You've had twelve years here." In and out of police cells. Mark always made him pay back the bribe money. Usually, I said 'don't worry.' Briefly, I glimpse the greyness around him. *How many more times will it be?* But I shake my head, shake away these thoughts, come back to the immediate problem. We cannot, I cannot, leave this thing any longer. "So do you want to just curl up and wait for this curse to take over?"

He shakes his head miserably. "I want to see Rejoice, once more. I will go home before I die."

And so that's why we're in my car now, we're going up the hill to my own old doctor. I'm really pissed off. It's not the money, it's that this malaise of his is already soaking up so much time.

Doc Mendel sits behind his big mahogany desk just like he has for thirty years, only now he's a little more hunched. And there's less hair, not that there was ever much, pale strands plastered firmly from one side of his head across the baldness, to the other ear. His eyes protrude slightly, but there are still no spectacles. He smiles his small closed smile, then he leans forward over steepled fingers, like he always does, and he says what he always says: "So Maa-reee-na, what can I do for you today?"

He talks as if Gabriel is not in the room, and it does annoy me, the way Doc calls Gabriel 'he.' Soon tuberculosis comes up for discussion. 'He' really should go to the hospital and have the test. Doc's already starting his note of referral – I stop him. "Gabriel won't go to a hospital," At least I turn to look at him. "But it is contagious, isn't it? How would we treat it, if he did have it, I mean? And where would he have got it in the first place? And now Gabriel is always complaining about being tired. Aren't you, Gab?"

The old man looks at us very calmly, then he sighs and he looks out the window, which is in fact the entire southern wall of this consulting room on the ground floor of his Observatory mansion. It's a good view, a serene cascade of greenery into a steep valley and up again to the shining roofs of Kensington on the other side. "Maa-reee-na," he sings, but he turns to Gabriel. It's only time Doctor Mendel addresses him directly. "I think you have to have a blood test."

Suddenly the whole room folds in on us. Grey mist almost obscures Gabriel's face, then it slips over his shoulders, squeezing in around his neck. Damn it, this inconvenient second sight. My old doctor just sits there gazing at us, but it's the first time since all this started that my chest goes tight. "Are you sure?" I ask.

"Just do it now, Marina, go to Linksfield Clinic. It'll take five minutes." Doctor Mendel gives me the standard Lancet paper, dense green writing and square boxes. I don't even want to see which one's he's ticked. In the car the only thing I can manage to say the whole way, is the same thing I know I say every time we've gone to see the doctor these last twelve years: that I have known him since I was six years old.

The lab is not crowded, thank god. I can't help it, looking at my watch. The whole morning has gone. I pay the nurse and I stand at the first door near the administration. Gabriel shuffles through the second door, to the blood booth. His backward glance is so stricken, he looks like he's entering another cell door about to close on him. The nurse greets him. He can barely get a sound out of his mouth in response. Her eyes narrow. Then she nods. He puts his arm out on the bench. The nurse straps the tourniquet around it, tells him to make a fist. She keeps talking, talking, all the time about silly stuff like the weather and what happened on *Isidingo* last night. Gabriel makes a grimace and turns his head away from her to stare at the wall.

Then she's telling him to stand up, she hasn't got all day. His arm is unstrapped, a neat wad of cotton wool and a plaster sit at his elbow crease and two thin glass tubes full of dark red blood lie neatly labeled on the bench. "How long have you been here?" The nurse asks him softly. Before he can answer she winks and pushes him out the cubicle.

Driving home we talk about him getting a license, it's a big dream of his, to own a car. The old red Renault, my first car that I bought with my inheritance from my grandfather, is still standing in the driveway. I know that's the car Gabriel wants. Perhaps that's why I keep it, even when Mark shouts back to me about who the hell is keeping a scrap yard in the house.

II

We've just sat down to supper when Mark's cell phone beeps. "Can't you ever turn that bloody thing off?"

Mark slides the phone across to me. "Gabriel's caught again." The text message says, *Can you bring my jacket to Norwood. R500. Plse.* Mark reaches for the corkscrew. He fills my glass without even asking if I want wine. He turns the pepper grinder over both our plates, in silence. Then he picks up his fork.

"We can't just leave him."

"The pasta's getting cold."

"And if we miss him? We don't know how long he's been there already." I've

185

just read an article about illegals, and rising xenophobia... "It's not his fault."

Mark's face gets quite red when he's angry. "Fuck it, Marina, it's not mine, either." But he pushes his chair away from the table. I hear the lock on the kitchen security door squeak, as it always does when you turn it. I hear his footfall moving outside towards Gabriel's rooms. Then he storms back past the dining room with Gabriel's jacket, grabs his keys on the tallboy. The front door slams. I sit on my own and stare at the two mounds of mushroom pasta, handmade by Mark, porcini and black pepper and cream, growing cold and sticky.

I was going to tell him the results of Gabriel's blood test over that supper.

By law a doctor's not allowed to disclose the test results to a person's employer – but as I say, I have known Doctor Mendel nearly all my life. So now, instead, I sat and pondered over CD4 counts, what I remembered about T-cells, trying desperately to recall the endless articles I had read, and failed to absorb. But I understood this: given his numbers, it was an absolute miracle Gab was still standing at all.

"Listen to me," Doc had leant forward behind his big desk, "You should give him long leave, Marina. You should let him go home."

"Why?"

Doc had shrugged. "He's going to die."

I cleared the plates into the bin. The phone rang. Mark actually sounded panicked. "He's gone. There's a new superintendent here." That article I'd read about illegals, it was really about stamping out corruption in the police force, especially coming down hard on policemen who took bribes. "There was only one guy I recognized." Mark went on, "They've all been shuffled around. Sergeant Dlamini came out, supposedly to tell me I'd parked illegally. But at the car he pointed to the jacket and said *Lindela now-now.*" There was a long pause. Mark didn't even sound resentful, just weary. "I suppose I'll have to go."

And maybe I surprised myself, because I shouted, "Don't go Mark. Not now. Best we remember that every time we get Gab out, we bloody break the law." The article had specifically referred to Lindela Deportation Camp. And people who offered bribes. Bribes? Us? But how many times *had* we helped Gabriel? Enough times to have a standard code: *can you bring my jacket to Norwood. To Sandton. To Hillbrow.* And always followed by R250. Or R500. Or even R750. And after that, Plse. Sometimes I went with Mark. We took the spare key to Gabriel's room and we always found his leather jacket hanging behind the door, as if he kept it there just for this purpose, to fold casually over a wad of banknotes. To be procured by ourselves of course, at whatever time of day or, more frequently, night, in the middle of a movie or dinner or once, when we'd just got onto the highway to spend the weekend away.

Mark had the routine perfected by now: "We've come to see Gabriel Ncube," he'd say. The policemen stared at us, stony-faced: "No-one here of that name," someone ventured after a suitable silence. "Sure there is," Mark started walking towards the cells, "He's just phoned me." It helps that Mark's a big man. He holds his arm up, with the jacket conspicuously draped over it, and keeps walking. In Norwood he knows exactly where he's going, in the other police stations, sometimes it's a guess. "He tells me he's cold." Gabriel was cold, in Autumn, or the heat of Mid-summer. The whole thing became a pantomime. The roles never varied. The cop, a cop, at Norwood we used to know them by name, maintained his sullen air, but somehow understood the drape of that leather jacket and leapt ahead of Mark, to lead the way. At Norwood I could actually hear the cell door clang open.

If we missed him at the police stations, we usually had four or five days to expedite a comfortable transaction at his next stop, before deportation. We'd only missed him completely four times in twelve years, times we'd been away. It took him about three weeks to make the round trip back. It had got harder, over the years. Usually Gabriel went home via Botswana although recently he'd been bitterly frustrated by centralized computer systems. Beit Bridge was practically impassable, bribes exorbitant and not guaranteed effective. But here, here, it was worth anything to keep Lindela at bay.

And now it didn't matter anyway.

"What's wrong?" Mark stood in the kitchen. I didn't realize I was crying.

In the morning, we sent his brother, Thursday, to Lindela with the money. We couldn't find him.

I was sure we'd never see him again. But we did. Gaunt and with a strange tinge to his skin, Gabriel arrived at the gate exactly three weeks later. He shuffled to his room. He slept for so long Mark went in to see if he was still breathing. When he emerged he complained of a headache; and that the sun hurt his eyes. He barely even kept up the pretence of working now. Everything in the garden had run to seed or withered from lack of water. The lawns stood un-mown, ankle high.

Gabriel refused to go to my doctor, refused, of course, to go to hospital. He even refused Zama's newest sangoma. "You need help," I said, "Let us help you." A sheen of sweat covered his face at 8 o'clock on a cool Autumn morning. He shaded his eyes and squinted. "Marina, long ago I told you," he coughed,

"Nothing can help me."

Thursday appeared soon after. It was the middle of a supposed work day but he dragged Gabriel off. Thursday re-appeared the same day and stood at the window. "Gabriel must come home now," Thursday's voice was deep and rumbling.

In his absence, I'd decided that if Gabriel got back, it would be a sign. If he got back – I could save him. I would clear all that greyness clinging around him. Not that I hadn't already been trying, I sent white light to erase the greyness, every day. Now I meditated, I chanted. I did holographic repatterning. I called on the angels. But it wouldn't budge. I had to get him anti-retrovirals.

Which I knew absolutely nothing about. Except that there was still no national rollout; and even if there had been, it came back to the thorny issue of Gabriel's legal status. Doctor Mendel shook his head at me and did his gazing out the window routine. "Marina," he said at last, "Listen to me, leave this alone, it's too big to take on." I glared at him. He returned my gaze, complacently. "These people don't see things the same way," he said mildly. At last he sighed and took a piece of paper and scribbled a name on it. "These drugs are not easy to come by. Try this doctor. I hope your bank account is in good condition."

After that everything happened very quickly. I phoned a friend who'd worked with AIDS orphans, who phoned some other friends and we got Gabriel a place on a privately funded program. We were that close to exorcising *this* beast.

If we could only find Gabriel. I phoned his sister. Priscilla informed me he was at his brother, Thursday's, and they were, indeed, preparing to take him home. "If you take him home you'll kill him," I shouted. "He needs to be in hospital."

The next day it rained. It rained and it rained, an out-of-season downpour, an unfortunate omen. I had a bad day, missing deadlines every way I turned, clients screaming, suppliers defaulting. In the middle of a phone call, the office bell rang. I wasn't expecting anyone. I hated it when people pitched up with no appointment. "Thursday," said the voice through the buzzer. The buzzer crackled. "Thursday here with Priscilla. We have come to talk about Gabriel."

And that's how I stood in the rain because Thursday didn't want to come in. We stood beneath the big old Prunus tree, me and tiny, wiry Thursday in his dust-covered building site shoes and overalls, eye to eye. And Priscilla, bigger than both of us, rocking from foot to foot, and struggling to keep back her tears. You see – I told them. "Gabriel has got AIDS," I said. "Not HIV, full-blown AIDS. You can't take him home. We have to get him anti-retrovirals, very quickly. Here," I knew I was shouting above the rain, "In this country, we can. In your country, he is truly a dead man."

Thursday, I would have believed, did not hear me, did not understand me. Except for the look on his face: it was as if I had damned him. As if I had personally crafted a curse and made sure it was accurately placed.

Priscilla folded her arms around herself and rocked harder. She was softly spoken, like Gabriel. "Madam, help us," It was almost a whisper. "To take him home, we need money."

Thursday looked at the ground. "No medicine can help Gabriel."

I stood there, shaking my head.

Epilogue

I sent my spirit out. Soaring, searching. Out there, somewhere, was a taxi moving north. *I moved over the vehicle, like a cloud. I waited.* In there, he was hot, hot, he complained. *The greyness moved swiftly now, swirling around him.* His body was wet. He moaned. He cried out that he was drowning, drowning in his own sweat. The air was full of voices shouting and petrol fumes and the screech of brakes. The vehicle was at the border post – *but he was elsewhere, caught in the dervish mist, raging through the body, claiming every cell, a stain spreading, that could not be stopped.* He cried out that his head was sore, that he could not lift his neck. He wanted to lie down but he could not do that either, because there were too many people, squashed close around him. Why were they screaming, all shouting so loudly, he demanded in a burst of strength. 'You hurt my ears.' *He collapsed forward. I, cloud overhead, observed something move out of the body, intact, free of the darkening mist, the obliterating stain.*

And then, freed also of the constraints of time and space, I watched him move away. Until the light became a gentle, golden colour. I watched a young man, striding up a winding road. The mud was red and soft. There was the fresh smell of rain. Water still pooled in fat drops on the leaves of the greenery, spreading out on either side. The road turned towards a huge pink rock, basalt formation. In its shadow was a clearing. In the clearing was a house. It was newly built. A small girl came towards the man on unsteady legs, smiling, smiling such a big smile. For a moment he stopped, seemed surprised she could walk already. But then he was running to pick her up in his arms and shouting "Rejoice, Rejoice."

And then I drifted away.

In memory of Raphael Sibanda, 1971-2004.

Elizabeth Pienaar is an architect and writer living in Johannesburg. She won the 2005 HSBC/SA Pen Award, and 2nd place in the HSBC/SA Pen Award 2006. Her novel *Ahkenaten's Garden* was one of five short-listed for the 2006 European Union Literary Awards. Her novel *The Gift* was on the long-list for the 2007 European Union Literary Award. She was placed in the Shell/*The Economist* Travel essay awards in 2001. Her work has been published in poetry anthologies *Over the Rainbow* (1996/7) and *Under African Skies* (1997) and short story anthologies *African Compass* (2005) and *African Road* (2006). Her work has also appeared in the International Pen Magazine.

Looking for Biko

Véronique Tadjo

AT FIRST, IT WAS not about Biko at all. It was about having a good time and discovering a region of South Africa they had never been to as a family.

Mark took out the map, his guide book and carefully planned the trip. The boys wanted to take Bella, the dog. Their parents said no, but they argued that she needed a holiday, too. Besides, it was going to cost them a lot of money to put her in a kennel.

So, one early morning, the day after the school break began, they all set off for Port Alfred. They were in high spirits. After a while Bella settled down and went to sleep at Christopher's feet.

A few hours later, they reached Bloemfontein, their first stop. Amina read what the *Rough Guide* had to say:

It isn't a place anyone actually visits, but because it lies at the cross-roads of South Africa many travellers end up here to break a journey cross country.

Not really encouraging. However, one of the main attractions of the city is a big art gallery set in beautiful gardens. They decided to go and have something to eat in the little restaurant. It was a nice day and the boys took turns to walk the dog. She was feeling restless and would not drink water from her bowl. They did not stay long as they had a lot more driving to do before getting to their B&B for the night.

Smithfield was a dead place. Not a soul in sight. The guest house had a splash pool but Barbara, the hostess, a former journalist who had a connection with Kenya, was unwelcoming. She looked at Amina as if she was trouble incarnated and immediately took an instant dislike to the dog. "We have two cats, you know," she said like a school mistress disapproving of her pupil's conduct. "Don't let your animal roam around."

They unloaded the car. Mark was upset about the woman's attitude. While unpacking in their room he remarked:

"But I don't understand, when I made the reservation on the phone, I specified

191

that we were bringing a dog. It wasn't a problem, then."

"And did you specify that you were bringing a black woman?" Amina asked tongue in cheek.

They laughed. His wife was determined not to let herself be bothered by someone who was obviously in the wrong job.

"Look, you are the white man here. Maybe you should deal with her from now on. There is no way I am going to go near the reception again."

The boys were watching TV but their father was adamant they should visit the town before dinner. He dragged them out of the door and they all strode towards the main road. They walked in the dusty alleys of Smithfield. Enraged dogs barked at them as they passed along one empty bungalow after the other. Where was everybody? Simon was kicking his heels with his big boots which annoyed his father tremendously.

"Stop that immediately! Can't you see you're stirring the dust?"

His younger brother was rubbing his eyes. Simon shrugged his shoulders and stayed behind for the rest of the time.

Bella was frightened by the fierce watchdogs. Further down, they met a silent dog which was sitting alone, just outside his master's house. He did not move an inch when he saw them. His eyes were just closely following their progress as they went past the house. Christopher took pictures of his parents in front of a war memorial. It seemed as if time had frozen, as if the many changes that had gripped the nation had not had any impact on the place. Except that when they came round a corner into what looked like the town centre, they saw a Chinese shop. The sign read: "Best Price Supermarket". The boys were very excited about it. It sold all sorts of imported goods. Christopher got some strange looking crisps and Simon bought a T-shirt with a big dragon on it for 40 rand. There were some Chinese pyjamas on sale that were too small to fit anybody in the family. Amina almost bought some Chinese slippers but thought better of it when she tried them on. The young Chinese woman at the till spoke very little English. She took Simon's money while a little girl, certainly her daughter, played next to her.

They had a light dinner in a local restaurant and retired early to bed.

The following day after a full English breakfast, they took the N6 heading towards Aliwal North. They crossed the Orange River which wasn't orange at all. Mark wanted to drive to the Spa, perfect for swimming and relaxation with pools and grassy surroundings. But after getting lost several times, he decided he could not find it and had an argument with his wife about her poor navigation skills.

Instead they visited the Boer War Concentration Camp Memorial, a camp cemetery which looked like a prison from the outside. Hundreds of Afrikaners died there, many of them children, killed by malnutrition and the appalling conditions in the tented camps set up by the British.

They climbed back into their car and did not speak for a while.

They stopped in Queenstown for some tea and cakes.

"We are now going to King William's Town. Do you know who is buried there, boys?"

"I don't know," said Simon. "I don't want to hear about any more dead people."

His father ignored him and continued:

"Christopher, do you know who Steve Biko was?"

"I know," he replied triumphantly. "He was a freedom fighter, wasn't he?"

"Yes, well done Chris, and a very important one at that. He died in detention. Amina, can you read for the boys what the guide book says about him?"

"Ok, but wait, first," she said as she was turning a page. "There's something interesting about the town itself:

"Off Albert Road, is the nineteenth-century Edward Street Cemetery, notable for the story it tells of the conflicts in the area. Besides a memorial to those killed in the innumerable Frontiers Wars against the Xhosa, there is an open piece of ground on the far side of the cemetery which marks a mass grave. This is where hundreds of Xhosa were buried, their bodies emaciated as a result of the 1857 Cattle Killing, when many Xhosa people destroyed their cattle at the behest of the prophetess Nongqawuse – she promised that this would finally drive out the British.

"I find this truly fascinating," said Amina when she had finished reading. "Can you imagine? Thousands and thousands of cows killed just because of a false prophecy. And people dying of hunger. It is incredible how we are always ready to follow those who claim to be able to offer us the moon. Boys, always keep an independent mind."

"Careful Amina, it is much more complicated than that. I guess it was an act of extreme desperation in the face of an imminent invasion," Mark remarked. "Now, I would like to know what there is about Biko."

"OK, it's a bit long but listen to it boys, you need to know these things." She turned round to look at them and saw on their faces that they were not thrilled. "What does it all mean for these young ones?" she suddenly asked herself. "All they want is to go ahead in life, to be free of the burden of History. They don't want to be told how messed up things were. They want to believe they have a bright future."

"Don't be like that kids; you live in a society that is still feeling the consequences of the past. If you try to ignore it, it will catch you up."

"We know, Mum, we are not dumb, you don't need to ram it in!"

"Don't speak to your mother in that tone. Do you want to be grounded?"

Simon shrugged his shoulders.

Christopher was keeping quiet. He could always sense when trouble was approaching. He was stroking Bella on his lap. He hated these constant fights between his brother and his father.

"All right," Amina cut in. "Let's calm down. I'll just read a small excerpt. If you don't want to listen it is up to you:

"Born in 1946 in King William's Town, Biko's political ascent was a swift one, due in no small part to his eloquence, charisma and focused vision. While still a medical student at Natal University during the late Sixties, he was elected president of the exclusively black South African Students' Organisation (SASO) and started publishing articles in their journal, fiercely attacking white liberalism."

Amina stopped for a moment.

"Do you understand what 'white liberalism' means, Simon?"

"I think I do," he replied. "It is when white people think they are being nice to black people but in fact they are still full of crap and they talk down to them."

"That's a pretty good definition." replied his father.

"Good. Let me continue reading, then.

"In an atmosphere of repression, Biko's brand of Black Consciousness immediately caught on. He called for blacks to take destiny into their own hands, to unify and rid themselves of the 'shackles that bind them to perpetual servitude'."

Amina stopped to look at her sons again. They were fine, seemingly interested. But when she went back to the book, she saw that it would take too long to read everything aloud. She decided to tell them the rest in her own words:

"He suffered greatly as a result of his political commitment. He was imprisoned many times and barred from leaving King William's Town. But he would regularly get out, defying the order. After the Soweto riots in 1976, he was stopped at a road block near Grahamstown. He was taken to Port Elizabeth, very close to where we are going, interrogated and tortured by the security police. He died of a brain haemorrhage in prison in September 1977. He was only 31 years old! His death triggered a change in public opinion all over the world. Sanctions against the apartheid regime were finally imposed by the United Nations.

"What do you think, boys?"

"It's a sad story," muttered Christopher, slightly confused. He was trying to work out in his head how much of all this concerned him directly.

"I think it is pretty cool," said Simon. "He was a freedom fighter. Like Mandela. Everybody loves Mandela."

"I propose we go and see his grave," announced their father. "It won't take us long and after that, we will drive straight to Port Alfred in time for a swim."

Finding Biko's grave proved to be harder than expected. The map of the town provided by the guide book wasn't precise enough. So, they went on through Alexandra road where the tourist information office was located. But when they got there, it was already closed. They asked a few pedestrians for directions. Nobody seemed to know. They were getting impatient in the car. But the father did not want to give up so he decided to follow the general direction given by the guidebook. It said that the way to the Memorial would be signposted. They saw nothing. After driving outside the town for several kilometres, Mark realized that they had missed it and turned round. The usual arguments about navigating started between husband and wife. The boys were bored, feeling hungry and the dog was jumping up and down obviously in need of a walk.

They stopped at a huge petrol station just outside the town. It was crowded with cars parked everywhere and streams of people coming in and out of the shops with food, ice creams or drinks. Dirty papers littered the space. They found a spot on the grass where they ate some fast food. The chips were limp.

Mark decided to abandon the search and go straight to Port Alfred. But he saw a security guard and asked him on the off-chance whether he knew where Biko's grave was.

"You mean, Steve Biko's Garden of Reverence? It is just opposite this petrol station. You go back on the road and take the next left which is a dirt track. You continue for a while and then you will see the entrance to the cemetery."

They followed the directions and got there in no time. They parked the car next to what must have been some sort of refreshment space where the mourners could sit with family and friends. There had probably been a shop or something like that, selling Biko souvenirs maybe. But now it was completely deserted and everything looked old and abandoned. There was nobody to tell them where Biko's grave was located. No guard at the entrance. The gates were wide open.

They proceeded to look for it in two groups. Mark and Simon went left and Amina and Christopher right. It was a paupers' graveyard and there were no markers, so they walked through the dusty alleys, their heads bent down trying to read the names on the tombstones. At times they inadvertently walked on graves, which were simply covered with sand. The sun was burning hot. There was a feeling of desperation. How could this be? How could someone who had given so much to his country be buried so anonymously? Then Amina remembered the time years ago when she had found herself in the same situation with Mark, miles away from South Africa. They had been to the Fespaco film festival in Burkina Faso and at the end of their stay in Ouagadougou had decided to go looking for Thomas Sankara's grave. It was a sad experience. At the time they were there the man's grave was at the edge of a cemetery bordering a dirt road. It was covered with the red earth that is so characteristic of the savannah landscape. They had both been shocked to see that here lay a former president and a revolutionary man who had come to symbolize the struggle against economic dependency and neo-colonialism.

"What is it with us?" Amina asked herself, irritated by what was becoming a fruitless search for Biko's grave. "Why do we abandon our heroes? How can we celebrate them publicly and then forget about them, forget what they were as real people?"

She noticed while walking around that a lot of the graves were just mounds of rocks or bricks. Some were made out of plain cement with bits of shelves, beads or broken glass stuck in them. Huge black ants crisscrossed the ground, busy looking for food.

"But perhaps we don't need heroes after all," she whispered to herself on the verge of giving up. "We certainly must not wait for any form of salvation."

"Over here, we've found it!" yelled Mark from the middle of the cemetery.

"At last!" thought Amina as she rushed with Christopher to the spot. Her husband was standing with Simon next to a brown tombstone. She looked at the small plaque that bore Biko's name and her heart sank. It was a neglected grave. The polish had long gone and the marble was turning grey with dust. A bunch of dried flowers were scattered on one side. Were there signs of desecration? She picked up some pebbles that were scattered on the tombstone and threw them away. She spotted a plant that was growing on the side of the grave. It had young tender leaves and it was very small. But Amina started imagining that over the years, it would grow into a tall tree bearing fruits, its foliage casting a cool shadow over the tombstone. In her mind, she was many trees scattered all over the graveyard, like a garden in full bloom. And there would be flowers sending perfume in the air and there would be grass soft under people's fee. She smiled. She took some tissues out of her handbag and started dusting the grave. She did it in slow movements. Her sons looked at her, puzzled and there was an awkward moment. They looked at their father but he had wandered off inspecting the surrounding graves. They looked at each other. Christopher said,

"Can we have some tissues, too, Mum?"

Amina gave them the last ones she had and they joined in.

"What did this man die for?" She asked aloud. "Was it not for his people?" Outrage was taking hold of her. She thought of her home, of elaborate funerals that lasted days if not weeks. Mausoleums that stood tall to tell the story of the men and women under the ground. Of course, she was aware of the excesses of such celebrations and in a sense she was grateful that Biko's grave was so humble.

But deep inside, she knew that the word "humble" wasn't the correct one. It was a case of neglect. Perhaps they had come in search of Biko's grave at the wrong time. Perhaps for the anniversary of his death it came alive again with fresh flowers and renewed attention. Perhaps...

She saw in the boys' eyes that they sensed her sadness, so she put the dirty tissues in a plastic bag, carried them to the car and straightened up.

They reached Port Alfred roughly when they said they would. It was a beautifully appointed guest house and everybody felt happy they had reached their destination. But Amina had already withdrawn into herself.

The next morning, she demanded to go to a bookshop to buy a copy of *I Write What I Like*. She had already read it but decided she needed to revisit it. She thought she owed it to him. She told her husband and the boys that she did not feel like a day at the beach. She stayed behind. Alone in the room, with Bella sleeping in the armchair, she sat down at the desk and started reading. She used her pencil to mark significant passages. Then she wrote them down neatly in her notebook.

Once the various groups within a given community have asserted themselves to the point that mutual respect has to be shown then you have the ingredients for a true and meaningful integration. At the heart of true integration is the provision for each man, each group to rise and attain the envisioned self. Each group must be able to attain its style of existence without encroaching on or being thwarted by another. Out of this mutual respect for each other and complete freedom of self-determination there will obviously arise a genuine fusion of the life-styles of the various groups. This is true integration.

She thought of changing the word "integration" to "transformation". Yes, it would work. After all, wasn't it the point of all this? Wasn't it the heart of the matter? But today, in the country of Biko's children, she felt that everything was moving fast and in all directions. She felt that society was spinning round and had lost its focus. Yet who was she to judge? She had come here with the preconceived idea that this country would change the face of Africa. Now, she realized that bits of hope were slipping away, that dreams were being cut down to size. She saw the relevance of what Biko had said decades ago and she surprised herself wanting to get deeper and deeper into his thinking. It struck a cord in her. At the same time, she had the impression that the strong currents that were sweeping the nation were engulfing everything.

"Biko's memory belongs to all of us," she thought, remembering when she first heard of him. She was just a young woman then, studying African literature back in her country in West Africa. After reading his book, she saw everything differently and thought she had found answers to some of her pressing questions.

"Why was there so much self-hatred around her? Why was it that many years after independence, the old mentalities still survived, people so desperately in awe of France? What sort of legacy had she inherited: 'oppression, denigration and derision'?"

She was so young but she already felt disillusioned. She, too, could not trust leadership. She wanted to take hold of her life. She wanted to be someone who could go anywhere in the world and be at home. No borders – just human beings treading the same ground. She was naïve of course, but was that not the normal order of things? However, what she was certain of was that if she did not harness her emotions and direct them in the right trajectory, she would lose herself and she would be alone in the world.

Maybe memory does not need graves and mausoleums. It flies in the sky and lodges itself in our subconscious selves. We are not just flesh and bones. Maybe it did not matter if his grave was not what it should have been.

It suddenly dawned on her that the title *I Write What I Like*, could have been one of the reasons why she became a writer. The enormous responsibility behind it. If when you first hear it, it sounds more like something a teenager would say, "I *do* what I like", in the context of the time, it was simply a death sentence.

"I write what I like. Even if you don't like it, I'll stand by it. That's what I want to say today. Now."

She kept thinking of Biko, lying in the back of a Land Rover being driven through the night from Port Elizabeth to a prison hospital in Pretoria. She kept thinking of his agony, being tossed around for 700 miles, his head fatally wounded. He must have known he was dying. What went through his mind? What were his last thoughts? Did he regret having sacrificed so much? Did he think about his young family and the pain his death would inflict upon them?

She felt ashamed. To which level would she be prepared to take her own writing? Her eyes were wide open and it pained her to see what was happening around her.

"Yes, there are no frontiers. Wherever we are, the story needs to be told."

She wanted fusion.

Amina read in one go, hardly lifting her head from the pages until she had reached the end.

And when she closed the book, she promised herself that she would tell the story of their search for a hero's grave and the terrible sense of loss she had experienced on that day.

The door opened. The three of them barged in, their feet covered in sand, their hair still wet and their faces bearing the sun. Amina hugged them as if they had been away for a very long time.

Christopher saw *I Write What I Like* lying on the desk. He picked it up, read the blurb and asked:

"Can I borrow your book for a while?"

Véronique Tadjo was born in Paris and raised in Côte d'Ivoire. Two of her works, *As The Crow Flies* and *The Shadow of Imana, travels to the heart of Rwanda*, are published by Heinemann. *Reine Pokou*, her latest novel, won Le Grand Prix Littéraire d'Afrique Noire in 2006. She is currently a Senior Lecturer in French Studies at the University of the Witwatersrand in South Africa.

Simon Said

Mary Watson

IT TALKED MUCH MORE than you would think, its Noddy hair and little boy blue shorts not really an indication of how old it was and how much it knew. The paint was coming off the shorts, the shoes scuffed and worn, but not from walking, not really. Its hair was painted brown in a schoolboy haircut favoured by long-ago children, now grown-up and grey or bald or dead. The mouth was fixed in a smile, one thin pink curve, and the blue eyes lit by a painted sparkle – dancing light on water. There was a splash of red on each of its fingernails which hinted at parties, or maybe bloody scratching. It was a perky looking thing; it looked like the kind of doll that should say things like "Righty-ho" or "Jolly good". But it didn't.

The doll had been christened three times, passed from one owner to another through mothers carelessly boxing up toys their children had outgrown, giving them to church sales or charities, not quite realising what they had done. The first child had called it Sebastian, which was a suitable name – the painted braces and bow-tied laces sat comfortably with that. The next time it was named was less considered: Moofoo, an indignity that made his fixed smile and eyes seem insipid, rather than Sebastian's more shifty look. And now, this time, for the last few years, it was Simon. Simon was good – simple and unpretentious. Simon looked like a nice boy.

Alicia had stolen Simon from the waiting room at the children's hospital. Her asthma, she had to go every few months. She found Simon discarded next to the toy-box, looking poor, hard and faded next to Barney the Dinosaur's velvety purple. She didn't know what came over her: she just had to have it. So when Crispin, skin crusted with eczema, was looking the other way, she slipped it under her pink T-shirt, walking slowly and purposefully to the toilet. There, she took a good look at the doll before putting it in her Lucy Locket pocket. As she leaned forward to breathe deeply while the doctor, through his strange earphones, listened to her lungs making their whispery wheezing music, she felt the doll hidden in the fold of her skirt.

The police came just after twelve, one hour after the armed response got there. They were all the same – men in grim, dark uniforms and guns nesting at their hips and speaking in loud hard voices, tracking dirt and leaves across Hayley's new beige carpet. They caught him in Mountain Road; he had run uphill, the other direction from home. He thought he could outrun them – at school they named him Lange because he was tall and wiry and ran very fast – but he miscalculated the gradient of the hill; maths was never his subject. Lange had heard the house alarm shrieking – someone hit a panic button – but didn't know that the car with its flashing sirens would be so close. He headed for the bridge beneath the highway – he could hide there. Where novice thieves and muggers always tried to hide. This was his third error in judgement, but then he had been the kind of child who only ever thought to hide behind the door or couch with some part of his body sticking out: hide-and-seek was not his thing either. Not like Alicia who once hid for two hours, cold and stiff, because the others had forgotten about her.

It was a stupid crime, hardened gangsters would laugh at him. It happened just one road up, in Chamberlain. One road away from where his mother and Carmen had just changed the sheets after Mosselino wet the bed again and where his Ma, in her pink brushed-cotton gown and teeth in a glass, was reading her Daily Bread (large print). Where his father was not. And where Alicia, under the duvet, talked to Simon, softly and earnestly. And where her doll spoke back. In his bedroom voice.

It was the widow from next door, Mrs Carlisle, who saw what was happening. She was, she said later, closing the blinds at the bay window in her bedroom when she saw the men with guns. They were hammering at the door but no-one opened. She noticed the van, then she saw that they had Lange. He was a tall sixteen, his body paused at an awkward moment in its metamorphosis from boy to man: his hands, feet, ears and shoulders had suddenly, as if sprouted werewolf hair, become alien and at odds with the rest of his thin boy body. Buttoning her jersey, Mrs Carlisle went outside to the two guards who were now thumping at the closed door, calling out something unintelligible. They were about to leave, taking Lange with them, when Mrs Carlisle, iron tits leading, marched over.

"You're scaring them." She pushed the guards out of the way. Mrs Carlisle stood at the door and called to the people inside.

"Hayley? Byron?"

They had been neighbours for four years. They held spare keys for each other, chatted about the wind – either that it was windy or that it was not – or gossiped if someone in the street been broken into or divorced. Or about gentrification. How the old community were leaving and how the new, young and professional, attracted crime: moths to flame, ants to sugar, bees to honey. But they did not know what to say to each other if it did not involve their houses, or details that were specific to the neighbourhood. It was a secret society, where the members identified each other by their house numbers, like some kind of code.

"It's Jane Carlisle, from number 75."

Shuffling from behind the door, whispering.

Mrs Carlisle added: "They've got Lange."

The door opened, quietly and slyly, the witch's marzipan door, but instead of a crooked finger, Hayley's small face peered out, "Is he hurt?"

"Is this your son, Ma'am?"

"Something's wrong," Hayley whimpered.

"He hurt someone. A girl."

One arm clutching her Woolworths peach satin gown (Christmas present from Carmen and Lange) Hayley wailed and, with a look of murder on her face, she launched herself at him. She got him across the head, hard vicious *claps* from such a small piece of woman, Mrs Carlisle would later gossip to the neighbours on the other side, shouting "stupid boy" again and again. Ma Windsor (named because she had been living in Windsor Park when Carmen was born; it distinguished her from Hayley's mother, Ma Lentegeur) was a thin, short pink bundle in the doorway who let out little yelps, "Yip, yip, yip" like a kicked dog. Carmen stomped off growling, "Oh for fuck's sake!" while Mrs Carlisle jumped about like a referee in a boxing ring. Alicia, holding Simon in the crook of her arm, stood just inside and watched.

The police were on their way, one of the guards must have said it. Lange's long bony hands – piano fingers, thief fingers – shielded his head as Hayley swatted at him. The guards looked on perplexed, they were only trained to handle criminals. They tried to explain: the German student, blonde and bloody, had walked home from Don Pedro's. Had to be from overseas, no local woman would walk alone that time of the night. Lange had been crouched down by the wheel of a car. He must have been sitting there in the sleeping street for ages, waiting. She didn't see him, and was about to open her front gate, when he came up behind, brandishing the knife. She didn't have a wallet, or a phone – she had nothing, just a five rand coin, change from the fifty she had taken with her to pay for two margaritas. She had screamed when she felt the tip of the blade, Lange panicked and stabbed, slicing her arm with one of his mother's steak knives – it was from a set of six; from then onward, there was always a missing knife whenever they braaied but it was okay because Hayley pre-cut the meat for Ma Windsor and Mosselino anyway. The German girl screamed louder and Lange, dropping the five rand, took off as fast as his famous long legs would go. The woman from number 137 heard the cries and hit the panic button while her husband – a big man with a gun – ran outside, his trousers not quite zipped. The armed response ("four minutes average response time!") were there in two – the guards had been down at the Kentucky Fried.

Now, Ma Windsor was crying, "Oh Jesus. *O Here help vir ons!*" Hayley stopped hitting Lange and was shrieking to the guards: "Arrest him. Lock him up and throw away the key. I don't ever want to see his face again."

"Where do you see a knife?" Lange was screaming, "Where do you see a knife?"

Carmen was back in the doorway, her face a thundercloud, "Shut up. Do you want all the neighbours to hear? You always fuck things up for me. If you're going to steal, don't do in the next road. Tit."

Contemptuous, Simon whispered delighted, *her voice dripped with contempt.* He said it in his TV newsreader voice. Alicia did not like it when he used that voice. But he would not say anymore because he did not like to talk too much when the grown-ups were around. In case they asked questions. Later as Alicia placed him on the desk next to her bed – legs stretched out in front of him – Simon said that, unusually for him, he agreed with Carmen: if you're going to be a criminal, there had to be more effective ways than blindly stabbing some cheap-assed student in the next road.

They kept Lange for the whole of the next day. He missed school, Alicia told Simon in a worried voice. Simon said that sometimes the best way to learn was through the school of hard knocks. Alicia asked where the school of hard knocks was. Simon said that it was any room that had bars and no windows.

After Lange came back from the school of hard knocks, he was different. He looked thinner, more angular and bony. He sat on his bed listening to music through earphones, and when Alicia came into the room in the afternoon, he would say, "Fuck off and play with your stupid fucking doll somewhere else."

Moody and surly, said Simon.

Hayley wouldn't talk to Lange. "Wait till your father gets back," was the only thing she said; Byron was at sea. But Carmen would not stop. She went on and on, scolding and scolding, you would think that she was his mother and not his sister. Ma Windsor insisted that he prayed and read the Bible with her for half an hour everyday. So that he would stay a good boy. As if the Daily Bread were an antidote for the bad boy poison fighting its way through his veins. Lange would just sit in her room while Ma Windsor prayed in her old lady voice, pointing out verses, saying, "See, child?". And Lange would look down, as if he was contrite, and intone, "Yes, Ma Windsor" to everything she said. But when he looked up, he looked bored.

Ma Windsor had her own box room on the side of the house facing Mrs Carlisle's wall. No light came in, but she said she liked it like that. The small barred window was too stiff to open, and it occurred to Alicia that this must be a remote campus of the school of hard knocks, so she and Simon fitted themselves into the cramped room during the Daily Bread, just to see. There were too many of them for that house. Carmen shared her room with Mosselino: they slept side by side in a three-quarter bed. Usually that worked well. Carmen would tell him stories so Mosselino liked her best. But when she woke to find the cold wet on the sheets, Carmen would get that sour spinster look about her face; she was only eighteen but was fast-tracking to a life of disappointed sighs.

Alicia (and Simon) shared with Lange. They had the biggest room. Two single beds were on either side of the room and each was like a different country: Alicia's bed and desk were neat and green, the colours of an empty field, without much adornment. Lange's half of the room was the land of the teenaged boy; dirty socks, stale T-shirts and smelly shoes were the flora and fauna of this strange place. His landscape was the rise of his head on his arms, elbows jagged, the gentle slope down to his tummy and then up his thighs to his bent knees, then down again to his feet: a boring rock formation. There was a sea between them, a carpet of deep mucky blue which they never crossed. Or else a no-man's land; the empty place between two opposing armies. Relations between the two took strain after Lange's botched attempt at becoming a criminal. Alicia perceived hostile missiles making their way across the patch between the two beds. She tried sending diplomatic emissaries (biscuits) but to no avail. She wanted him to disarm, but Lange simply increased his defences and became impenetrable, and ready to strike at any time. But he was a petty tyrant whose Secret Services amounted to nothing more than furtive masturbation in the small hours of the morning. Alicia knew all about it: Simon told her.

Hayley punished Lange for his crime. She placed him under house arrest until Byron returned from sea, and put him to work. He cleared the gutters, painted the front wall, cleaned out the kitchen cupboards and swept leaves which were soon scattered again by the south-easter. He would not say why he did it, why he mugged the German girl. Just did that irritating shoulder shrug as if to say, get off my back. Hayley surprised him with a visit to the clinic to test for drugs but it wasn't that. There were no syringes hidden beneath his mottled teen boy underpants, no burned light bulbs nestling between his rolled-up pairs of mismatched socks. Alicia checked, just to be sure. When Carmen nagged him about why why why, he said, "I just felt like it". Which got Carmen going again.

"You'll break your mother's heart," she said with passion. Lange ignored her.

Simon said: *My achy-breaky heart. I just don't think.*

In his country-singer voice.

But Carmen didn't hear Simon. She never listened.

There were meetings. Hayley and Lange went to the police, they went to see the German student, her forearm neatly wrapped in a white bandage. A bizarre present. Lange had to say sorry. He mumbled an apology, shiftily looking away. She took the downcast, hang-dog look as a sign of remorse and, shiny-eyed and beneficent, she forgave him. Then he had to say sorry to the people from 137 Chamberlain Street. They did not forgive him. The man grabbed Lange's shirt and said, "I know your type, you dirty drug-dealing gangster. Come near Chamberlain Street again, and I won't call the police this time." He mimed a gun to Lange's head.

It wasn't over, Simon said. Alicia should watch and observe. Lange was up to something. He, with his doll's eye view of the world, he knew that Lange was up to something. Alicia asked him, what do you mean? Simon said: *all work and no play makes Jack a dull boy, all work and no play makes Jack a dull boy, all work and no play makes Jack a dull boy.*

In his mechanical doll voice.

He said it again and again until Alicia begged, stop. And then he clammed up. That maddening smile. Alicia hated it when he got like that. His moods. Then he wouldn't say anything for ages, sometimes days. He could be a very frustrating little toy boy.

Lange had new friends. But he pretended he did not have them. He'd meet them on the way back from school, stretching out the walk home for as long as possible. Carmen was the afternoon warden, on duty from when she got home from tech, and she kept a tight watch – she timed it when Lange took a piss. Alicia saw Lange and his new friends smoking outside the Balmoral when she went to buy bread. Everything they wore looked new and shiny, branded with big labels: Diesel, Adidas, Tommy Hilfiger, CK.

Simon said that she must ask, while they were having supper, who those two guys were. So she did.

"Do you know them from school?"

"Do I know who from school?" Lange said, hunching over his plate.

"The two guys."

"What two guys?"

"The ones you were talking to there by the shop."

"Did your doll tell you this?"

"How come they don't have teeth?"

"They do have teeth."

"So there are two guys."

"I dunno what you talking about." Lange stuck his head in the sand.

One of them came to the house on Saturday morning, through the back alley. Lange was meant to be weeding between the brick paving in their small backyard when Alicia saw him hoist himself onto the wall and talk to someone in the alley behind. The alley was gated and locked.

Go, go, go, said Simon.

Alicia ran out the front door, to the end of the street and around to the entrance of the alley and saw Diesel Jeans dropping down from the top of the locked gate. He brushed his Diesel jeans and strolled off.

The next Saturday Lange was told to remove the old layers of varnish from the kitchen lino with a Stanley knife. Hayley and Carmen had taken Mosselino to a birthday party. Ma Windsor always did the church flowers on Saturdays. Lange took Mrs Carlisle's spare keys from the third kitchen drawer. Alicia watched from behind the lounge door. He grabbed a screwdriver from the tool box and slipped out the back.

Simon said, *Let him dig his own grave.*

Lange climbed over the dividing wall into Mrs Carlisle's backyard, tramped through her roses, and unlocked the back door. Mrs Carlisle was out shopping; three weeks of house arrest meant that Lange knew that she left at nine, and came home at one, every Saturday.

Fifteen minutes later, after returning the keys and slipping something in the bedroom, he was back at the lino, scraping, scraping as if nothing had happened. When they came home, Mosselino in his Batman outfit charged towards Lange kneeling on the kitchen floor, thrusting his wooden sword.

"Leave me," Lange barked. Mosselino froze, sword awkward in hand.

While Carmen was shouting at Lange – Why do you have to be like that? He just wants to play with his big brother. Must you always be so selfish? Can't you think of anyone else for once in your life? They should have kept you in jail – Alicia seized her moment.

He had hidden it in one of his drawers.

Simon sighed, *that boy has no imagination.*

The ring was pushed into the box of condoms at the back of the bottom drawer.

Simon said, *don't put all your basket in one egg.*

It was Mrs Carlisle's engagement ring. The one with the big diamond that she wore on her pinkie on the days that she wore her light blue satin dress. Special days. Alicia put it back. She took out the condoms. Still eleven left. Lange had been ambitious to buy the twelve-pack, and now, here they were slowly ticking towards their expiry date.

And the used one wasted on a practice round in the bathroom.

Over the next weeks, Diesel Jeans and CK would pop up unexpectedly. Lange was not allowed to go out or use the phone, but seemed to communicate with them through some kind of secret skelm grapevine. If Carmen and Hayley went out, there would be a tap-tap on the alley wall. If Lange was sent to the Balmoral to get milk or garlic or dhania, Diesel Jeans and CK would be there first, leaning against the wall of the shop. They would hunch together, their complicity made evident through the touch of a shoulder, the way they leaned forward to each other when lighting their cigarettes, that in-the-know handshake.

Well, well, well. Lange has found his tribe.

During his house arrest, Lange began to take more and more baths. Carmen would knock on the door and say, "There are other people in this house who need to use the bathroom." She would rattle the handle of the door as if it would make him come out sooner. But since the toilet was in a separate room, she couldn't force him out.

"What are you doing in there?" It drove Carmen crazy, because she couldn't get at him when he was in the bath.

"There's a water shortage, you selfish bastard."

But Lange, in silence, attached the hose-pipe to the dirty water and siphoned it to the plants.

Simon said, *clever, clever.*

When Lange took his endless baths, Alicia did her weekly search of his things. Nothing new in the drawers, nothing in his shirt pockets, nor at the back of the cupboard behind his shoes. But, between the mattress and the wall, she found, set to silent, a cell phone tucked away.

Simon said, *aha aha aha.* If he could, he would have hopped up and down with delight.

Everything on the phone had been deleted, even the sent messages.

Sneaky. Very sneaky, Simon said in his spy voice.

Five weeks into playing prison warden, Carmen began to get bored. Her small cruelties were misdirected poison arrows; she just kept aiming in the wrong direction. He was immune to the shrill orders (put those crisps down, I'm watching *Days of our Lives* so you can't watch TV, get out of that bath, *now!* I mean it!). None of it mattered to him, while Carmen just cared too much. Lange would just back off and retreat to his bed, arms folded behind head, knees bent. And sit quietly, biding his time.

Carmen lost interest. So it became easier and easier for Lange to slip over to

Mrs Carlisle's while the others were out on Saturday mornings. Lange would listen for the sound of the car driving down the road. Alicia would pretend to be immersed in the cartoons. Maybe Lange knew that she was not really watching, maybe he thought that his secret was safe with her. He would sneak out the back door, over the wall and into Mrs Carlisle's house. When they returned from the shops, Carmen would ask Alicia if Lange left the house. Alicia, eyes glued to the TV, wouldn't bother replying. She was not going to spy for Carmen.

It became the Saturday morning routine: Ma Windsor did the church flowers, Carmen and Hayley did the weekly shop. And Lange did a bit of alternative shopping, why not. He would select things from Mrs Carlisle's home: slim pickings, there was not that much for a teenage boy in the widow's house. He'd take things that wouldn't immediately be missed: an unused digital camera in a drawer in one of the darker rooms in the dingy house; jewellery, she had so much; an accordion packed away on top of the cupboard in the spare room. He would also move things around, just for the hell of it, so that the widow could persuade herself that she'd absent-mindedly misplaced things: he put the milk in the cupboard, the butter in the bedroom. It was funny. Not very funny, just mildly amusing, enough to ease his creeping boredom.

Alicia did not follow him. She could guess what went on inside Mrs Carlisle's dark, over-furnished house. Simon said, *follow him*. And Alicia said no. Simon got cross. But Alicia simply did not jump over walls. It would dirty her dress.

Simon sulked.

To cheer him up, Alicia said that they would go and look at Lange's porn magazines. So they headed off to the bedroom.

In Mrs Carlisle's house, Lange went through the dark rooms at the back. The mine was drying up – he couldn't find anything. He checked under the bed, moved boxes that hadn't been touched for years, shifting the dust. He did not fold the clothes in the drawers as neatly as they had been. He'd left a trail behind him, like a mouse in a kitchen. Nothing.

Alicia set Simon on the desk. The magazines were under the bed. Lange stashed them in a shoebox labelled "school books". Textbooks. At the school of hard knocks. Alicia lay flat, tummy side down, on the blue carpet so that she could pull the box from beneath the bed.

In Mrs Carlisle's bedroom, Lange looked in the drawers, through the heaps of costume jewellery, in the underwear drawer, then her pantyhose, then her big woolly jerseys. Into the bathroom, smelling strong of Dawn body lotion and rose soap. Water splashed onto the floor just outside the shower. Huge beige panties and bra drying over the bath. Nothing.

As Alicia pulled the shoebox towards her, it jammed against something tucked in the mattress springs. Something small, something soft. Alicia tugged, but it was fastened to the springs. Alicia belly-crawled under the bed. A spring caught her hair and she yelped, but she stretched until she had it in her hand.

Simon said, *what is it? What's going on?*

Leaving Mrs Carlisle's bathroom, a glint of shiny caught Lange's eye. A perfect round circle. A wedding ring. What did she need it for? Nothing at all. He picked it from the ashtray on the shelf and put it in the small pocket of his jeans.

Nothing, Alicia said to Simon. Still under the bed. She opened the envelope. There was more money than she had ever seen. *What, what?* Simon was hissing. Just caught my hair, gimme a minute. She needed quiet. She needed to not hear Simon speak. There was something else. That same thing she had before, that made her take Simon from the children's hospital. It came over her again: she had to have it. So she took it, and Simon didn't say.

Through the dark passage with its nasty plastic runner, into the bright kitchen and – Lange stopped. Mrs Carlisle stood at the kitchen door holding her grandson's cricket bat.

"Put it on the kitchen counter."

She was blocking his escape route. A big woman, and backlit, she looked fierce. He made a run for the front door. It was locked. She ran after him, closing off his return to the kitchen. A rage overcame him – how dare she – and he went for her, arms around her neck, then grabbed the bat from her hands, then swung up and then –

Can't find the magazines. Alicia had never lied to Simon before. She tucked the money in her pocket. Later. She would tell him. In a bit.

When Lange came tearing into the house, Alicia and Simon were in front of the TV again. Twelve Dancing Barbie princesses. She could have all the Barbies in the world now. But Simon could be a bit jealous sometimes. He would always be her favourite but it would be nice to have a dancing princess Barbie. And maybe some Bratz. But he would always be her favourite.

Lange threw some clothes in a bag. He grabbed the phone from behind the mattress, the condoms from the bottom drawer, and got flat onto his belly, one hand feeling the wire coils for the cash.

He was murderous as he charged into the lounge.

"Where's it?"

"What?"

"I don't have time for this. Just give it."

"I don't have it."

He grabbed her shoulders. "I'm gonna moer you."

"So do it. What you waiting for?"

He shook her. "Don't make me do this."

"Stop. Let go. Ow."

"Give. Me. The. Money."

"Make me."

"It's my money."

"It's mine now."

He let go of her shoulders. Suddenly there was a knife.

"Don't make me do this, Alicia. I need that money."

Alicia began to falter. Is this how the German girl felt? Maybe she should scream. But she just didn't feel like it.

Simon said, *wanker.*

Lange looked up. It could have been the VHS clicking to a stop. He looked towards the window. Sirens wailed in the distance.

As he turned back to Alicia, his eyes fell upon Simon. They both looked at the doll perched on the edge of the couch.

"Don't," Alicia said in a strangled voice. She was getting that tight feeling in her chest. As if Lange had grabbed her by the lungs. She scrabbled for Simon. But Lange was, well, longer. He grabbed Simon and held the doll out of her reach.

"Do you want your dolly back? Does the little baby want her dolly back?"

Simon said, *put me down.*

Alicia said, "My pump, I need my pump."

Lange said, "Give me my money."

The sirens were getting closer. Lange held Simon by the hands. For one second, it looked like he was dancing. Then Lange ripped first one arm, "Give", then the other "It". "To me now." The plastic was soft and yielded easily. His hands were poised to pull the head from the body. "No?" He tore the head off. Then he picked up the knife again. "And now?"

"No. Stop!" Alicia cried.

Lange dragged the knife, one long gash down the centre of Simon's tummy. Then he stopped.

"You – sneaky – bitch!"

Lange pulled the wad of notes hidden inside Simon's tummy.

The sirens stopped outside the house. Lange dropped two hundred over the scattered doll parts.

"Buy yourself a new doll." He dropped another hundred. "Keep the change."

He went to the bedroom, took his bag, and headed for the kitchen. He had his hand on the back door just as Hayley and Carmen were entering through the front.

"Lange!" Hayley went straight to the kitchen.

Lange paused for a moment, looking at his mother. Then he left. Out the kitchen door, over the wall and down the alley.

Alicia stayed on the couch, breathing in bursts through her inhaler.

"Your doll!" Carmen cried in dismay, looking at the remains of Simon.

"There are other dolls," Alicia said.

"But you won't get another talking doll. We can try to fix this one."

Alicia considered this carefully.

"You know, I think I've outgrown dolls."

Alicia picked up the pieces of Simon, his arms, his head, then his torso with the deep-long gash, and wrapped him in yesterday's newspaper. She went out back, stepping over the clean bricks, raised the black lid of the wheelie bin, and dropped.

Mary Watson was born in Cape Town, South Africa. Her collection of interlinking stories, *Moss* (Kwela 2004), explores themes of innocence, human cruelty, loss and belonging, distorted through the prism of apartheid Cape Town. Watson is currently lecturing Film Studies at the University of Cape Town where she received a Meritorious Publication award for *Moss*. She completed her Master's degree in Creative Writing under the mentorship of Andre Brink in 2001, and studied Film and TV production at Bristol University in 2003. Her film, writing and research interests all arise from an obsession with stories and with alternative ways in which reality can be represented through art. She has contributed several short stories to published anthologies (including in translation in Afrikaans and German). She is currently working on her first novel and on a collaborative novel together with a group of other South African authors.

Rules

The prize is awarded annually to a short story by an African writer published in English, whether in Africa or elsewhere. (Indicative length is between 3,000 and 10,000 words).

'An African writer' is normally taken to mean someone who was born in Africa, or who is a national of an African country, or whose parents are African, and whose work has reflected African sensibilities.

There is a cash prize of £10,000 for the winning author and a travel award for each of the short-listed candidates (up to five in all).

For practical reasons unpublished work and work in other languages is not eligible. Works translated into English from other languages are not excluded, provided they have been published in translation, and should such a work win, a proportion of the prize would be awarded to the translator.

The award is made in July each year, the deadline for submissions being 31 January. The short-list is selected from work published in the five years preceding the submissions deadline and not previously considered for a Caine Prize. Submissions should be made by publishers and will need to be accompanied by twelve original published copies of the work for consideration, sent to the address below. There is no application form.

Every effort is made to publicise the work of the short-listed authors through the broadcast as well as the printed media.

Winning and short-listed authors will be invited to participate in writers' workshops in Africa and elsewhere as resources permit.

The above rules were designed essentially to launch the Caine Prize and may be modified in the light of experience. Their objective is to establish the Caine Prize as a benchmark for excellence in African writing.

The Caine Prize
The Menier Gallery
Menier Chocolate Factory
51 Southwark Street
London, SE1 1RU
UK
Telephone: +44 (0)20 7378 6234
Fax: +44 (0)20 7378 6235
Website: www.caineprize.com

About the *New Internationalist*

The *New Internationalist* is an independent not-for-profit publishing co-operative. Our mission is to report on issues of world poverty and inequality; to focus attention on the unjust relationship between the powerful and the powerless worldwide; to debate and campaign for the radical changes necessary if the needs of all are to be met.

We publish informative current affairs titles and popular reference, like the *No-Nonsense Guides* series and the *World Guide*, complemented by world food, fiction, photography and alternative gift books, as well as calendars and diaries, maps and posters – all with a global justice world view.

We also publish the monthly *New Internationalist* magazine. Each month tackles a different subject such as Trade Justice, Iran or Ethical Consumerism, exploring each issue in a concise way which is easy to understand. The main articles are packed full of photos, charts and graphs and each magazine also contains music, film and book reviews, country profiles, interviews and news.

To find out more about the *New Internationalist*, subscribe to the magazine or buy any of our books take a look at: **www.newint.org**